"And are you really and truly a fool?" asked Tom,-Page 56.

TOM PLAYFAIR;

OR

MAKING A START.

BY

FRANCIS J. FINN, S.J.,

Author of " Percy Wynn," " Harry Dee," etc.

TWELFTH EDITION.

NEW YORK, CINCINNATI, CHICAGO:

BENZIGER BROTHERS,

Printers to the Holy Apostolic See.

Tom Playfair

THE   vicissitudes of the "Tom Playfair " manu-I script would alone make a story. How itwas written over seven years ago, for the sake of acollege class, and with no ulterior thought of publi-cation; how portions of it gradually found theirway into print; how the writer hesitated for yearswhether to consign the remaining parts to the bookpublisher or to the waste-basket; how the cordialreception of " Percy Wynn," and the kind words con-cerning " Tom Playfair" from critics and from read-ers inspirited him to take the venerable manuscript—done at all manner of odd times, in lead penciland ink, upon all sorts and conditions of paper—from his trunk, and subsequently devote no smallpart of his vacation days (July, August, 1891) to itsrevisal; how the valued advice and kind words ofliterary friends served him in the revision—are notall these things indelibly impressed upon the author'smemory ?

And now he ventures to offer this story to theboys and girls of the land, in the hope that it mayafford them healthful pleasure.

Advancing the figure learnedly styled hysteron-proteron from sentences to volumes, he has published

3

4 PREFACE.

1 Percy Wynn' first, although Percy's adventuresare subsequent to Tom's. The reason for this pro-cedure may be gathered from what has been said ofthe "Tom Playfair" manuscript.

St. Maure's is a pseudonym for a certain collegein the West. Besides inventing incidents, theauthor, to suit his purpose, has on occasion takenliberties with the local surroundings; but in themain he has adhered to the prototype.

It is almost needless to say that the real collegenever suffered from the effects of a thunderbolt; infact, the "cupola," upon which turns a catastropherecorded in these pages, was erected, not by an archi-tect, but by a few strokes of the pen.

Near this Western college there is a village—athriving, happy community. This village the au-thor has eliminated from these stories. The villageof St. Maure's, which takes its place, is a fiction.

In drawing, with certain necessary reserves, uponhis three years' experience at this Western college,the author has, perhaps, made too little of one strik-ing feature—the manly piety of the students. In allhis experiences there he could count upon his fingersthose who, while in attendance, had evidentlychanged for the worse; and they were markedexceptions.

It is hard upon seven years since the writer lastsaw " St. Maure's." Then it was just on this side ofits pioneer days. Now it is a college with a historyof which it may well be proud. The " old churchbuilding," the little boys' dormitory and wash-room, the long, low frame structure used as an in-firmary, are gone; new and nobler piles have arisen

PREFA CE. 5

in their place so that the college of to-day, as Peg-gotty remarked, I believe, of her nephew, Ham, hasu growed out of knowledge"; and yet the sweetspirit of faith and prayer has abided unchangedamid all changes.

The author has not seen these changes he isblessed in believing. Nor can he doubt, aside fromall testimony, that the same spirit pervades themall. The Dialy a college paper conducted by thestudents, reaches him every month; and he can readin the lines and between the lines that the collegeof to-day and the college of seven years ago are onein that closest and most sacred ot

moral unions—atrue, devout, Catholic spirit.
FRANCIS J. FINN, S. J.October 19, 1891.

Father Francis J. Finn, (October 4, 1859 – November 2, 1928) was an American Jesuit priest who wrote a series of 27 popular novels for young people. The books contain fun stories, likeable characters and themes that remain current in today's world. Each story conveys an important moral precept.

Life:

The son of Irish immigrant parents, Francis J. Finn was born on October 4, 1859, in St. Louis, Missouri; there he grew up, attending parochial schools. As a boy, Francis was deeply impressed with Cardinal Wiseman's famous novel of the early Christian martyrs, Fabiola. Eleven-year-old Francis was a voracious reader; he read the works of Charles Dickens, devouring Nicholas Nickleby and The Pickwick Papers. From his First Communion at age 12, Francis began to desire to become a Jesuit priest. Fr. Charles Coppens urged Francis to apply himself to his Latin, to improve it by using an all-Latin prayerbook, and to read good Catholic books. Fr. Finn credited his vocation to this advice and to his membership in the Sodality of Our Lady.

Jesuit:

He entered the Society of Jesus in 1879 after graduating from St. Louis University. Francis began his Jesuit novitiate and seminary studies on March 24. As a young Jesuit scholastic, he suffered from repeated bouts of sickness. He would be sent home to recover, would return in robust health, then would come down with another ailment. Normally this would have been seen as a sign that he did not have a vocation, yet his superiors kept him on. Fr. Finn commented, "God often uses instruments most unfit to do His work."In 1881 Finn was assigned as a prefect of St. Mary's boarding school or "college" in St. Mary's College, Kansas (which became the fictional "St. Maure's"). Francis was ordained to the priesthood in 1891, and after some time at Marquette University in Milwaukee, Wisconsin, he came to St. Xavier College (now Xavier University) in Cincinnati. Fr. Finn spent many years of his priestly life at St. Xavier's. There he was well loved, and it is said that wherever he went—if he took a taxi, ate at a restaurant, attended a baseball game—people would not take his money for their services, but instead would press money into his hand for his many charities. During the 1920s Fr. Finn served as a trustee of Xavier University.In 1904 he served as the first director of the St. Xavier Commercial School for girls, which offered a two-year course of study including stenography, book-keeping, and typesetting.Father Francis J. Finn died in Cincinnati, Ohio, on November 2, 1928.

Children's author:

Before 1865, most American Catholic Literature was either translated from French, German, or Flemish books, or reprints from English and Irish works.

At St. Mary's College Finn learned how to teach and discipline boys. If they promised to behave, he promised to tell them a story. He began with Oliver Twist. One afternoon while supervising a class busy writing a composition, Mr. Finn thought of how they represented to him the typical American Catholic boy. With nothing else to do, he took up pencil and paper. "Why not write about such boys as are before me?" he asked himself. In no time at all he had dashed off the first chapter of Tom Playfair. He went on to write 26 more.According to the American Catholic Who's Who, Fr. Finn is "universally acknowledged the foremost Catholic writer of fiction for young people." It was Fr. Finn's lifelong conviction that "One of the greatest things in the world is to get the right book into the hands of the right boy or girl. No one can indulge in reading to any extent without being largely influenced for better or worse."

CONTENTS.

Tom Playfair

CHAPTER I.

IN WHICH THE HERO OF THE STORY IS REPRESENTED

IN A DOUBTFUL LIGHT.

"""TOMMY!'

1 No answer.

' Tommy—do you hear me ? Get up this moment,sir. Do you think this house is a hotel ? Everyone's at breakfast except yourself."

Miss Meadow, Tom Playfair's maternal aunt, stoodwithout the door of Master Playfair's sleepingapartment. She paused for a moment, partly to gainher breath (having come up three pairs of stairs toarouse Tom) and partly to await some reply fromour sleeping hero.

The silence, however, was simply emphasized bythe ticking of the great clock in the hall.

' Tommy!" she resumed at length, in a higher key,' do you hear me?"

Her strained ears caught the dull sound as of someone turning lazily in his bed. " Now you're awake,sir, jump right up, and dress for your breakfast."

"Sho! scat!" came a yawning voice from the room.

'Dear me!" cried poor Miss Meadow, "the boydoesn't mind me in the least."

"What's the trouble, Jane?" queried Mr. Playfair,who just then issued from his room.

'' I can't get that Tommy out of bed. He's grow-ing worse every day, George. Last week he was latefor school five times."

"I'll fix that, Jane," said Mr. Playfair. And hetook one step toward Tom's sleeping-room, whenthe door of that apartment opened a few inches, dis-covering a young face peering anxiously from beneatha mass of tangled hair.

'`Pa," said the apparition, "I'm dressing just asfast as I know how. I heard you, auntie, and I'mcoming right away."

Then the door closed. Tom, it must be explained,had been composing himself for another nap, whenthe whispered dialogue between his aunt and hisfather had brought him out of bed with most un-wonted celerity. The wily lad deemed it best notto wait for an order from his father. Hence theapparition.

' If you are not at the breakfast table in two min-utes, sir, you shall hear from me," and with thesesternly delivered words Mr. Playfair conducted MissMeadow to breakfast.

Little more than a minute later, a stout, healthy,dark-complexioned lad of ten emerged from his roomready and eager for the labor and heat of the day.His rosy face and jet-black hair gave token of ahasty toilet. His shoes were partially buttoned, hissturdy legs were encased in a pair of bright red stock-ings and rather tight knickerbockers, and his chubbycheeks wore an air of serenity, which coupled with.

his naturally handsome features made him a pleas-ing sight to all lovers of the genuine Americanboy.

Hastily descending the stairs (which he did bytaking from three to four steps at a bound), Tomvery quickly presented himself in the dining room,and ignoring the presence of the cat, in the teasingof which he spent a considerable portion of his valu-able time, he seated himself at table, and fell to withgreat good will. But trouble was brewing.

Besides Mr. Playfair and Miss Meadow, there wasat table a young man, brother to Tom's aunt, andthe bane of our hero's life. Mr. Charles Meadowwas not a bad young man, but he had, despite thisnegative good quality, a large and constantly in-creasing stock of small faults, one of which was aninordinate delight in teasing and browbeating Tom.It is fair to say, however, that in the indulgence ofthis fault Mr. Meadow did not always come off withflying colors. Tom contrived to gain a victory nowand then, and thus added a zest to the domesticwar, which would otherwise have been too one-sidedto be interesting. Strangely enough, Mr. Playfairheld himself, in general, strictly neutral; and it wasonly when the campaign gave signs of unusual bit-terness that he felt himself called upon to interfere.

On the present occasion young Mr. Meadow hadbeen awaiting with ill-concealed anxiety Tom'sappearance.

" Oh, so here you are at last, are you ?" he beganas Tom seated himself at the table.

In the tranquillity of a healthy appetite appliedto its proper purpose, Tom ignored the enemy'shostile flag.

14 TOM PLA YFA1R.

" Look here, young man," continued Mr. Meadow," were you at my room again last night ?"

" How could a fellow get in your old room whenyou had it locked?" queried Tom with virtuousindignation.

"Never mind the 'how,' but did you go into myroom last night?"

" Say, Aunt Jane, please put a little more sugar inthis coffee. You never do give me enough."

"What I want to know," pursued the unrelentinguncle," is, whether you went into my room last night."

" If you stayed at home, and went to bed early,instead of running round the town nights," answeredTom, still desirous of shifting the battle-ground,"you wouldn't be asking such questions."

At this moment Mary the cook entered the dining-room with a plate of pancakes.

If Tom had a preference, it was for this dish.

"Whoop!" he cried, and his eyes glistened.

A smile of triumph passed over Mr. Meadow's coun-tenance; just as Tom was about to help himself lib-erally to the food of his preference, his persecutortook possession of the plate, and having helped Mr.Playfair and Miss Meadow to several cakes, he placedthe rest upon his own plate.

Tom waxed angry.

"Oh! you think you're funny, don't you? May beyou don't use hair-dye for that straw-colored mus-tache of yours—I spelled it on a big bottle."

Mr. Playfair smiled, Miss Meadow tittered, Mr.Meadow blushed deeply. Recovering himself, hereturned to the charge.

"Aha!" he cried, directing his forefinger at Tom." So you have be'en in my room ?"

It was Tom's turn to blush; he was fairly caught.

" How did you get in, sir ?" continued Mr. Meadow, pursuing his advantage.

"Button-hook," answered Tom, with the falling inflection.

" Exactly—that's just what I thought, and that's just the way you ruined the lock of the pantry last week."

Mr. Playfair's face took on an air of concern; he glanced severely at the culprit.

"Well," drawled Tom, "I guess it isn't fair to lock up ripe apples. They don't give a fellow any show in this house."

" Tommy!"—an electric shock seemed to convulse our little pantry-burglar at the low, stem tones of his father's voice,—" Tommy, have you been forc-ing locks with a button-hook again?"

The roses in Tom's cheeks grew out of all bounds, till the " roots of his hair were stirred "; he dropped his knife and fork, and with a despairing expression hung his head.

" This is getting too bad," Mr. Playfair continued. "I don't like to say it, but such conduct is more fit for a young thief than for a little boy whom his father wishes to make a gentleman." At the word " thief" there was a subdued boo-hoo, followed by the sound of heavy breathing.

"You may well cry, sir," pursued the parent," for you have every reason to be ashamed of yourself."

"I j-j-just d-d-did it for f-fun," he sobbed.

"Oh, you're exceedingly funny!" broke in Mr. Meadow with infinite sarcasm.

This last remark filled his cup of sorrow to over-flowing; stifling an incipient sob and muttering that

he "didn't want no breakfast," he departed into the welcome solitude of the hall. The word "thief" still rang in his ears, and sigh upon sigh bursting at short intervals from his passion-racked bosom testi-fied his appreciation of the term.

Presently Mr. Meadow, on his way down town, where he held the honorable position of assistant book-keeper in a St. Louis hardware store, issued from the dining-room. At the sight of him, Tom's grief hardened into the sterner form of anger.

'You'll pay for this, Mr. Give-away," he mut-tered, shaking a diminutive fist at Mr. Meadow.;' I'm going to see Miss Larkin to-day—I will, I will!—and I'll just tell her all the mean things you say to me, how your mustache is dyed—see if I don't,—I'll spoil your chances there."

Mr. Meadow, who had a soft spot in his heart (devoted almost exclusively to said Miss Larkin), was taken back not a little at this threat.

'You young scamp," he roared with more earnest-ness than dignity, " if you go near that young lady with any of your wretched stories, I'll give you a cowhiding."

' Ugh! you give-away!" cried Tom with ineffable disgust.

"So, sir; that's the language you use to your uncle," said Mr. Playfair, who as he opened the din-ing-room door had caught these words. " Go up to your room, sir, and don't leave it till nine o'clock. Jane," he continued, looking into the dining-room,'*please tell Tommy when it is nine."

Mr. Playfair left the house with a stern cast of countenance. Tom was scarcely five when his mother died. The boy was good—but the want of a mother's

care and refining influence was very evident. Then too, Mr. Playfair reflected, the child stood in great danger of having his disposition ruined. Petted by Miss Meadow, he was growing selfish; teased by Mr. Meadow, he was becoming bold.

"Yes," he muttered, "I shall have to take some decisive step, or the boy will be spoiled."

CHAPTER II.

IN WHICH TOM BY A SERIES OF MISADVENTURES BRINGSDOWN THE WRATH OF HIS FA THER IN SUCH WISE THA TTHE A UTHOR, FOR FEAR OF FORFEITING TOM'S CHANCESOF BECOMING A HERO IN THE READER'S EYES, DIS-CREETLY VEILS WHAT ACTUALLY HAPPENED WHENJUSTICE WAS ADMINISTERED.

THE mournful wail that swept at dismal intervalsthrough Mr. Playfair's house touched the sym-pathetic chord of compassion in the heartstrings ofgentle Aunt Jane. Stealing softly up to Tom's room,she entered on tiptoe. Master Tom, his hair di-shevelled, and the channels of grief plainly tracedupon his cheeks, was lying prone upon his bed. Thesight of her compassionate face opened a new flood oftears.

"Don't cry, Tommy," she said softly.

"I wish I was dead," cried that young gentleman.

" Now, now, Tommy," exclaimed the horrified andtoo credulous aunt, "don't talk that way: it is sin-ful, and I'm sure you don't mean it."

"I'll bet I do," he howled. "And I wish I wasb-b-buried too under the ground. And I'll tell youwhat, Aunt Jane, I'll run away."

2

11 Oh, Tommy, how can you say such wicked things ?Come, now, can't I bring you up some breakfast?"

'Don't want any breakfast. I'll runaway, andsell newspapers, and have a jolly time."

' Dear, dear, where did you get all these notions ?"queried Miss Meadow, whose confiding spirit receivedthese exaggerated expressions of grief as so muchgospel truth. ' Tommy, what do you say to somebuttered toast, and a bit of cake?"

In spite of himself, Tom could not help showing,at this stage, some interest in sublunary affairs.

"No," he said, sitting up in bed, "but I'd like tohave some pancakes."

: They're all gone, Tommy, and it's so muchtrouble to make them."

'Well, then, I don't want any breakfast," he said,throwing himself back on the bed, and relapsing intosobs.

This last exhibition of tactics won the victory.Miss Meadow descended to the kitchen, and put her-self to the elaborate work of making pancakes for theworld-worn youth of ten.

Upon her departure, Tom smiled in a manner notentirely devoid of guile; and the smile runningcounter to his tears formed a sort of facial rainbow.

Presently Aunt Jane appeared with the pancakes,and other delicacies, and very shortly, indeed, Tomfell to in a manner most encouraging to behold.

' I say, Aunt Jane," he said, speaking with as muchdistinctness as the crowded state of his mouth wouldallow, " you're a real genuine, old fairy-grandmother,you are."

He intended this for a magnificent compliment, butAunt Jane did not look particularly gratified. To a

miss of thirty the epithets " old " and " grandmother "were rather suggestive.

Perceiving that he had made some mistake,Tomadded:

"I'll tell you what, Auntie, I won't bother yourpantry, or scare the cook for—well, for a week."He spoke as if he felt how handsome his offer was.

"That sounds better," said Miss Meadow. "Soyou'll be a good boy now, wont you?"

" Honor bright, Aunt Jane." And Miss Meadow,with this consolatory assurance gladdening her heart,departed to attend to her domestic affairs, havingfirst given him his liberty.

Availing himself of this, he was presently engagedin the back yard in constructing a chicken-coop.

'Halloa!" said a voice directly behind him.

' Halloa yourself; is that you, Jeff?" he madeanswer, as a boy of about his own age, with a dollishface, and clad in soft garments, met his view.

;'Got any chickens yet?" asked Jeff, ignoringTom's question as being superfluous.

'Not yet, but I guess I'll trade off my base-ballwith Tom White for one." And master Tom pickedup a pine board which he proceeded to split intosmaller sections. In the midst of this interestingoperation, a chip flew up, striking Jeff rather sharplyupon the lobe of his left ear.

" Confound you!" shouted Jeff, rubbing the injuredmember with pathetic earnestness.

'You needn't curse," said Tom resentfully.

' That aint cursin'," retorted Jeff in a sharper key.

"Well, it's vulgar all the same," insisted Tom,unwilling to give in entirely.

"It isn't."

"It is."

"I tell you it isn't."

"I tell you it is."

" I guess my pa uses it."

"My pa doesn't, and he ought to know."

Their voices "took a higher range."

" See here, Jeff Thompson, do you mean to say thatyour pa knows more than mine?"

"Yes, I do."

Tom seemed to think that the conversation hadreached a point where argument should be advancedby other means than mere verbal expression, for hesuddenly struck out straight from the shoulder, andbefore his astonished opponent could hold up hisbands to ward off the blow a sturdy little fist cameinto forceful contact with Jeff's nose.

As stars gladiatorial flashed before Jeff's eyes, hisyell of anguish broke upon the silence.

"I'm killed," he shrieked, as the blood gushedfrom his injured member.

The fast-flowing stream frightened Tom exceed-ingly.

" Oh, Jeff! " he cried, clasping his hands, " I didn'tmean to hurt you so much—cross my heart, I didn't,"and he rubbed his thumb so as to form an invisiblecross upon the right side of his sailor jacket, suppos-ing, in his ignorance, that he had precisely locatedhis heart.

"Go 'way, don't talk to me, "said Jeff, suspendinga howl to deliver this important communication." I'll never speak to you again."

"Oh, Jeff, don't stand bleeding! " implored Tom."Come 'long to the pump and I'll help you washyourself."

"I wont go to the pump," roared Jeff. XT11 juststand here and bleed to death, and you'll be hungfor a murderer."

This threat, coupled with the sight of the flowingblood, filled Tom's soul with horror.

"Good gracious! Jeff, I believe you will die, if youkeep on bleeding."

" Do you think so?" inquired Jeff, paling a little,for he was not so very anxious for death.

" Yes, Jeff, I—I'm afraid you're gone, and you'll becold and stiff, and a big policeman will come andgrab me, and a judge will hang me in a black cap—Oh, gracious!" And at this dismal prospect Tomblubbered.

" I guess I'll go to the pump," said Jeff. And twomournful little lads sought together the coolingwaters. Despite the wholesome application of thewater, the bleeding still continued. Their looks ofdismay deepened. Suddenly Tom's face lighted up.

"Oh, Jeff! I've got it! I heard Aunt Jane read inan almanax that if you hold your arm up when yournose is blooded it will stop."

Forthwith, Jeff's right arm reached madly towardthe sky. To the intense gratification of both partiesthe bleeding soon began to subside.

" I say, Jeff, hold up both arms, that ought to makeit stop twice as fast."

With equal docility, Jeff struck the new attitude.The bleeding was now almost imperceptible.

"And, Jeff, what's the matter with your leg?"

"How?"

"Suppose you hold that up too."

There was a returning twinkle in Tom's eye, whichJeff failed to notice.

"How'll I do it?"

" Lean up against the pump, and I'll fix the rest."

Jeff obeyed, and Tom catching hold of the patient'sright leg lifted it up, up, up, till Jeff shrieked withpain.

"Drop it, you goose!"

" You needn't get excited. I didn't mean to hurtyou," said Tom, apologetically, and he lowered Jeff'sleg a few inches.

It was a funny sight—Jeff leaning against the pumpwith his two arms raised perpendicularly, and his legsupported at a right angle to the rest of his body byhis sympathetic friend. The bleeding soon ceased,and Tom showed his sense of the humor of the situa-tion by giving the leg such a twist that Jeff shriekedlouder than ever.

'You're a.mean fellow, and I wont speak to youagain," vociferated Jeff when he had recoveredspeech.

' You oughtn't to sass a boy in his own yard," saidTom argumentatively.

'Who's going to stay in your old yard?" and Jeffin high dudgeon made his way into the alley.

Tom now devoted himself for the next five minutesto the construction of the chicken-coop. Presentlywearying of this lonely occupation he clambered overthe fence into the alley in search of some compan-ion. To his great disappointment not a single boywas to be seen except Jeff Thompson, who was por-ing interestedly over a kite. The loneliness whichhad come upon Tom caused his heart to soften.

" I say, Jeff, got a string for that kite?"

" You needn't mind about this kite," answered Jeff,without raising his eyes.

"Because, if you haven't," went on Tom in gentletones, "I'll lend you mine."

Jeff's countenance softened somewhat. Tom, see-ing his advantage, followed it up.

' Oh, Jeff, you ought to see my new flint!"

"Where'd you get it?" This with awakened inter-est.

' Bunkered it off Sadie Roberts; come on up, andI'll show it to you."

This ended all hostilities; and within five minutesJeff and Tom had entered into a solemn contract tobe " partners " thenceforward and forever.

An hour or so after this binding contract, AuntJane called up at Tom's room to ascertain what waskeeping that young gentleman so quiet. His tran-quillity was easily explained; neither Tom nor Jeffwas there. Miss Meadow made a careful examina-tion of the house, paying special attention to Mr.Meadow's room, and the pantry; but finding not evena trace of her graceless charge in these places, shehurried into the yard. Her eyes swept anxiouslyover the limited view. The yard was deserted.

"Tom!" she cried.

"Yes'm."

"Good gracious! where in the world are you?"

"Up here."

Miss Meadow raised her eyes, then gave a shriekof horror; on the slanting roof of the house Tomwas busily attending to a dove-cot with one hand,while the other was held by Jeff, who was standingon the top rung of a ladder, his little nose, " tip-tiltedlike the petal of a flower," just appearing over theopening in the skylight.

" Tommy, get down out of that this very instant.

Good gracious! do you want to slip off and kill your-self?"

;' I want to put some feed in for my doves. Idon't care about falling and killing myself," camethe tranquil answer.

' Tommy, I want you to get down from that dan-gerous position instantly."

' Oh, Auntie, just one minute; I'm all right."

Miss Meadow was ready to cry with anxiety.' Tommy, if you don't obey me this very—"

Miss Meadow paused on seeing the look of anima-tion that suddenly appeared upon Tom's features.

"Did you hear it, Jeff?"

" What ?"

;< It's the fire bell,—hurrah!" and with a quickspring through the trap - door Master Tom dis-appeared.

' Now, he thinks he's going off to the fire," solilo-quized Miss Meadow; " but out of this house he shallnot stir one step." And she hastened in, constrain-ing her mind to the proper degree of firmness. Butalas! as she passed through the kitchen and dining-room into the hall, four sturdy little legs twinkleddown the front door steps; and two treble voicesraised to their highest yelling key completelydrowned her command to come back.

Miss Meadow sank into a chair and wiped hereyes. It was mortifying to confess even to herself,but she had to admit that Tom was fast slipping be-yond her control. The mild, timid little lady wasno match for the wild, impetuous, thoughtless boy.If Tom could have understood the pain and anxietyhis conduct had wrought in her gentle bosom, hewould have thought twice before taking so abrupt a

departure. But her tears (so far as he was concerned)were as dew upon the naked rock ; and, shouting withexcitement, he hurried away through the streets tothe scene of the fire.

The dinner hour came, but no Tom; and the poorlady with aching eyes peered long through the parlorwindow hoping to catch some glimpse of the return-ing adventurer. As the quarters passed on, MissMeadow became more grieved.

" I must give up," she said to herself. " The boyloves me, I am sure; but I cannot take the place ofhis poor dead mother. He does just what he likes.Unless something decided be done, he will growup to be self-willed and undisciplined. Thank God!to-morrow's a class day. But even at school he isnot under the proper charge. Miss Harvey teacheswell; but in Tommy's hands she is powerless."

At length, wearied with waiting, and vexed withthe disagreeable train of thought Tom's recent esca-pades had occasioned, she endeavored, with poorsuccess, however, to eat a little dinner. As she wasabout to leave the table, a light but slow tread washeard without. The tread drew nearer; the dooropened, and Tom, his stockings bespattered withmud, his shirt-collar crushed out of all shapeliness,his hat gone, and an expression of shame upon hisdirt-smeared features, entered the room.

"Well, sir," began his aunt, who, in spite of thejoy she felt at his reappearance, was determined tobe severe, " how are you going to account for your-self?" Tom hung his head, fell into a close consid-eration of his feet; and, having no hat to twirl, be-gan pulling his fingers,

"Aren't you ashamed of yourself?"

Tom appeared to consider this a difficult question.

"Do you hear? Aren't you ashamed of yourself?"

'Yes'm," this in a subdued tone, and after duereflection.

'* Now, sir, you needn't think to escape a flogging.Let's hear your story, and then I'll attend to you inyour room, where you may remain fasting till supper."

Healthy boys as a rule are not pleased with theprospect of losing their dinner; nor is the numbergreat of those boys who entertain no prejudicesagainst flogging. Tom saw that matters had cometo a crisis; and that nothing but a masterly strokewould win the day. Quick as thought the younggeneral had planned out his campaign. Advancingto his aunt's side in all humility, he suddenly caughther hand, and said:

'* Auntie Jane, I'm sorry," and before Miss Meadowcould become aware of his intention, he threw hisarms round her neck and kissed her.

Under the warmth of this greeting, her icy stern-ness melted away, and flowed off in a gentle streamof kindness.

'Poor boy! you must be tired and hungry, too.Indeed you don't deserve any dinner. But sit down;I haven't the heart to see you go to your room inhunger."

Tom was not slow to avail himself of this permis-sion; and while Miss Meadow, her bosom agitatedby a conflict between duty and affection, helped himto the various dishes, Tom plied knife and fork withno small earnestness.

For the rest of the afternoon he distinguished him-self by his conduct. In fact, he was trembling onaccount of the wrath to come, His unusual excur-

sion would be reported to his father, and then itwould require more than Tom's address to avoidserious consequences.

Nor were his forebodings without foundation.When Mr. Playfair heard from Miss Meadow's lipsthe account of his son's doings, he compressed hislips tightly, knit his brow, and then, after some seri-ous reflection, called for the culprit.

'Sir," said the father sternly, "you have gone thelimit of your tether."

Tom did not know what "going the limit of one'stether" meant; but entertaining the idea that it wassomething very horrid indeed, he set up a dismalwail.

:' Sir, you need to learn obedience and respect toyour elders. Next September, just five months fromnow, you start for St. Maure's boarding-school, andremember this—if you give any trouble there, I'll notallow you to make your First Communion for anotheryear. Now, sir"—

But as Tom Playfair is to be the hero of this vera-cious story I cannot bring myself to put on recordwhat his father said further; still less have I theheart to chronicle what Mr. Playfair did. Tom wasvery noisy on the occasion. Up to this hour he hadknown the force of his father's hand only from thefriendly clasp. But over that occasion, which Tomnever forgot, and ov.er the ensuing five months, youand I, dear reader, drop a veil which shall not bewithdrawn.

CHAPTER III.

IN WHICH TOM LEAVES FOR ST. MAURES, AND FINDS ONTHE ROAD THITHER THAT FUN SOMETIMES COMESEXPENSIVE.

interval of five months taught Tom several1 years, as it were. The prospect of preparingfor his First Communion, and of going to a schoolwhere he would be thrown upon his own resources,put a touch of earnestness, hitherto lacking, intohis life, in such wise that there came a changeso perceptible as even to attract Mr. Meadow'snotice.

During the vacation, strange to say, Tom gaveso little trouble that Aunt Jane entertained seriousfears for his health.

About thirty minutes past seven, on a Mondayevening in September, Master Tom, enveloped in alinen duster which reached nearly to his heels, look-ing rather solemn and accompanied by his uncle,aunt, and father, stood silent in the Union Depot ofSt. Louis.

Bells were ringing, engines were puffing, hissing,and shrieking, tracks were rumbling and quivering;cars were moving in and out; newsboys, hackmen,and depot officials were shouting, porters were hurry-ing in every direction throwing trunks and otherbaggage, now here, now there, in a manner most con-fusing to the inexperienced eye; women and childrenwere standing near the ticket offices, or sitting rest-lessly in the waiting-rooms, some indulging in a hasty

lunch, many looking hopelessly lost: while the mul-titudinous electric lights flared and sputtered overthe whole scene.

As train after train moved away for its long jour-ney, and Tom realized that he too would soon be onhis way to another part of the world, his heart grewheavy.

"I say, pa," he suggested, "I guess I don't wantto go."

Pa smiled.

"Mr. Don't-Want is not a member of our family,"volunteered Mr. Meadow very smartly.

Tom shot an indignant glance at the speaker ofthese cruel words.

" Keep up your courage, Tommy," whispered AuntJane, quietly pressing a silver dollar into his hands."It's for your own good, dear, and in ten shortmonths you'll come back a little man."

The prospect of ten short months, and the result-ant of a little man afforded him small consolation,but the silver dollar had a reassuring effect. Absent-ing himself from the family group, he immediatelyexpended one quarter of his aunt's gift on a paperof caramels and a cream-cake; and he was thinkingvery seriously of laying out twenty-five cents more inthe purchase of a toy pistol, when a crowd of boysof all ages and sizes came pouring into the depot.

Tom gazed at them in amazement.

'* I say," he said, addressing one of the boys abouthis own age, "what's broken loose?"

Instead of answering this question, the boy stoppedand considered Tom attentively. ' Don't you belongto our crowd?" he at length said.

" What crowd ?" asked Tom.

"The St. Maure's fellows."

'What!" cried Tom in amazement, "are all youfellows going there too?"

"That's what they say."

' Why, then, things aren't so bad as I thought theywould be. I say, let's be partners. My name isTommy Playfair: What's yours?"

"Harry Quip."

'Here, take some candy," said Tom, opening hispackage.

Harry embraced both offers. Henceforth he andTom were "partners."

While the two were thus exchanging small-boycourtesies, a clean-shaven gentleman, somewhat be-yond middle age and attired in a clerical suit, walkedup to them.

Harry raised his hat, and endeavored to composehis features.

"Well, Harry," said the new-comer, "who is thislittle friend of yours?"

Tom, perceiving that the eyes of the gentlemanwere fixed upon him, became nervous, and in endeav-oring to bolt a caramel which he had recently placedin his mouth, nearly choked himself.;This is Tommy Playfair," said Harry.

' Oh, indeed! so this is the boy that runs after fire-engines, is it?"

' Only did it four or five times in my life, father."

' And gets himself on top of slippery roofs."

Tom only remarked:—

'Please, father, I wont do it again."

Upon this the reverend gentleman who had chargeof the boys laughed cheerfully, shook his new ac-quaintance's hand, and, cautioning both to take their

places in a car which he pointed out, hurried awayto see to the safety of the luggage.

'What's his name?" inquired Tom.'That's Father Teeman, he's prefect of disciplineat the college."

'Discipline!" echoed Tom, with a vague idea ofa cat-o'-nine-tails running through his head; "whatdoes that mean?"

'It means that he does the whipping."

'Whew!—But he doesn't look so savage."

' He doesn't have to. But just wait till he catchesyou cutting up. He'll thrash you so as you will pre-fer standing to any other position for a week after."

Tom was appalled. His companion, could heonly know it, was exaggerating grossly for the sakeof enjoying the new-comer's surprise and terror.

" Does he thrash a fellow often?" was Tom's nextquestion.

'Well, I should say so! last year I got whippednearly twice a day, and there was scarcely a weekthat I didn't go to the infirmary to lay up for repairs. *

"Gracious!" ejaculated Tom. 'I wont stand it.Harry, you and I are partners. I'll tell you whatlet's do. Nobody's watching us. Let's slip out.I've got a dollar, and we can support ourselves onthat: and when we get broke, we'll sell newspapers."

Harry had no idea of encouraging Tom to runaway. In his school-boy idea of a good joke, hemerely wished to put him in a state of dismal sus-pense. So he said:

"Oh! you needn't get scared! There's lots of funout there."

' I don't see any fun in getting strapped once ortwice a day."

"You wont get a strapping at all, maybe. I wassuch a dreadful hard case, you see; that's why I gotit." Notwithstanding this avowal it is but just toremark that Harry Quip's features, in their normalstate, wore a very mild expression.

Still, Harry's explanation did not succeed indisarming Tom's fears. If there were to be anywild boys at St. Maure's, Tom, like Abou BenAdhem, had substantial reasons for believing thathis name would lead all the rest. He was aboutto press his proposition of running away withstill greater earnestness, when he heard his namecalled.

" Coming directly, sir. I say, Harry, you keep aseat for me next you on the car," and Tom patteredoff to bid adieu to his father.

"Well, my boy, "said Mr. Playfair, catching Tom'shand, " I am about to put you into good hands.But you must be careful. You will now be thrownamong all kinds of boys—bad, good, and indifferent.Remember, that on your choice of company dependsin great part your piety. Teachers may instruct,priests may exhort, but if your company be bad youwill be no better. And don't forget that every dayyou are preparing for your First Communion. Thatshould be the day of your life. If you make a goodFirst Communion, you're sure to get on well; so lookout for your company, and try to be as good a boyas you can. Now, my dear child, be watchful onthese points. As to the rest, I hold no fear.Here's something to keep your courage up—butdon't spend it all at once."

Tom took the advice in good part, and the five-dollar bill with effusive enthusiasm. Then kissing

his father, he turned to Aunt Jane. The kind ladycould not repress a few sobs.

"God bless you, my boy!" she faltered. "Besure and write every week; and I'll pray for youevery morning and every night as long as you'reaway." And she handed him a basket laden withhis favorite delicacies. Tom's eyes filled at theseexhibitions of his aunt's kindness.

'I've been awful mean to you, Aunt Jane, lots oftime; but I didn't intend anything, you know; andI'm sorry. And when I come back I hope I'll bebetter—honor bright."

Even Mr. Meadow, yielding to the solemn influ-ence of a parting scene, had purchased his nephewa red-covered book, concerning an impossible boy,who met with all kinds of impossible adventures inan impossible country.

"Chicago-ooo-and Alton Railroad; all aboard forKansas City!" shouted a voice.

"That's for you, Tommy," Mr. Playfair said.

They all moved towards the cars indicated. Anegro in the official garments of the road met themhalf-way.

' Is he a college boy, sah ? Step jes dis way, sah.I have de high honaw of taking chahge of all ofthem. Come on, young gemman. Now, up yougo." And without giving our hero an opportunityof making a farewell speech, he quickly raised Tomupon the platform, and, in a manner quite gentle,yet effective, pushed him into the reclining-chaircar.

'Here you are, Tom!" shouted Master Quip, whofaithful to his promise had kept his friend a seatbeside him.3

Tom hastened to occupy the vacant chair, andseated himself as the train began to move out fromthe depot, while the boys gave three vigorouscheers.

"Ah! I like this," said Tom, throwing himselfback in his seat, and yielding to the luxury of thehour.

"Jolly, isn't it?" Harry observed. "Take asmoke" and he offered Tom a cigarette.

"Well, no," said Tom with some hesitation.

" Why not ?"

"Well, I'll tell you," answered Tom, in a burstof confidence. " I hate anything like humbug.And if I was to smoke now, it would only be to lookbig. You see I've got no liking for it. I've smokedonce or twice up in papa's hay-loft, but it's alwaysmade me feel bad. So you see I don't like it; andI'd be a humbug if I pretended I did."

This was one of the Jongest speeches Tom hadever made; and it produced its impression.

"Well, you've got true grit, Tom. And I likeyou the better for what you've said. I like a smokemyself once in a while, but I'm pretty sure that halfthe little chaps who smoke do it to look big."

" I'd rather be little than big," said Tom.

"Why?"

"Oh, pshaw! a man's got to shave, and has todress stylish, and can't play, nor eat candy in thestreets, and lots of things."

"That's so."

'Yes; and then half of them get stuck up. Andthey wear stiff hats, and are afraid to run, and don'tplay any games at all."

"Yes," assented Harry; "and then when chaps

grow up, they've such a lot of worry about bringingout their mustaches."

Both considered the subject pretty well exhausted.

" I say," continued Tom, " they're all boys in thiscar."

'Yes; it's been chartered for our crowd."

" Do you know them all ?"

' I know some of the old boys."

'Who's that fellow with his coat collar turnedso's to hide his ears, and his hair stickin' up likebristles, trying to smoke a cigar as if he was usedto it?"

'That's Johnny Shoestrings."

" Who ? "

'Johnny Shoestrings. That's his nickname, youknow; he's such a slouch. I can't think of his right

name."

Who's that boy with hair like a carrot bangedall over his forehead, and a pug nose, and an aw-fully big mouth ?"

"That's Crazy Green."

' Crazy Green?"

"That's what everybody calls him. He hasn'tgot any sense, and doesn't know how to behavedecent. In fact, I think he's a real bad boy."

"Do all the fellows have nicknames?" askedTom.

;'All the old boys have, except one."

"Who's that?"

" His real name is Black, and it fits his color sowell we thought we'd let him keep it."

'Who are those five fellows down there, who looklike each other's sisters, they're all so timid andpretty?"

"New-comers," answered Harry.

Tom's eyes were fascinated by this group; and,not being satisfied with the information Harry hadvouchsafed, he went to the other end of the carwhere he could interview them personally.

Having first satisfied himself by taking a deliber-ate survey of the five, much to their uneasiness andmanifest discomfiture, he opened the conversationthus:—

"I say, halloa!"

The largest of the group, a boy about fourteen,answered timidly:—

' How do you do, sir?"

"I aint a sir: my name's Tom Playfair. What'syour name?"

"Alexander Jones."

"Whew! five Joneses. Are any of you twins?"

"Harry and Willie are twins, sir." "There aint any triplets among you, are there?"

"No, sir; not this time," answered Alexander Jones, who in his timidity was accidentally face-tious.

"Well, good-by; take care of yourselves." And bestowing a genial grin upon the Jones brothers he returned to his seat.

The train, having now crossed the great bridge that spans the Mississippi and passed out of the city of Alton, was speeding along through the open country. Without it was pitch dark, and the sable solemnity of the night was enhanced by an occasional light that flashed before the eyes of the passengers at the windows, and then as quickly disappeared.

'I say, what kind of a place is it?" asked Tom, resuming his conversation with Harry.

TOM PL A YFAIR. 37

" What place ?—the gravy station ?"

"Is that what you call it?"

'Yes; they feed us on corn-bread and gravy."

" And don't you get any meat?"

"Oh, yes! they give us meat on Christmas; and at New Years every one gets a small piece of pie."

'Gracious!" cried Tom, absently placing his hand upon his stomach. " But I suppose you have lots of holidays?"

' Not so many, I can just tell you; and then even we've got to stay cooped up in a little yard that isn't large enough to swing a cat in."

'They're not going to treat me that way. When no one is looking I'll slip out every chance I get."

'If you do," said Master Quip, who was bent on scaring Tom to the utmost, "you'll get collared by a prefect and then posted."

'What do you mean by 'posted' ?"

' Why, a great big prefect bangs you up against a tree-box, or a post, or a stone wall; and tells you that if you move from it before three hours are up he'll petrify you."

Tom groaned.

'I guess my fun is all over," he muttered in a faltering voice.

"Oh, we have fun sometimes, you know."

' How is that ?" asked Tom anxiously.

' Why, we go out walking in ranks—two abreast—on recreation days, with a big prefect walking in front and another big prefect behind us. Then we walk six miles or so; that is, we keep on walking till most of the little tads aren't able to stand any longer. We sit down, then, and rest for five min'

utes, before we start to walk back again. And while we are sitting down to rest, we are allowed to talk,

you know."

"Why, can't you talk while you're walking?"

"Not much," said Harry emphatically.

"And do you mean to say," cried Tom excitedly, "that after resting five minutes, they're all able to walk back again?"

"I didn't say any such thing."

" Are they left behind, then ?"

"No, indeed; they always have a big hay-wagonalong; and when a fellow can't walk they tumblehim in. But he's got to be mighty tired before that happens."

"So," said Tom, after a moment's reflection,"that's what you call fun?"

"Certainly; it's the jolliest kind of fun."

" I suppose you fellows consider a funeral a goodjoke." Tom did not know that he was sarcastic.

"You're talking now," said Harry. "Whenevera boy dies we get off night studies."

" Does a boy die often out there?"

Harry ignored the literal meaning of this ques-tion as he answered:—

"Well, no; not as many as we would like. Onlytwo or three a month."

"What do they die of?"

"They don't die at all; they get killed by beinghit over the head with a loaded cane."

Tom jumped up from his seat.

"Take it back," he said, with considerable fierce-ness.

" Take what back ?" inquired his astonished friendrising from his reclining position.

TOM PLA YFAIR. 59

"You've been telling me yarns. Take it back,will you, or you and I aren't partners any more."

"' Well, I'm willing to take it back. I only did itfor fun, just wanted to rattle you a little. Youneedn't get mad about it."

Whither the conversation would have drifted it isimpossible to say; for, as the train stopped just thenat a station, Harry and Tom, with that natural curi-osity to see and know all things which is the proudprerogative of the American boy, dashed out uponthe platform. So satisfied were they with this newposition, that they resolved to keep it for a timeindefinite, and accordingly squatted down on theside steps. They were not long there, however,when Father Teeman ordered them inside.

'Harry," suggested Tom when they had gainedtheir proper positions, "let's have a little fun."

"What are you thinking of now?" asked Harry.

'* Let's play conductor."

Harry glanced around the car dubiously. It wasnow after ten o'clock ; and most of the boys, weariedwith the excitement of the day, were asleep.

"What's the use," he said, "nobody's awake."

"All the better."

"Well, how'll we do it?"

" Did you see that lantern on the platform of thecar?"

"Yes."

"Well, that's the idea. Come on."

Accompanied by Harry, Tom sallied forth, ob-tained possession of the lantern, and again walkedinto the car. Stealing up to a boy who was lockedin slumber, he thrust the lantern into his face and,jn as deep a voice as he could assume, said;—•

1 Tickets, please."

' I haven't got it," cried the boy, jumping up andrubbing his eyes. I gave mine to Father—
"

He broke off when he perceived the grinningface of an unknown boy behind the lantern, and ingreat rage he levelled a blow at the joker. Tomvery naturally held up his hands to protect him-self, not taking into account that a lantern wasin one of them. Crash! out went the light,down clattered the glass in a hundred fragments.He had guarded himself very well; but the lanternwas the worse for it. The youthful conductors stoodaghast.

'* Let's put the old thing back," said Tom.

'Yes; and we'd better hurry," counselled Harry.

But before they could carry out their purpose, theporter came hurrying in.

' Young gemmen, who done tuk my lantern fromthe platform?" And as he spoke he glanced sternlyat the discomfited culprits.

" I did," said Tom. " Here's the old thing; lookslike it's exploded, don't it?"

;'Oh, muffins!" cried the porter, "it's ruined, andI'll be discharged. You young bantams, what didyou go and spile my lantern for?"

Tom, remembering the words of Scripture that asoft answer turneth away wrath, put his hand intohis pocket, came out with it filled, and said:—

'Here, old fellow, take some candy."

'Sah! I doesn't want none of your candy. Un-less I can get a lantern at the next station I'mruined. Can't you pay for it? 'cos if you don't, I'llreport you to the company."

" How much do you want?" asked Tom sadly.

"Foah dollars, sah," said the negro, smiling, andmuttering that he " knowed they was gemmen."

" I'll give you fifty cents," said Tom.

" Does you want to ruin a poor man?"

" How does a dollar suit you ?"

"Can't afford it, sah, for less than two dollars."

"Well, I'll give you a dollar and a half; andwe'll call it square."

" Seein' you're such a puffick gemmen, 1*11 take it,sah." And the negro went his way rejoicing in aneat bit of profit.

"Boys, "said Father Teeman coming upon themfrom behind, " suppose you go to sleep, or at leastgive the others a chance to rest. Get your chairs,and keep them."

"I don't want any more fun to-night," said Tomruefully.

"Neither do I," said Harry.

And the two innocents falling back in their chairssoon slept the sleep of the just.

CHAPTER IV.

TOM A RRIVES AT ST. MA URE1 S A ND MA KES THE A CQ UA IN T-ANCE OF JOHN GREEN UNDER CIRCUMSTANCES NOTENTIRELY GRATEFUL TO THAT INTERESTING CHAR-A CTER.

"T OOK out, Tom; that's Pawnee Creek."

L/ Tom thrust his head out of the window and sawa small picturesque stone-bridge passing over theghost of a stream of water. He had hardly time tocatch one glimpse of it, when his hat blew off, drop-ping straight down into the bed of Pawnee Creek.He drew in his head mournfully.

"I guess travelling is pretty expensive," hegrowled. " There's twenty-five cents for caramels,one dollar and ten cents for railroad candy thatmade me sick, eighty-five cents for oranges, a dollarand a half to that nigger for his old lantern, and anew hat to Pawnee Creek."

' Oh, you can get your hat back easily enough.It's only a short walk from the College.

Now,keep your eyes open one minute," continued Harry,' See," he added a few minutes later, "see that roadleading along by the hedge? Many's the time I'vetaken a walk on it. Holloa, there's the good oldwhite fence. Now we are passing the Collegegrounds."

Tom had scarcely time to take a fair look at thefence, when the train came to a standstill in frontof a large four-story brick building with the words'* St. Maure's College," crowning its brow.

Fronting the building was a spacious garden,diversified by several winding and shady walks;fronting the garden was a high white fence, andfronting the high white fence were some hundredand odd boys, with a few professors, awaiting theold scholars and new from the train. But Tom tookno notice of all these things; his eyes, ears, feel-ings—his whole being seemed to be concentratedon the Professor standing nearest him. The longblack cassock and cincture were something new tohim; and so great was his astonishment that theloud cheers of the boys, the fierce whistling of thelocomotive, the sharp cry of "All aboard," followedby the departure of the train, might, as far as hewas concerned, have happened at the other end ofthe world,

Harry, who had left him to shake hands with someof his friends, found him,a few minutes later, stand-ing in exactly the same position.

'Wake up, Tom," he cried, slapping his friendon the back.

This touch snapped the charm.

1 I say, Harry," he at length burst out, " for good-ness' sake, look at that fellow with the gown on.Isn't he a sight?"

' Oh, what a greenhorn you are!" said Harry, withan easy air of superiority; "that's not a gown, it's acassock, and the man in it is your boss: he's theprefect of the small boys."

Tom's face expressed about two closely writtenpages of astonishment.

' Does he always wear that—that thing?"

'Yes, come on up, and I'll introduce you."

' But does he really wear it all the time?"

"That's what I said."

; Gracious! I'm glad of that. I'd like to see himcatch me, if I want to run. Pshaw! he looks for allthe world like an old lady."

"You'll find out, pretty soon, whether he can runor not," retorted Harry a little sharply; "and as tobeing an old lady, you'll change your mind mightysoon if you try any of your tricks on him. Mr.Middleton," he continued addressing himself to thesubject of these remarks, "here's another St. Louisboy, my friend Tommy Playfair."

The prefect, with a smile and a word of welcome,cordially shook Tom's hand, at the same time be-stowing such a clear, penetrating look upon thechubby upturned face that, as Tom afterwards de-clared, " Mr. Middleton seemed to see clear through

his sailor shirt way back to his shirt-collar on theother side."

"You're a wild colt, I suppose."

"Not so very wild, sir," said Tom in his gentlesttones.

"Is he lively as you, Harry?" asked the prefect.

" I'm not going to be wild any more, Mr. Middle-ton," returned Harry in all meekness.

Indeed the subdued air that had come over Harry,now that he stood in the presence of his prefect, wassomething wonderful.

"Well, Harry," continued Mr. Middleton, "youmay take care of your new friend yourself for thepresent; I see some new-comers over there who ap-pear to be very timid and ill at ease—they are quitelost." And he hastened away to do the honors tothe five Jones boys.

Tom and Harry, left to themselves, sauntered lei-surely up the garden-walk, the former all eyes for hisnew surroundings.

" What's that long, low, frame shanty to our right ?"asked Tom.

" That's the infirmary; when you get sick you gothere and lay up for repairs."

" It looks kind of snug."

"Yes; but when a fellow's getting just well enoughto enjoy the jam and buttered toast, they turn himout. This large four-story brick building in frontof us is the house where the fathers and prefects havetheir rooms. The lower floor of it on the east side,though, is the refectory for us little boys. You knowthere are two yards, two refectories, two study-halls,and two wash-rooms and four dormitories, so as tokeep little boys and big boys apart; the large room

TOM PLAYFAIR. 45

just above the refectory is our study-hall; now comeon over to our washroom and we'll wash and brushup before dinner."

They turned to the right on reaching the railedsteps leading up to the brick building, and passedbetween the infirmary on one side and on the other asubstantial three-story structure of stone, which, asHarry informed Tom, was the class-room building.

Continuing straight on, they passed through adouble gate—generally ajar, by the way—and foundthemselves in an open play-ground about four hun-dred feet long by two hundred wide.

"This is the small boys' yard," volunteered Harry.

"Yes?" queried Tom plaintively. "Does a fellowhave to stay around here all the time?"

"All the time, if he doesn't behave himself. Butcome on; let's hurry in before the rush."

Beside the gate, at their right, and next to theclass-room building, stood a two-story frame house,the upper floor of which was a dormitory and thelower a wash-room.

On entering, a novel scene presented itself to Tom'seyes. With the exception of one plain and two shovel-board tables, and a few benches, the main body ofthe room was devoid of all furniture or other obstruc-tion. But lining the four walls all around was aseries of small boxes with hinged doors, each box di-vided into an upper and lower partition, used for thekeeping of soap, brushes, toilet articles, and the like;and above the boxes were scattered towels, soap, andtin basins in all manner of ungraceful confusion; thetowels, for the most part, dangling from a water-pipe,ornamented with here and there a faucet. At thetime that our two friends entered there were a few

boys in the room, engaged at their ablutions, whilea prefect, note-book in hand, was giving each boy onhis entrance one of the many boxes.

" Howdo, Mr. Phelan," said Harry, tipping his hatand shaking hands with his superior.

"Why, Harry! So here you are again."

"Yes, Mr. Phelan, I'm like a bad penny."

"In one sense, yes,"said Mr. Phelan; 'butyou'retoo modest. I'm delighted to see you again. AndI see you have a new friend. Who is this?"

" This is Tommy Playfair, Mr. Phelan. And I say,can't I have my old box again, same as last year—itwas near that window, you know—and can't TomPlayfair have the one next to me ? I'm the only boyhere that he knows."

Mr. Phelan, who had, in the mean time, taken Tom'shand with a smile of welcome, assented to MasterHarry's requests.

"Thank you, sir," said Harry effusively; and he conducted Tom to box number twenty-nine, near the window he had pointed out in the making of his petition.

' This is number twenty-nine—my box, Tom—am i here's your's next to mine, number thirty."

But Tom was not satisfied.

' That little bit of a box for me!" he exclaimed.

'Why, of course," Harry responded. 'You don't want the earth, do you?"

Without making any answer to this important ques-tion, Tom walked over to the prefect.

'I say, Mr. Phelan, can't I have another box, be-sides the one you've given me?"

' Why ? What have you to say against the box I gave you?"

;'Oh, that's all right! but I want two boxes."

* Indeed! what do you want two boxes for?"

'Well, you see, I want one for my books, you know."

'Oh! "said the prefect, breaking into a smile,'you'll get a desk in the study-hall for them!"

" Oh! that's it—is it ?" and Tom, satisfied with this information, rejoined Harry Quip, who with his eyes bulging out of his head had been watching Tom's proceedings in utmost astonishment.

In the mean time the wash-room had been rapidly filling. Every other moment witnessed the appear-ance of new faces. Among those that entered, some, notably the Jones boys, were timid beyond descrip-tion; others, like Tom, were quite tranquil and self-possessed; others again were rather bold and un-doubtedly noisy. This latter class aroused Tom's curiosity.

' I say, Harry," he inquired, " who are those fellows in here that talk so loud, and lift up their shoulders when they walk around, and go on as if they owned the whole place?"

'Sh! don't talk so loud, Tom," said Harry, with unaffected seriousness. "They're a few of the old boys. You see they're perfectly at home. They're apt to be pretty hard on new-comers."

"Are all the old boys that way?" was Tom's next question.

'Well, not all. But a great many are."

These queistions and answers afford considerable insight into the economy of boarding-school life. We hear and read a great deal about the easy confi-dence,— nay boldness—of old servants, old clerks, and the like; but what are they all compared to the

old student at boarding-school ? As a new-comer, he may be the most timid, the most meek of mortals. The first few weeks of his changed life he may rarely speak above a whisper. But with the rolling months, as he picks up a friend or so, evidences of ease and natural bearing insinuate themselves into his address. At the end of the term he departs, it may be, a quiet, gentlemanly boy. But, vacation over, lo! he returns as one of the owners of earth and sky—with al) the as-surance and arrogance attributed by the American press to a plumber in mid-winter. Every look, every tone, every gesture proclaims in terms unmis-takable that he is an old boy; that he knows more about life in any phase than a new-comer; that he is up to every conceivable turn of school-boy fortune; that a new boy, how naturally gifted soever, is but an inferior sort of creature; and that, in fine, there is nothing, humanly speaking, in the heavens above or the earth beneath, or in the waters under the earth, that can compare with that supremest of mortals—the old boy. It would be an injustice, however, to let the reader suppose that all old boys belong to this class. Not so; quite a goodly number are as polite, unpretending, gentlemanly, and sensible as the most refined new-comer.

Johnny Green was an old boy of the former class.

For the last five or six minutes he had been mak-ing himself very conspicuous in the wash-room, bytalking in a raised voice—whenever the prefect wasout of hearing—of the way he had " got ahead of theold man," as he irreverently termed his father, of thegreat and disgusting number of " new kids" that hadalready appeared in the wash-room, and of their un-commonly disagreeable appearance, which MasterGreen put down as being " rather green."

Having completed his toilet, which consistedchiefly, and indeed almost exclusively, in so arrang-ing his hair as to conceal almost entirely his freckledforehead, John Green stationed himself at the narrowdoor of the wash-room, where he amused himself, atsuch odd times as the attending prefect's preoccupy-ing duties allowed, by tripping up various little new-comers, as they chanced to leave or enter.

Tom and Harry were now going out; and Greenwas anxiously awaiting his new victim. Harryadvanced first, and, being an old boy, was allowed topass unmolested; then came Tom, who, by the way,had been watching Master Green's little practicaljoke for fully five minutes. As Tom was vergingupon the threshold, Green put out his foot; suddenlya howl arose from the bully's mouth.

'Why, good gracious!" exclaimed Tom, turningon his steps, "did I walk on your foot? But really,what a big foot you've got!"

'You wretched little fool," roared the bully, whowas now hopping about with a combination of earn-estness and liveliness, exhilarating to see; "you'vestepped on at least five of my corns."

"That's too bad," Tom made answer, with hisface screwed into its most serious expression. " Butall the farmers say there's going to be a large corncrop this year."

With this consolatory reflection he passed on armin arm with Harry Quip, who was struggling, butwith sorry success, to keep a straight face, leaving thediscomfited Master Green to continue or conclude hisdance as he pleased4

50 TOM PLAYFAIR.

Adjoining the end of the wash-room there was—-and is yet, doubtless—a small shed, under whoseprotecting cover were a turning-pole, a pair of par-allel bars, a few other articles of gymnastics, and aline of benches. Upon one of these latter our twofriends seated themselves, calmly awaiting the wel-come sound of the dinner bell. But the calm—ho\vhistory repeats itself!—proved to be the forerunnerof a storm.

Scarcely had they composed themselves in theirseats, when John Green, who was wearied of dancing,and was anxious to meet Tom in a place beyond sightof all prefects, turned the corner. Leisurely leaninghis head on his left arm, his left arm on one of theparallel bars, and placing his right hand on his hip—he had made a special study of this special attitudeduring vacation—he fastened a stern gaze upon Tom.Notwithstanding, our hero seemed to be oblivious ofGreen's presence.

'I say," began the bully, when he realized thatboth pose and gaze had shot wide of the mark, " arethere any more like you at home?"

"I don't know, I'm sure," answered Tom withsuavity; "but if you wish, I'll write home andask."

At this retort three or four new-comers who weresitting near by, and had been gazing about listlessly,broke into a titter. The bully glared at them fero-ciously, whereupon their faces fell into length again,and a far-away look—the symptom of home-sickness'—came into their eyes. Harry had laughed too;but his laugh met with no rebuke; he was an old boy,and in consequence was entitled to the privilege.

Encouraged by the power of his eye, Master Green

turned it in full force upon Tom, and again addressedhimself to that unterrified youth. 'What's your name, Sonny?"

Tom's face assumed a troubled expression; hepassed his hand over his forehead and through hishair—then, after a pause, made answer:

"Can't remember it just now. My memory's badwhen the weather's warm. It's an awful long name.It took the priest over five minutes to get it in, theclay I was baptized."

Another titter from the listeners, and a loud laughfrom Harry. But Green was too astonished at thecoolness of the new-comer to check this outburst.

'I suppose," continued Green, with excessiveirony, "you think you're funny?"

"I guess I do, "answered Tom blandly. "All thefamily say I am; and when I was home they'd neverlet me go to funerals, for fear I'd make 'em laughin the solemn parts."

A prolonged giggle and a louder laugh.

" You're terribly smart," exclaimed the witheringGreen, who, forgetting his pose, was now quite stiffand bolt upright.

"Smart!" echoed Tom, "why, now you're hittingthe nail right on the head. The fellows at the schoolI 'tended last year said they wouldn't come back ifI did, because I always carried off all the premiums;and that's why I came here."

" You'd better shut your mouth or I'll hit you one,"vociferated the bully, drowning the laughter evokedby this last retort; and as he spoke he pulled up thearms of his coat, revealing in the act a pair of cuffswith many-flashing cuff-buttons.

" Oh! if you're going to strike," pursued Tom with

all the placidity of a midspring zephyr, ' I think Ihad better shut my mouth, or you might poke yourfist down my throat, and then I'd be sick for life."

In this quick rejoinder there was to the spectatorsgazing upon Green's clenched fists a certain obvious-ness of point; consequently it aroused mirth in allthe listeners and rage in the heart of the bully.

"You're a coward!" he foamed.

'That's whatjvw say," said Tom,

"And a sneak."

"That's what;w/ say."

"And a mule thief." '

" I never stole you."

This was too much for Green; he made a spring4t Tom. But Harry caught his arm.

' Hold on, Green," said Harry. " Just take a boyof your size."

Harry and Tom, it should be remarked, were each4 year or two younger than Green.

'Let go of me, will you?" shouted the bully.

"No; I wont."

Suddenly John Green became very quiet, jumpedupon the parallel bars, and began swinging up anddown; Mr. Middleton had just turned the corner.Harry broke into a whistle, while Tom maintainedhis blandness to the end. Before hostilities could berenewed the bell rang for dinner.

' You took him up in great shape, Tom," observedHarry on the way to the refectory. "

Where did youget that cool way of saying things?"

" Oh, I used to have a great many rows with myuncle; and he got me so's I couldn't get excited."

"All the same, you'd better keep your eyes open.Green will pay you back for your talk before long.

Anyhow, if I'm around, or any decent old fellow,you'll be all right. He's a coward and a mean boy,and if he caught you alone he'd be sure to take itout on you. But he wont tackle us together."

They were now at the door of the refectory; aseach student entered Mr. Middleton assigned him hisplace at one of the ten tables, each of these beinglaid for twelve.

To their regret, Harry and Tom were placed atdifferent tables. Dinner passed off quietly. Beforethanks had been returned, Mr. Middleton announcedthat each boy should, immediately on leaving therefectory, go to the room of the prefect of studies,where he would learn his class and obtain a list ofthe books which he should procure from the procura-tor, or (being translated) the buyer.

Tom and Harry, who contrived to have their inter-view with the prefect of studies at the same time,were both assigned to the class of Rudiments—a classwhere the student is prepared to enter upon the studyof Latin. They managed to get their books aboutthe same time, too; and so, to their undisguised de-light, Mr. Middleton appointed them seats next eachother in the hall of studies.

"Tom, this is just glorious!" exclaimed Harry,as they emerged from the study room. 'We're inthe same class; and we're right next each other forstudies. But look here!—while you were gettingyour books, and I was outside waiting for you,I heard something. Do you know the first thingGreen's going to do to you?"

"No; what?"

"Why, the first chance he gets to-day he's goingto pin a paper on your back with 'KICK MEI AM A FOOL' on it. He's waiting his chance now in the yard, Ithink."

Tom stood still, and gave himself up for a few sec-onds to reflection; then he resumed his walk andobserved:—

" We'll fix him, if he tries it, Harry. I'll tell youwhat: we'll let him go pretty far with his joke. Iwont notice him. But when he gets behind me, andis pinning it on, you take out your handkerchief—will you? Of course you'll be standing in front andfacing me."

"What'll you do?"

'You'll see. He wont enjoy the joke very muchanyhow."

No sooner had the boys entered the yard, thanthey noticed that John Green was eyeing themclosely.

'He's waiting his chance," whispered Harry.

'Just so," answered Tom. "Say, let's go downby the hand-ball alley."

Harry acquiesced, and both made their way to thefurther end of the yard. Harry, with his hands in hispockets, leaned against the body of the alley so as totake in the whole playground, while Tom, also handsin pockets, stood facing Harry, commanding a vietfof nothing save what was included in the two walls ofthe alley. Green, in the mean time, was following intheir wake with stealthy steps; even Tom could di-vine this from the expression on Harry's countenance.At length Green had secured a suitable position forpinning on the placard. He stooped. ForthwithHarry drew out his handkerchief.

'Talking of jumping," exclaimed Tom at once,"how's this?" and he gave a sharp backward kickwith his right foot.

Green received the full force of this on his shins—the tenderest part of him, perhaps, by the law of com*pensation; for his head was within a little of beingactually impregnable both as to blows and as toideas.

On the moment, Green testified his presence by aprolonged howl.

;' Good gracious!" Tom exclaimed, turning aroundand addressing Green, who with both hands was hold-ing one knee, and hopping enthusiastically with theonly foot he had at liberty: " Why how in the worlddid you come to be behind me? You're terriblyunlucky—aint you?"

A crowd of boys, who had been watching Green'sill-timed attempt to fasten on the placard, were nowshouting and laughing, as they hurried down the yardto take in, in fuller detail, the victim's lively andnovel dance.

" Does it hurt ?" asked Tom compassionately, as hepicked up the placard, which Green had allowed tofall to the ground.

"Does it hurt?" bawled Green, suspending hisdance to give full effect to his answer. 'Oh no! itdoesn't hurt at all. It's awful pleasant, you fool!"And with this burst of eloquence, he resumed hisdancing.

"I say, what's this?" enquired Tom, holding theplacard at arm's length, and scanning it critic-ally. " Is this your paper?"

"Yes; and I wish you and that paper were inHalifax."

The intense devotion of this sentiment was beyonddoubt.

"But," pursued Tom, "you've got 'kick me* writ-ten on it. So you've got what you want. And areyou really and truly a fool ?"

This question so angered Green that he lost sightof his pain. Releasing his injured leg, he made asavage rush at Tom. But this time, too, his inten-tions were frustrated. George Keenan, a boy whohad attended St. Maure's for several years, and who,judging by his modesty, didn't seem to know it,caught the aggressor's arm with a grip which elicitedanother howl.

"Let him alone, Green; he served you right.You've no business to be picking on boys under yoursize every chance you get. And look here,—you'dbetter not touch him when John Donnell or I amaround." And George walked away.

The bully was too crestfallen to face his fellow-students. Scowling and shame-faced, he hobbledoff to the infirmary to get his leg " painted " withiodine.

George Keenan, who has here entered upon thescene, merits a few words. He was a model boy; notthe kind of a model boy that figures in many tales forthe young; but such a model as you may expect tomeet with occasionally, nay—God be thanked forit—oftentimes in real life.

At baseball, running, handball, football, and allmanner of athletic games, no one was more skilledthan George. He was small, undergrown for hisyears, and slightly made; still his strength was un-questioned. And yet no one had ever known Georgeto exert his strength for mean or low purposes, no

one had ever known him to use his influence for aughtsave what was ennobling. He was everybody's friend—with him the bad were, for the nonce, good; andthe good were better. Withal, he was cheerful, jo-cose, and a bit of a wag. He made his way throughlife with the brightness and wholesomeness of a sun-beam. Nor is George, among the general run ofboarding-school students, an isolated character.

In every well-conducted boarding school there arehearts as warm and minds as noble. These boysare themselves the least self-conscious of mortals.Though they know it not, they are doing work, andgood work, too, for the Lord and Saviour whom inthe nobility of their hearts they love with manlytenderness.

CHAPTER V.

IN WHICH TOM IS PERSUADED TO GO TO SLEEP.

NO doubt many of my readers have been askingthemselves what manner of hero is Tom Play-fair. Couldn't the author have selected a better, orat least a more refined character ? This Tom is bold,given to slang, rather forward, self-willed, and—butstay, reader, let us get in a word. We throw up ourhands, and grant the full force and truth of all thesenaughty adjectives. Indeed there are faults, andgreat faults, to be found in Tom. There are manyflawstin the crystal. But what then? These littleflaws, after all, are not irremediable. Tom may bea real gem—even if it be that the gem is in the rough.Some of his flaws, indeed, are simply untrimmed vir-

tues. His boldness is an exaggerated manliness—*certainly it has nothing of the bully in its ring; hisslang is that ineffectual struggle for humor so notice-able in many young people; and in them,at least—wespeak not for maturer sinners in this line—pardona-ble; his forwardness is the exaggeration of what weall love and hold fast to—American independence.But enough on the score of excuses. Let us hopethat the edges may be rounded; that the gem in therough may sparkle unto the admiration of many, thatthe exaggeration of American virtues may be subduedto that golden mean which we all admire so muchand practise so little.

Tom's dialogue with the shin-worried Green, whiledrawing our hero into prominent notice, gained hima host of admirers and a few friends.

As he and Harry were taking a stroll about theyard, shortly after Green's departure in quest of thatboarding-school-boy panacea, iodine, he was accostedby a little lad in knickerbockers, his expression amixture of timidity and wistfulness.

'Well, my son," said Tom, who was about half aninch taller than the stranger, "what can I do foryou?"

'I'm so glad you didn't let that Green get aheadof you. He's mean; he pinched me for nothing, andasked me whether my mother knew I was out—and—and I don't want to stay here. My baby sister"—here the little man began to cry—"wont know mewhen I get home."

'He's homesick—got it bad," whispered Harry ina kindly tone.

'Here," said Tom; "take some candy."

The youngster accepted the candy, and tried to

cheer up; he ceased crying, though he gave vent atintervals to deep sighs.

;< Come and sit down here," continued Tom.'Now, what's your name?"

"' Joe Whyte. My pa is a doctor in Hot Springs,and he's got lots of money, and rides round in a horseand buggy."

'* It must be fun riding round in a horse," observedHarry. " Does he do that often ?"

Joe relented into a smile.

'* Haven't you any friends here?" pursued Tom.

'No; and I want to go home," sobbed Joe, in afatal relapse. 'The boys are all mean here; andnothing is good."

"Oh, you don't know 'em well enough)%t," saidTom; and he added with ingenuous modesty, " Harryand myself are good fellows. You just wait, Joe,till you grow up to be a man, and then you wont haveto go to boarding-school, you know. Then your papawill die, and you'll have all his money, and go ridinground in a horse and—"

'Boo-oo!" interrupted Joe, appalled by this ill-directed bit of word-painting. "I don't want mypapa to die."

" Don't get so excited," put in Harry. " He isn'tgoing to die now."

"I don't want him to die at all," blubbered thewretched victim of homesickness. " I want to gohome right now, and see him and mamma and Sissyand little Jane and all of 'em."

"I tell you what," said Tom; " let's be friends,and then you wont be lonesome. What do you say,Joe?"

With one hand rubbing his eyes, Joe extended the

other first to Tom, then to Harry. Each of theseyoung gentlemen shook it warmly.

Master Joe's case is a fair specimen of the maladywhich attacks almost invariably the new boy—home-sickness. Like measles, whooping-cough, or sea-sickness, few escape it and, still true to the likeness,it seizes upon its victim with various degrees of ma-lignity. Under an ordinary attack, the patient feelsfully convinced that life outside the home-circle isnot worth living. Games, meals, even candies losetheir zest. Like the quality of mercy, homesicknessis "mightiest in the mightiest"; the large boy whenafflicted with it is a piteous sight indeed.

After five o'clock supper, the students took recrea-tion till six, when a bell summoned them to the hallof studies. Here they were at liberty to sort andexamine their books, and write their parents assuranceof their safe arrival.

Tom on entering noticed that the older boys, in-stead of seating themselves at once, were all stand-ing in silence. Following their implicit guidance,he too stood beside his desk, and fixed an inquiringlook upon Mr. Middleton, who from a raised platformcommanded a view of the entire study hall.

Whilst Tom was still wondering why the old boyswere so slow about sitting down, the prefect madethe sign of the cross and recited the " Veni SancteSpiritus" This beautiful prayer concluded, all ad-dressed themselves to their work.

Instead of beginning to study, Tom sat for sometime curiously watching the movements of thoseabout him. The old boys, with scarce an exception,were inscribing their respective names in their newbooks, the new-comers were rummaging in their desks

in a vain attempt at appearing easy and self-possessed.Mr. Middleton seemed to have his eyes on every one.

Presently a professor entered the study hall, andMr. Middleton retired. This professor was the reg-ular study-keeper.

Tom gazed at the new official for some moments,and then turned to Harry.

" I say, what's the name of that man?"

"Sh!" said Harry.

Throwing a look of disgust at his admonitor, Tomturned to Joe Whyte, who sat at his left side, and re-peated the question.

"I don't know," returned Joe.

"Say, what are you going to do this hour?"

" I'm goin' to write home and ask them to take meaway from this place."

"Oh, don't be in a hurry about that!" whisperedTom; "after a few days you will begin to know thefellows better and—" Just then a hand was laidupon his arm, and Tom on lifting his eyes saw thestudy-keeper before him, looking rather stern thanotherwise.

"Keep silence in here, Playfair," he said, "notalking; take out your books and paper and go towork."

"Say, Mister, how did you come to know myname?"

The study-keeper bit his lip to restrain a smile andmoved to another part of the hall. The secret of hisknowing Tom's name was very simple.

A map is made of each boy's place in the study-hall, wash-room, refectory, dormitory, and chapel.One glance at the map will inform the presidingofficer whether each boy be at his post, and, in conse-

quence of this system, a boy cannot absent himselffrom college for any period beyond an hour at themost without being missed.

Thus admonished, Tom opened his desk, took outhis writing materials, and after great effort, muchblotting of paper, soiling of fingers, and intellectualtravail, delivered himself of the following letter:—

ST. MARS COLLEGE,

Sept. 5, 18 8-.MY DEAR AUNT JANE:

I take my pen in hand to let you know that i am well, hope-ing this leaves you the same. St. Mars is a pretty jolly sortof a place; and i am not one bit home sick; lots of new kidsare. Tell Jeff Thomas I will write to him soon. Who is tak-in care of my pijins? Tell papa my love. Is my rooster withthe long tale all rite ? My money is nearly all gone. I had anaxident on the car comin here, and I had to pay the niggerporter for an old lantern. Good bye. I am goin to study ritehard. Your lovely nephew,

THOMAS PLAYFAIR.

While he was addressing the envelope destined tocarry away this choice bit of literature, he felt someone poking him in the back. On turning, he per-ceived a hand extended from under the desk behindhim, holding a bit of paper. Tom received the note.It read as follows:

MISTER PLAYFAIR:

Say will you fite me at recess, behind the old church bilding.

Yrs.,

JOHN GREEN.P. S. You're a sneak.

To which Tom elaborately replied:

DEAR MISTER GREEN:

How did you come to be called green? and why do the boyscall you crazy ? How is your knee ? does it hurt much ? You

don't spell well. Fife is wrong; it ought to be fight. You arebiger than i am and older. Insted of fighting you ought tostudy your speling book. Fightin' is low and i don't want toand you ought to be ashamed of yourself. When you rite homegive my love to your papa and mamma.

Yrs.,

THOMAS PLAYFAIR.

After passing this note, he took a leisurely surveyof the study-hall, stretched his arms; then concludedto go out. Taking up his cap, which, by the way, hehad borrowed from Harry Quip on losing his own,he walked toward the door. Just as he was openingit, his progress was arrested by the study-keeper'svoice.

' Playfair, go back to your seat." This in a veryimperative tone.

'I'm going out, sir," said Tom, pausing with hishand on the door-knob to impart this information.

;' Go back to your seat."

With a look of patient unmerited persecution Tomreturned to his place, casting wrathful glances on theway at several who were grinning at his mistake.

A little later the bell rang; and all repaired to theyard to enjoy a few minutes of recess.

This over, they recited night prayers in common,and retired to their dormitories for the night.

The novel sight of a hundred boys undressing asone struck Tom as being rather funny than otherwise.Indeed he was so absorbed in a humorous survey ofthis spectacle that he stood stock still, grinningbroadly and incessantly for some minutes. A handupon his arm called him down from his humorousheights. It was Mr. Middleton.

;'Playfair," he whispered, "have you anything onhand just now?"

'No, sir," answered Tom, wondering what wouldcome next.

'Well, then, you had better undress, and get tobed." And Mr. Middleton resumed the saying of hisbeads, as he continued his route up and down thepassage formed between the beds.

"Pshaw!" growled Tom. "A fellow can't lookcross-eyed here, but he gets hauled up for it. I don'tsee any harm in looking around." And sadly heproceeded to pull off his sailor-shirt. He had justsucceeded in getting this garment free of one arm,when he perceived Harry Quip some ten or elevenbeds further off. Harry caught his glance and smiled.The smile brought sunshine back into Tom's heart;suspending further operations on the sailor-shirt, heplayfully put the thumb of his right hand to his nose,and made the popular signal with his fingers.

Instead of taking this friendly and jocose demon-stration in the spirit in which it was given, Harry'sface lengthened into dismay, while his eyes glancedapprehensively in the direction of Mr. Middleton.Tom, following the movement of Harry's eyes, turnedand—yes! there it was again—saw Mr. Middletonbearing down upon him.

'Well, I'm switched," he thought, as he slippedout of his clothes with marvellous speed, " if he isn'tmakin' for me again." And leaping into bed heburied his face in the pillow.

'Young man," whispered Mr. Middleton, bendingdown over him, ' we want no levity in this dormi-tory."

"No what, sir?"

"No levity."

"What's that, sir?"

;' Sh! don't talk so loud. I mean you mustn't talk,whisper, laugh, or make signs. Do you understandme?"

"Yes; but—"

"That'll do; go to sleep now; and if you haveany objections to make I'll hear you in the morn-ing."

"He's a nice one," grumbled Tom to his pillow.'He wont give a fellow any chance to explain."

Two minutes later he was sleeping a dreamlesssleep.

CHAPTER VI.

IN WHICH GREEN AND TOM RUN A RACE WHICH PROVES DISASTROUS TO BOTH.

CLANG—clang—clang—clang—clang!"Halloa! what's the matter ?" cried Tom, in themidst of this clatter, as he jumped out of bed andrubbed his eyes.

The cause of the din was a large, iron-tonguedbell, which Mr. Middleton was ringing right lustily.

Tom looked about him; all the students, with theexception, of course, of several of the old boys, whowere quite accustomed to this unearthly sound, wereup and dressing.

"It's a little too early for me," thought Tom; and, satisfied that the horrid bell had become silent, heturned in again. He was peacefully dozing off whena hand was laid upon him.

" Playfair, did you hear the bell ?"

" Did I ? I should think I did! That's all right,5

Mr. Middleton; but I guess I don't care about get'ting up just now."

The sentence was barely out of his mouth, when,as it appeared to him, there was a mild form of earth-quake in the vicinity; and before he could realizethat anything had happened at all, he was sprawlingon the floor with his mattress on top.

"I say, what did you do that for?" he sputtered;but Mr. Middleton was already half-way down theaisle.

" If that's the way they treat a fellow the first day,what'll they do on the last ?" he murmured. " I don'tthink this school is much account anyhow."

On rising, the boys were allowed half an hour forwashing and dressing. Then came Mass, followedby studies and breakfast.

At nine o'clock—on this particular day—they hadwhat is technically termed ;' Lectio brevis "; that is,the teachers of the respective classes gave theirboys a short talk, and appointed lessons for the nextday.

Tom was mildly surprised, and a trifle dismayed,when he discovered that his teacher for the year wasnone other than Mr. Middleton. But after listeningin silence for some minutes to his professor's openingspeech, he concluded that perhaps things might notbe so bad.

The " Lectio brevis " was compressed into an hour,and the students had the rest of the day free.

Shortly after dinner Harry Quip, accompanied bya strange boy, approached Tom.

"Tom, here's a particular friend of mine, WillieRuthers; and I'm sure he'll be a great friend ofyours."

Willie and Tom shook hands, while Will murmuredsheepishly, " Happy to see you '

" Wont you take some candy ?" inquired Tom.

The candy was gratefully received, and the friend-ship of the two was firmly based.

" Have you been out walking yet?" asked Willie.

"No; and that's a fact; Harry, we ought to go andget that hat of mine at Pawnee Creek."

Obtaining permission from the prefect, they setout on their walk along the railroad track, and incourse of time discovered the hat partially embeddedin the mud. When on their return they came nearthe college, Harry proposed that they should passthrough the "Blue-grass." The "Blue-grass" is afavorite resort of the boys. It lies just beyond thecollege yard, and is well shaded with large, gracefulpine trees.

It chanced on this particular day that the only oc-cupants of the " Blue-grass" were John Green andthree lads of similar taste.

Green caught sight of our trio from afar.

"Oh, I say, boys," he exclaimed, " here comes thefunny man. Come on here, you young sneak," headded, addressing himself to Tom, "and we'll settleour accounts."

"Tom," whispered Harry earnestly, "let's run;those fellows with him wont let me or

Willie helpyou; and Green has been acting like a bully sincehe's come back from vacation."

"I'm not going to run, unless I've got to," answeredTom; and he walked straight on, intending to passby Green and his following. But Green put himselfsquarely in the trio's path.

"Where are you going, funny man?" he inquired.

"I'm going to St. Maure's this year. How's yourshin ?"

"You've got to fight me, you sneak," pursuedGreen, reddening with anger at the retort.

"But I don't want to fight, you see."

" I don't care a cent what you want. Put up yourhands. I'll teach you to sass me. You can't getout of it!"

" Can't I though ? Catch me," and as Tom spokehe dashed away in the direction of Pawnee Creek.

It took some seconds for Green to realize this sud-den and utterly unexpected change of front; thenwith a shout of wrath he gave chase.

Before leaving home, it may be explained, Tomhad made a solemn promise to his Aunt Meadow notto engage at fisticuffs under any circumstances.

He was a good runner for his age; but he lackedthe speed of his older and longer-legged pursuer.Although he had obtained a start of some twenty-fiveor thirty feet, he perceived presently that he was los-ing ground rapidly. For all that the serenity habit-ual to his chubby face did not diminish one whit;and as he turned his head from time to time to makea reconnoissance, his expression was as tranquil asthough he were racing for amusement.

The scene was an interesting one. Tom was fol-lowed by Harry and Willie, while Green was cheeredon by his three cronies, who were also hot in pur-suit.

Before Tom had got clear of the " Blue-grass"trees, he saw that he was sure of being captured, un-less he could introduce some new feature into hisflight. His invention did not fail him. Suddenlyhe wheeled sharply, and, assisted by a tree which he

caught hold of, turned at aright angle to his formerline of retreat.

In nimbleness Green could not compare with Tom;

•

and so, before he could adjust himself to the change,our hero obtained a new lease of flight. All werenow speeding towards the line of low bluffs whichfronted the" Blue-grass," and divided it off from theprairie land beyond.

But it seemed quite evident that Tom could nothold out long enough to gain the bluffs.

Nearer and nearer panted Green. ' He was com-ing along in short pants," Harry Quip subsequentlyremarked to some of his schoolmates; who rousedhis indignation and cut short his narrative with theirlaughter over his remarkable bull—in his case, orig-inal. Well—nearer and nearer came the pursuer.The interval between the two was scarcely twelvefeet.

"You're gone, Tom!" cried Harry.

" It's no use," added Willie Ruthers, as he ceasedrunning, "you can't get away."

Tom was now within twenty yards of the bluff,while his pursuer was but six or seven feet behind.Suddenly Tom came to a full stop, turned, and ashis pursuer shot on, whisked aside, and put out hisfoot.

Green took the foot offered him, and went right on,not as a runner, but more after the manner of a fly-ing squirrel. He came down all-fours on a soft bankof earth, and in no wise injured picked himself up.

But before he was well on his feet, Harry Quiphad come to the rescue with a suggestion.

"Tom, Tom!" he cried, running, as he spoke, at anangle toward the bluff, "run this way for all you're

worth. We're near Keenan's cave; and if we canmake it, we'll bar them out."

Long before Harry had ceased speaking, Tom wasmaking for this prospective sanctuary. The cave inquestion was fronted by a rough, clumsy, woodenstructure, in general appearance not unlike a storm-door.

Tom's eyes grew brighter. He felt sure of him-self now. Once within the cave, Harry, Willie, andhimself might bid defiance to all outside.

Nearer and nearer loomed the cave; one hundredand fifty feet more, and all was well. Green wasfar behind, and was not running as at first.

But alas! as Tom with his eyes fixed on the refugewas making bravely on, he struck his foot against astone and fell violently to the ground. It was anugly fall. But Green did not pause to make any in-quiries. Throwing himself upon Tom, he proceededto strike him blow after blow upon the partially up-turned face.

In falling, Tom had incurred an ugly cut on thehead. The pain was intense; more than enough tobear without the savage attacks of Green.

' Give up—will you?" roared the young savage.

'Give up what?" groaned Tom, who, dizzy andweak and suffering as he was, could not take histormentor seriously.

The bully continued his brutal work. Tom's con-dition was becoming serious. Harry and Willie,who had attempted to come to his assistance, wereforcibly held back by Pitch and his companions.

'Now will you give up?" asked Green, againpausing.

Tom felt that he was fainting; lights flickered

It

u

fore his eyes, strange noises rang in his ears;—forall that he had no idea of " giving up." Summoningall his strength, he said, almost in his natural tones:—I think you asked me that before."Well, I'll punch you so's you wont know your-self next time—"

Green never finished his speech; a vigorous jerkat this juncture brought his jaws together with asnap, and sent him to grass with almost lightning-like rapidity.

George Keenan stood over him. But even whe'ireleased, Tom made no move; he had fainted.

' Quip!" cried Keenan, " run over to our cave andget some water—quick!—Look at that, you low-livedbully," he continued, addressing Green. "Do yousee what you've done?" And as George spoke heseized the terrified boy by the collar, and shook himwith the energy of boiling indignation.

' He wouldn't give up," howled Green.

"Ugh!" growled George, casting an anxious lookat the pallid face of Tom. " If I had nothing betterto do, I'd be glad to spend my life in shaking youup. That's it, Harry," he continued, as Quip witha jug of water bent over Tom, " throw it over hisface; he'll be all right in a moment."

George seemed to be quite absent-minded. Withhis eyes fixed anxiously on Tom, his hands and armswere working to and fro with such energy that it wasimpossible to say where

Green's head was at anygiven moment.

He made no pause even, when, a second later,Tom's face twitched.

"Hurrah! he's comin' to!" cried WillieRuthers,who had just thrown open Tom's collar.

Willie was right. Tom opened his eyes; then withan effort raised himself on his arm. He gazed abouthim in a dazed manner, till his eyes fixed upon thetear-stained face of Harry Quip. He brightened atonce, put his hand in his pocket, and said:—

' Here, Harry, take some candy." And Tom arose,feeble but smiling.

'Green," said George, "before I let you go, youmust beg this boy's pardon."

"I'll not."

' You wont—eh ?" and George annotated this re-mark with a shake.

'Ow! stop! Yes! I beg your pardon."

'Much obliged," said Tom seriously.

'Now," continued George, "I want you to prom-ise me not to interfere with smaller boys. Do youhear? We want no bullies this year."

"Oh yes!" cried Green, now shaken into a ball.' I promise, upon my word. Oh, George, please letme go."

George acceded to this earnest request, and Greenhastened away to rejoin his friends, who, at the firstapproach of danger, had fled.

Morally speaking, Tom had won the fight.

CHAPTER VII.

IN WHICH TOM USURPS MINOR ORDERS WITH STARTLING RESUL TS.

ONE Sunday morning toward the end of Septem-ber, the president preached a sermon to thestudents, taking for his subject our Lord's castingout of the devils. He proceeded to show how

Church has established certain forms of prayer, calledexorcism, for the casting out of unclean spirits; andhe dwelt at some length on the pitiable condition ofa soul possessed by the evil one.

Then, turning to the allegorical side of the sub-ject, he declared that perhaps there were in that verystudents' chapel some who were in the toils of Satan;some who were profane, impure, unjust; some whohad blackened their souls with mortal sin, and drivenout the Holy Spirit from His proper temple.

So engaging was the style, so impressive the man-ner of the speaker, that all listened with eager atten-tion. But no one was more interested than TomPlayfair. That young gentleman, it must be con-fessed, had scarcely ever heard a sermon during thedecade of years that summed up his life. What lit-tle knowledge he had of his religion had been gleanedfrom an occasional flash of attention to his aunt's ex-hortations. Hence it is not surprising that Tom didnot fully take in the speaker's remarks; it is notsurprising that he confounded fact with fancy, theliteral with the figurative.

Mass over, Tom remained in the chapel, and pro-ceeded to make a careful examination of all theprayer-books scattered about on the benches. Atlength the gratified expression which came upon hiscountenance evinced that he had found what he de-sired. Gravely seating himself, he read and pon-dered, pondered and read. Finally seeming to besatisfied with his researches, he closed the book andhurried away to the yard, where he at once soughtout his three confidants, Harry, Willie, and Joe.

" I say," began Tom, " take some candy." Candywas Tom's pipe of peace. All accepted the peace-

offering, whereupon the young chief unfolded hisideas in the following conversation:—

'I say, did you fellows mind what the presidentsaid at Mass?"

"Yes; what about it?" inquired Harry.

'Why, just this,—one of the boys in this yard ispossessed by the devil."

'What!" exclaimed all in a breath.

'That is just what," returned Tom, in a decidedmanner. ' Didn't he say that any one who cursesand acts vile is possessed by the devil ?"

"That's so," assented Willie.

" Now, boys, I ask you—what fellow in the yardis it who curses and talks vile?"

"John Green," put in Harry.

"John Green," echoed Willie.

"Just so," added Joe.

"Well, now," resumed Tom, "'I've been lookingthis thing up, and I guess we must— what's thatword the President used ?"

"Exercise," suggested Willie.

"7'hat's just it; we must exercise him."

" Chase him round the yard or something of thatsort," said Joe, imparting to his voice a tone half ofsuggestion, and half of inquiry.

Tom rewarded this remark with a glance whichwas almost severe.

"Joe," he said, reproachfully, "exercise is some-thing religious, and you oughtn't to talk that way.To exercise means to drive the devil out, and that'swhat we're going to do for Green."

" But seems to me," observed Harry, the best theo-logian of these youths, " we ought to get a priest todo it,"

"I've thought of that, too," answered Tom, withan impressiveness which carried confidence. ' Butyou see here's the trouble; no fellow likes to giveanother fellow away. And if we told a priest, we'dhave to say all the bad things we know about Green.Anyhow, we can try our hands first, and if our pray-ing don't do good, we can get a priest at it."

Strangely enough, these three boys began to lookupon Tom's proposition in a serious light. Our herohad a boyish eloquence which persuaded where it didnot prove. Had any other student of the yard madethis proposal, Harry Quip would have laughed himinto silence; but Tom was a born leader.

" Well, how are we to go about it ?" inquired Willie.

"I'll tell you," answered Tom. 'Fasting andprayers is what does it."

"Fasting?" echoed Joe.

"Yes; wre must go without supper to-night."

The members of the little band looked at eachother doubtfully.

"It's got to be done," said Tom, with decision." I read about it in a prayer-book."

" And what else ?" asked Harry.

"Then we've got to pray over him."

The prospect of these duties was inducing a feelingof awe upon all.

"What will we say, Tom?" whispered Willie.

" That's just the trouble; it's got to be in Latin,'cause I saw in the prayer-book a lot of Latin prayersthey use for exercising."

"Whew!" exclaimed Harry. "We can't get overthat."

" Yes, we can," said the ever-ready Tom. " There'sa lot of Latin hymns at the encl of my prayer-book,

and I'll practise saying them during the day. Then,when I read them out loud, all you fellows need dois to answer, ^ Amen.'

"We can do that easy enough," assented Harry." But when is all this to come off?"

"That's another thing I've settled," Tom madeanswer. "At twelve o'clock to-night. You needn'tlook so scared. I'll keep awake till twelve, andthen I'll call you fellows. You see, we must prayover him; and when he is lying in bed, we can do itas easy as not. I'll stand at his head reading theverses, and you three be ready to grab him, if hewakes, so as to make him behave while he's gettingexercised."

" Oh, Tom!" suddenly exclaimed the ingenious Joe." How can you read at twelve o'clock without alight?"

For the first time during the proceedings Tom wasnonplussed. The question of illumination had notoccurred to him.

" Gracious! I didn't think of that. Let's all tryand get up some scheme."

"Halloa! I'll tell you what!" cried Harry tri-umphantly, breaking in upon the silence which hadensued: "we can get some candlesticks out of thesacristy."

"You're a jewel, Harry!" exclaimed Tom, enthusi-astically. "That'll make it more religious-like,still."

"What's the matter with a few surplices?" askedWillie.

"I don't know," mused Tom. 'Do you think itwould make the thing more piouser?"

"Qf course," rejoined Harry,

"Then we'll get surplices, too; and, Harry, I'llleave all that to you, because you know more aboutthe sacristy than I do. Get 'em at last recess to-night. Hide the candlesticks behind the door goingup to the dormitory. Each boy can keep his surpliceunder his pillow. Now, don't speak about this affair,and we'll put it through in style."

At supper that evening four little boys took noth-ing; and before retiring Harry procured candles andsurplices, and bestowed them according to direc-tions.

As Tom slipped into bed he felt confident of suc-cess. Indeed, he found less difficulty in keepingawake than might have been expected. With hiseyes fixed on the presiding prefect, Mr. Middleton,he watched anxiously to see him retire. But Mr.Middleton sat at his desk, calmly reading, till a coldperspiration came upon Tom, who feared the prefectmight stay up all night. Finally, to Tom's greatrelief, the prefect arose and set about preparing forbed; but before retiring he knelt beside his bed, andkept this position for an interminably long time, asit seemed to Tom.

"Pshaw," growled the impatient sentinel; 'thisisn't the time to pray. He ought to do that whenthe boys are awake instead of watching 'em."

At length Mr. Middleton did go to bed, and therewas silence for an hour. Then arose Tom, donnedhis garments, and, tiptoeing from bed to bed, arousedhis fellow-conspirators.

All dressed, they stole noiselessly out of thedormitory. Presently a solemn procession enters.Tom, surpliced, and with prayer-book, at the head,followed by his three friends, each bearing a lighted

candle. Solemn and silent they range themselvesround the bed of the unconscious victim.

"Don't touch him," whispered Tom, "unless hewakes. But if he does, grab him, and hold himdown till I'm done expelling the devil out."

"What if he shouts?" asked Joe.

"He wont shout," said Harry; "I'll see that he'squiet."

" Very well," said Tom. " Now, are you all ready ?"

General assent.

"All right; here goes:

4 Dies ine, dies ilia,Solvet sseclum in favilla,Teste David cum Sibylla.'

i n

Here Tom looked up from his book. Generalsilence.

"Answer, will you—it's the end of the verse."

"A—men," came the solemn answer. The sleep-ing innocent did not appear to be affected in theleast.

Tom went on:

1'' Quantus tremor est futurus,Quando Judex est venturus,Cuncta stricte discussurus.'"

"Amen" was the prompt response. Green moveduneasily, and gave a groan.

"Go on, Tom, it's fetching him," observed Harrygravely.

"Oh!" cried Joe, "maybe it's the devil comingout. Do you think he'll hurt us?"

"Not if we behave properly," said Tom, thoughhe paled a little. "Come on, now. Here's onethat's got a sound to it:

' Tuba mirum spargens sonumPer sepulchra regionumCoget omnes ante thronum."

"Amen."

Green moved and groaned again.

"Grab him boys; he's waking!" exclaimed Tom.

As Green opened his eyes to find himself in theclutches of four white-robed figures, his terror knewno bounds. "What's the matter?" he gasped. "AmI dead ?"

"No; but you will be," answered Tom, "if youdon't lie still. Keep quiet, you goose, while youare being exercised."

Green's terror, now that he came to appreciate thesituation, fast gave way to rage. He attempted tocry out, whereupon Harry Quip promptly stuffed atowel into his mouth. Green was a strong lad; andhe made violent struggles to escape from the graspof his persecutors. But his efforts seemed to beunavailing.

Suddenly there was a great crash. The bed hadcome to pieces. Panic stricken, Joe, Harry, andWillie rushed from the dormitory. Quick as thought,Tom extinguished the lighted candles, which thedeserters had left on the field, and with a skip and abound tucked himself snugly in his bed.

Nor was he too quick. Mr. Middleton, oncomingto the scene of action, found Green standing besidehis dismantled bed, looking the embodiment of guilt.

" Take that vacant bed over there, Green, and we'llsettle this matter in the morning."

But, sir—" remonstrated the innocent victim—but, sir—"

"That'll do now; go to bed."

«

u

And Mr. Middleton, glancing about the dormitory,took down the names of the absentees.

Next morning Tom confessed the whole affair,taking all the blame upon his own shoulders. Mr. Middleton was secretly amused at Tom's ideas of diabolical possession; none the less, he kept that young gentleman very busy for some time commit-ting lines to memory; and with this exercise termi-nated Tom's career as an exorcist.

CHAPTER VIII.

IN WHICH TOM GETS INTO MANY DIFFICULTIES, AND HOLDS AN ASTONISHING INTERVIEW WITH MR. MIDDLETON.

TOM'S first five or six weeks at St. Maure's, like the course of true love in fable and history, did not run smooth. His troubles, some of which we have narrated, were not confined to the yard alone. They followed him into the class-room.

Tom thought, like many other students, that he would pick up the class matter by easy studying. But on this point his professor did not agree with him.

It must be confessed, too, that Tom was at times overbold in his manner of deporting himself in the class-room.

On one occasion, Mr. Middleton put himself to much trouble to explain a long and complicated sum in fractions. He went over the problem step by step in such wise that no one not absolutely feather-brained could fail of following the process. Mr.

Middleton was the soul of earnestness in teaching; and so at the end of half an hour's explanation he was covered with chalk, while beads of perspiration—it was by no means a warm day—stood out upon his brow.

" Now, boys," he said, turning full upon the class, "do you understand it all?" The head of each and every boy nodded assent. Suddenly a hand went up. It was Tom's.

"Well, Playfair?"

"Yes, sir," said Tom soberly.

Mr. Middleton was puzzled.

"What do you mean, Playfair?"

"I understand it, sir."

Mr. Middleton smiled; there was a slight titter among the more thoughtless boys; yet somehow Tom felt that he was out of order; he was sensible in a dim way that Mr. Middleton's smile carried a reproof with it. But the words had been spoken, and were beyond recall.

A day or two later, Mr. Middleton was hearing recitations. Alexander Jones was called upon to answer some questions on the geography of Vermont.

"What is the nature of the land, Jones?" asked Mr. Middleton in a kindly manner.

Jones arose, one quivering bundle of nerves, his eyebrows twitching, his knees bending under him, his lips quivering, and his fingers in a fury of motion. He grew intensely pale and gave several gasps.

Mr. Middleton, with a few encouraging words, repeated the question.

"It's a con-continent," gasped Jones.

"I'm afraid you didn't catch my question," said

Mr. Middleton. "Now don't be afraid. I'm sure

you know it. Listen; what is the nature of the land ? Is it rocky, or mountainous, or sandy, or what?

Poor Jones gasped again, but gave no answer. Here Tom (who knew nothing about the lesson) came bravely to the rescue. He was seated just behind Jones.

'It's mountainous," he whispered. 'It's m—mountainous," Jones stammered. 'Yes," said Mr.

Middleton, as if expecting more."Go on," growled Tom, "and tell him it'srocky."

'It's rocky," repeated Jones.But even this answer did not seem to satisfy Mr.Middleton.

'Tell him it's sandy," continued the prompter."It's—it's sandy."

But Mr. Middleton, for some unknown reason,failed to come to the rescue of the hapless boy. Hestill waited.

' Hang it," growled Tom, unwittingly speaking soloud as to be heard by the professor and the entireclass, " tell him it's very mountainous, very rocky,and very sandy."

" It's very mountainous, very rocky, and verysandy," blurted forth Jones, and as a burst of laughtersaluted his remark he sank back into his seat misera-bly conscious that he had cut a very ridiculous figure."Playfair, after class," said Mr. Middleton sen-tentiously.

"I didn't do anything," exclaimed Tom with vir-tuous indignation.

But the professor very wisely ignored this dis-claimer, and continued the recitation.

In consequence, then, of bad conduct and faulty

TOM PLAYFA1R. 83

recitations, it was not an uncommon sight after classto see our little friend, book in hand, patrolling theyard, endeavoring to make up at the eleventh hourwhat he had failed in at the first. And so, naturallyenough, Tom came gradually to imbibe a disgust forstudy and class-work, which in the course of threeor four weeks culminated in an almost entire neglectof studies. Tom felt in his heart that he was actingwrong; but he was a thoughtless boy, and his senseof responsibility was but poorly developed. Yet herealized with growing unhappiness that, should hecontinue in his present courses, he would soon be atthe foot of the class.

Mr. Middleton, indeed, had no trouble in diviningthe state of Tom's mind; but he resolved to wait tillsome favorable opportunity should present itself forturning the pupil from his ill-chosen path. The op-portunity soon came. An incident in the yard broughtit about.

It was a gloomy morning in early autumn. Tomwas straggling along moodily from the refectorytowards the yard, when he perceived lying upon theground two ready-made cigarettes, dropped, probably,by one of the senior students in the rush and shockof a game of foot-ball. Quickly picking them up,he hurried to his yard and sought Harry Quip. Tomwas rather out of spirits on this morning—he wastotally unprepared in lessons, and he looked forwardwith unpleasant feelings to the day's recitations.There was unhappiness awaiting him in the line ofduty. He would seek happiness in the line ofmischief.

He found Harry without difficulty, and drew himaside.

84 TOM PLAYFAIR.

"Look here, Harry," and Tom produced the twocigarettes, "what do you say to a smoke?"

' Halloa! what's up now ?" Harry exclaimed. " Onthe road here you told me you didn't care aboutsmoking, and I liked what you said first-rate."

"Yes; but just for fun," pleaded Tom.

Harry placed his hand affectionately on Tom'sshoulder, and with his honest face and eyes beamingearnestness, said:—

'Tom, old fellow, I'm afraid you're going wrong—just a little bit, you know. Of course there'snothing bad about smoking—but—but—well, I aintno philosopher, but it's so anyhow."

This speech was incoherent enough. Harry hadendeavored to tell the truth and at the same timespare the feelings of his " partner." But honest wordsare more than grammar and rhetoric; and long, longafter, the sympathetic face and kindly voice of Harryhaunted Tom, and helped him in the path of duty.

But at the moment he was in no mood to be softened.He added in extenuation:—

'You see, Harry, I've got to do something or I'lldie. Come on and take a few puffs."

"Nixie," responded Harry, shaking his head andgrinning, "and I tell you what, Tom, don't you getin with the smokers on the sly. It doesn't pay."

Seeing Harry's determination to behave well, Tomrespected it; and forthwith sought in his stead anold and tried smoker, John Pitch.

' You're just the fellow I wanted to see!" exclaimedJohn Pitch enthusiastically, when Tom had made hisproposition. 'You see the old church-building?Come on over to that corner between the walls of thehand-ball alley. It's a safe place now. Mr. Middle-

ton is taking his breakfast, and Mr. Phelan has tostay in the playroom—and I've got any amount ofmatches."

" Now," resumed Johnny a few seconds later, whenthey had nestled close together in the corner, " unlessyou want to get caught, don't blow your smoke outahead of you, so's it can be seen. Every time youtake a puff, turn your head round this way, and blowit here right through this chink into the old church.It's a great trick; I found it out myself."

Tom gave audible approbation to this advice, andproceeded to carry it out to the letter; and for someminutes the two smoked in silence.

"Isn't it immense?" John at length inquired.

" Isn't it though ?" answered Tom, repressing acough.

"Say," resumed John, a moment later, "can youmake the smoke come out of your nose?"

"Oh! that's nothing," responded Tom; and heexecuted the required feat.

"You can't inhale—can you?" pursued John.

"Of course I can, if I want to; but I don't caremuch about it."

"Well, I'll tell you what you can't do; you can'ttalk with smoke inside of you and then blow it outafter you're through talking."

"Neither can you."

"I'll bet lean."

"Let's see you do it, then!" exclaimed Tom withincreasing animation.

In answer to this, John gravely inhaled a mouth-ful of smoke; then said:—

"See! that's the way to do the thing," and blewit forth.

86 TOM PLAYFAIR.

"Gracious, out that's immense. I want to learnthat trick too; let's see you do it again."

Both were now absorbed—Tom, cigarette in hand,intently eyeing John; and John, cigarette in mouth,determined to heighten his disciple's admiration.

John now took two or three vigorous puffs, theninhaled the triple instalment.

Just at this most interesting juncture, Tom's quickear caught the sound of approaching footsteps.

'* Caz>e, look out," he whispered, and as he spokehe dropped his cigarette by his side and crushed itunder his foot.

But John was not so quick, his lungs were stillfilled with smoke, and his cigarette was still in hishand, as Mr. Middleton, the terror of smokers, turnedthe corner. But the young rogue was not withoutresource; he and his companion, as has been said,were nestled together, and the open pocket in Tom'ssailor-jacket was convenient to the hand in whichJohn was holding the cigarette. There was no re-sisting the temptation. Deftly, quietly, he droppedthe burning cigarette into the yawning pocket. Un-conscious of this, Tom, with his eyes full upon Mr.Middleton, was inwardly congratulating himself uponhis lucky escape. Not so John. Although free ofthe tell-tale cigarette, it could hardly be said that hewas in a happy frame of mind. The smoke withinhim imperatively demanded an outlet; and therestood Mr. Middleton, confronting him with the evident intention of opening a conversation.

"Good morning, boys," the prefect began.

"Good morning, Mr. Middleton," answered Tom,Who, aware of John's predicament, was resolved todo the talking for both.

"There's a strange smell about here," continuedthe prefect, with a peculiar smiie.

"Yes, sir, there is," returned Tom gravely. 'Iwonder if there arn't some skunks in this old build-ing. Some of the old fellows says there are."

" I hardly think it a skunk. But what's the mat-ter with you, Johnny? are you ill?"

The question was pertinent. John was now in apartial state of suffocation, his eyes were bulgingout of his head, his mouth was closed tight, and hischeeks were puffed out as though he were a cornet-player executing a high and difficult note.

It is superfluous to add, then, that John returnedno answer. Tom made an awkward attempt to divertMr. Middleton's attention. A number of boys hadjust issued from the play-room; Tom made the mostof it.

"Oh! Mr. Middleton, what's that crowd of boysoutside the play-room up to? Looks as if there'sgoing to be a fight or something."

"Johnny, you must tell me what ails you;" andMr. Middleton, regardless of Tom's eager remark,fixed his penetrating eyes on John.

A moment of painful silence followed.

One moment and the victim of asphyxiation couldhold in no longer—a gasp and a choke, and out camethe smoke.

"Dear me! you appear to be on fire inside,"remarked the prefect.

" I guess you're pretty sick, Johnny," put in Tom,becoming bolder under stress of desperation. ;< Any-how I hope it aint catching. I've been sittingalongside of—"

He finished this interesting address with a shriek

of pain, as he suddenly jumped to his feet and clappedboth hands to his bosom—smoke was streaming fromhis pocket.

'It looks as if it was catching," remarked Mr.Middleton. "You are on fire outside."

With some rubbing and slapping—accompaniedby a round of hopping and wriggling—Tom savedhis jacket pocket from utter destruction; then as hegrew calmer he threw a reproachful eye upon John.

With a smile the prefect walked away, leavingthem to conjecture the nature and extent of theirpunishment.

During six o'clock studies that evening, Tom wassummoned to the room of Mr. Middleton.

'Well, Tom," began the prefect when the culprithad presented himself, " how are you getting on ?"

Tom became lost in the contemplation of his feet.'Take a seat," continued Mr. Middleton, indicat-ing a chair. ' I want to have a talk with you. Now,my boy,"he resumed when Tom had seated himself," I have had a good chance to watch you in class andin the yard, for some weeks, and I have come to theconclusion that you are a very stubborn boy. Isn'tthat so ?"

"Yes, sir," said Tom mildly.

'You don't seem to mind anything I tell you.Day after day, it's the same old story, bad lessons,careless exercises, and then when I call you to ac-count, your manner shows that you have little or nointention of doing better. Do you deny that?"

'No, sir," answered Tom, beginning to feel veryuncomfortable and very wicked.

" And don't you think that a stubborn dispositionis a bad thing for a little boy ?"

"Yes, sir."

"Well, I don't," said Mr. Middleton.

'You don't!" exclaimed Tom in surprise.

:' Not entirely. Columbus, Washington, St. FrancisXavier were in a sense stubborn men. Indeed, I thinkall truly great men must have a fair share of stub-bornness in their composition.

Tom's face betrayed no less astonishment thaninterest.

'Columbus," continued Mr. Middleton, "by stub-bornly clinging to one idea in spite of rebuffs anddisappointment, discovered a new world. Washing-ton in the face of most disheartening difficulties—difficulties from friends and from foes—held to hispurpose, and created a nation. If Columbus had notbeen stubborn he would have given in; and Americamight have been undiscovered for years and yearsafter his death; if Washington had been less stub-born, perhaps our country might have never achievedher freedom. Did you ever read the life of St.Francis Xavier?"

' I don't read pious books very often, sir."

'Well, he was just such another man—stubbornas could be. When he was a young student nothingwould satisfy him but to become a great philosopher.So he studied away, week after week, year after year,till he became one of the learned doctors of his age.Then when St. Ignatius converted him, he becamejust as stubborn in converting souls .to God, as hehad before been stubborn in acquiring philosophy.Nothing could divert him from his new work. Labor,pain, hunger, abandonment of home and friends—allwere bravely endured to this end; and Francis Xavierbecame the great apostle of modern times."

90 TOM PLA YFAIR.

"Well, it seems to me, Mr. Middleton, that if stub-bornness were a good thing, it wouldn't make a boyact wrong."

"Oh, it may," answered Mr. Middleton with asmile, " if it be misused. Isn't bread a good thing ?"

"Yes, sir."

" But it wouldn't be good if you were to pave thestreets with it. Stubbornness is good too, but onlywhen used the right way. Stubbornness is merelythe sign of a strong will—a strong determination.If you exert your stubborn strength of will to doingwhat is good, you are all the better and nobler foryour stubbornness. But if you exert it for a badpurpose, then you are so much the worse. And whata pity it is that boys misuse so good a gift of God!Why, my dear boy, I have known not a few collegestudents who bent all their energies to getting offtheir lessons without being punished, and who withthe same energy might have acquired such an educa-tion as would have reflected honor on themselves.And you too, Tom, must guard against misapplyingthis energy, this determination, this perseverance,this stubbornness—you see it has many names—towrong purposes. It is a gift to you from God Him-self; and you must show your gratitude by using thegift aright. Do you remember when Green attackedyou, how steadfastly you bore his blows till youfainted?"

"I guess I do."

'You were determined not to give in. Now takeyour lessons the same way. Don't let trouble, weari-ness, memory-work scare you; just hold on tight toyour lessons. Never give in or yield to them; make them yield to you. Then, indeed, you will see that

your stubbornness is a gift of the good God. By the way, you intend making your First Communion this year, don't you?"

"Yes, sir; I'm awful anxious to make it. I'm going on eleven, sir,"—here the boy's lips quivered, and he caught his breath—"and—and—well, when-ever I think of Holy Communion, I—eh—think of my mamma, sir. She died when I was only seven. But I remember how she was always speaking to me about my making a good First Communion."

Whilst speaking these words, Tom repeatedly shifted from one foot to the other. This was his expression of strong emotion. And he had reason to be affected. For, as he spoke, the sweet, pure face of his departed mother came back vividly to his memory, and while her deep, dark, tender eyes kindled into love, her lips moved in a last prayer for the weeping child whom she strained in a dying clasp to her bosom; moved in a prayer that Mary the Virgin Mother might guide the ways of her dar-ling son. Then the strain relaxed, the sweet eyes closed, a shadow seemed to pass over the pallid face, and, as he covered the stilled features with kisses, he knew that his mamma was with God. Poor mother-less boy!

Mr. Middleton was touched. From Tom's halting words and shifting of position he had caught some glimpse of the little lad's heart.

"In general," said the prefect quite gently, ;<a boy is a great loser if his mamma dies before he grows up. The reason often is that he forgets. But you do not forget, Tom."

"Sometimes I do, Mr. Middleton; I've been for-getting a heap more than I ought to."

"Well, Tom, I have great confidence in you."

Mr. Middleton said these words in a tone so im-pressive, so earnest, that Tom felt more and more humbled.

"I haven't done anything to deserve it, sir."

" But you will do much to deserve it, or I am sadly mistaken in you. Now, I'm going to tell you a secret, Tom; but mind you keep it to yourself. Three weeks ago, I received a letter from your father in which he asked me to give him a report of you."

Tom's cheeks lost their color.

'* He said that you had given much trouble at home, that you seemed to be very thoughtless even for your age, and that he doubted strongly about your fitness to make your First Communion this year."

Tom caught his breath.

" And he added that, unless I could assure him that you were giving perfect satisfaction, he would defer your First Communion till you were twelve."

The listener turned away his face and gazed through the open window.

" I answered your father's letter half an hour ago."

'O! I'm a goner, then." Tom's expression was really pathetic.

'* Listen to what I've sent him.

DEAR MR. PLAYFAIR :

In regard to your son's conduct, it is too early in the year to say anything definite. But from the data already afforded me by what I have seen of him in the class-room and in the play-ground, I feel quite certain that he will develop into a thoroughly good and noble boy,

Yours sincerely in Xt.,

FRANCIS MIDDLETON, S. J.

Tom's lips quivered, and a softness came into hisdark eyes; he made no attempt to speak. The firm,noble head bowed low. He could have fallen atMr. Middleton's feet.

"Now, Tom, I'm quite sure that I have not beendeceived in you. Perhaps I was over harsh withyou at first—"

"No, you weren't. Hang it,"blurted forth Tom," if you'd kicked me once or twice, I'd feel better

now.'

Mr. Middleton held out his hand; Tom caught itin a fervent grasp.

" Now my boy, we will forget the past. Take awalk in the yard for a while, and think over what Ihave said. Then make your resolutions carefully,and ask the blessing of the Sacred Heart."

Tom departed, carrying a new range of ideas inhis little brain; up and down the yard he paced,buried in thought. The seed had fallen on goodground. Finally, going to the chapel, he knelt fora long time before the tabernacle and prayed withall the earnestness of his soul, that he might turnover a new leaf. Nor was his prayer unheard; fromthat hour Tom became a more faithful student, amore earnest Christian.

It was twelve of the night, when Harry Quip wasaroused from slumber by a hand which was shakinghim in no gentle manner.

On opening his eyes, he discerned by the dim lightof the dormitory lamp Tom Playfair.

"What's the matter, Tom?"

" I say, Harry, isn't Mr. Middleton a brick ?"

" Oh, go to bed," growled Harry, turning over andburying his face in the pillow.

Tom complied with this sensible advice, and layawake for full three minutes, building golden visionsof the great day now assuredly near at hand.

Ah! if he only knew what difficulties were to arise,and under what tragic circumstances he was to makehis First Communion, I am quite sure that he woulc?have lain awake for at least six minutes.

CHAPTER IX.

IN WHICH TOM CONCLUDES THAT VINEGAR NEVER

CATCHES FLIES.

FOR the ensuing two or three weeks the currentof events at college flowed on with scarcely aripple. Every day Tom seemed to gain new friends.Indeed, with the exception of John Green, he hadnot a single enemy among his playmates; and evenGreen's enmity had grown less demonstrative.

As a fit preparation for his First Communion,Tom had resolved to put himself at peace with thewhole world. He now regretted that he had madea laughing-stock of Green on the occasion of theirfirst meeting; and he was on the alert to do some-thing towards closing the breach between them.

A slight change in the routine of school-life gavehim the desired opportunity.

Towards the end of October, it was found neces-sary to make some repairs in the western corner ofthe small boys' dormitory. In consequence, seven-teen of the students occupying beds in that part wereassigned temporary accommodations in the attic ofthe main building, a structure towering high aboveall its fellows.

It was Wednesday afternoon when Mr. Middletonannounced the names of those who were to changetheir sleeping quarters. Tom, Harry Quip, Alex-ander Jones, John Pitch, Green, and others withwhom our story has not to do, composed this privi-leged number.

To add a zest to the privilege, he allowed thehappy seventeen to explore their improved dormitoryimmediately after class, and very quickly after classthe brick building resounded to the tramp of multi-tudinous feet scampering nimbly up the stairs asthough on a mission of life and death.

"Whoop-la!" cried Tom, as he burst into thegreat room, seamed and ribbed overhead with heavybeams. " It's like the attic of a haunted house,only bigger—isn't it, Green?"

"It's an immense place for fun," responded hiscompanion. "Look at all the corners and hiding-places. We can play 'I spy' here, if we don't feelsleepy."

"Yes," assented Tom, "and at night we mightclimb out on the roof and count the stars. Did youever count the stars, Johnny ?"

"Naw; did you?"

" I tried it one night at home, when I was lying inbed and couldn't sleep. I got as far as fifty-seven,and then I went off sound asleep. But there arelots more than fifty-seven."

"I guess there's over a trillion," said Greenreflectively.

Both felt that their remarks had fairly exhaustedtheir astronomical researches.

" Come on," said Tom, " let's get out on the roof."

As he spoke, he pointed toward a ladder which led

g6 TOM PLA YFAIR.

up to a cupola, rising some seven or eight feet abovethe roof of the building. This cupola gave accessto the roof by means of a small door, which openedat the side and was secured from within by a strongbolt.

Followed by Tom, Green ran up the ladder, shotback the bolt, and made his way upon the roof.

" I'd like to live on a roof," said Tom tranquilly,as he walked over to the eastern verge, and gazeddown upon the yard below.

"Come back, you idiot," cried Green, in what heconsidered his most persuasive accents, "you'll getdizzy and keel over."

"I'll bet I wont," answered Tom. "Don't youthink I've ever been on a roof before? This oneisn't steep like ours, but it's a heap higher. I say,how'd you like to stand on top of that lightningrod?" and Tom motioned with his index fingertoward the tip of a rod, which rose above thecupola.

Green ran over, caught hold of the rod and shookit.

" I wouldn't like it at all, unless I wanted to breakmy neck; it's loose. What'll you bet I can't pullit down?"

'It isn't ours, Johnnie."

"I'd just as soon pull it down as not," continuedGreen. Nevertheless, he relinquished his hold uponit, and turned away.

Tom had occasion to remember this episode sub-sequently, though at the moment both he and Greendismissed the subject so lightly.

Some seven or eight others now found their wayto the roof, and the conversation, made up in great

part of "ohs" and " ahs," had become quite generaland very noisy, when Mr. Middleton appeared andsternly ordered all down.

Tom and Green were the first to descend, followed by the others in Indian file. The last to re-enter shut the door behind him, but neglected to bolt it. The omission passed unnoticed.

' I say, Mr. Middleton, "' observed Tom solemnly,;'I thought you didn't believe in slang."

"Indeed! I wouldn't advise people to use it in ordinary."

'Well, sir, you gave us bad example."

"How?"

"You told us to 'come off thereof,' sir."

And satisfied with his little joke, Tom was about to hurry away, when he was arrested by Mr. Middle-ton's voice.

"Well, sir."

'You'll have to do penance for that joke, Tom. I want four or five willing boys to bring over pil-lows and bedding; the workmen will attend to the beds and mattresses. You might get Quip and Donnel to help you."

"All right, sir; that'll be fun." As Tom spoke, he saw an eager look upon Green's face. " And I say, Mr. Middleton," he added, " can't Johnny Green help us? he's willing."

" Of course," was the cordial answer, accompanied by a kindly look at Johnny.

Poor Green! there was a real, wholesome blush upon his face as he blurted forth some disjointed words of thanks.

'Well," commented Mr. Middleton to himself, as the lads went pattering down the stairs, u that Play-7

fair has unconsciously taught me another lesson. I mustn't forget to notice the hard cases now and then. Unless I'm mistaken, Green will be in a better mood for a week."

'He's a good fellow," Green observed, as they were trotting across the yard.

"Isn't he?" said Tom.

;'And so are you," added Green, growing very red as he spoke.

Tom laughed; he had succeeded. His only enemy was won over.

Tom had brought a diary from home having made a promise on receiving it to write something in it every day. That night at studies, he opened it for the first time, and made this his first entry. It hap-pened to be the last also.

OCT. 3OTH.—Since coming to college I have notised that vini-ger never catches flys. To-day I am eleven years old. This year I am going to make my First Communion. His name is Green. I don't believe there is anything near a trillion stars.

CHAPTER X.

IN WHICH TOM GIVES GREEN A BIT OF ADVICE, WHICH, AIDED BY A STORM, IS NOT WITHOUT ITS EFFECT.

ON the afternoon of the following day, Tom, Harry, and Alexander Jones were engaged in an earnest consultation.

"I don't think he'd allow it," said Harry. "What do you think, Alec?" asked Tom. 'I'd be afraid to ask," responded Alec. 'Well, he can't more than refuse, and I guess I can stand that. Yes, fellows, I'm going to ask."

TOM PLA YFAIR, 99

And without further ado, Tom walked over towards Mr. Middleton, who was acting as umpire in a game of hand-ball between Donnel and Keenan.

'Well, Tom," said the prefect, as he caught the anxious eyes of our hero fixed upon him, " what do you want ?"

'If you please, sir, I'd like permission to take a walk with Harry Quip and Alec Jones."

"Certainly; you are all on the good conduct list. Be back half an hour before supper."

"And, Mr. Middleton, can't Crazy—that is, can't Johnny Green come along with us?"

" He's not on the conduct list. You know the rule."

"Yes, sir; but he hasn't had a chance to go out since the first week of school."

" That's not a sufficient reason for his going out now.'

" But, Mr. Middleton, yesterday you told me you'd make it all right with me for carrying over the bed-clothes and things. Let Green come along, and I can't ask for anything I'd like more. You know, sir, we haven't been friends up to yesterday." And Tom gazed at the prefect wistfully.

"Tom," answered Mr. Middleton, after a few moments of consideration, "please tell Green that I'm very glad to have an excuse for letting him out, and that I hope he'll have all the privileges of the conduct list next month."

"Thanks, Mr. Middleton; I know every word you said just then by heart, and I'll tell it to him exactly as you said it." And touching his cap Tom hurried away.

;'Say, Green, wont you take some candy?" he in-

i* '

v .-

I

quired of that young gentleman, whom he found engaged in furtively carving his name on a corner of the little boys' building.

Green closed his knife very promptly, and accepted the candy with silent enthusiasm.

" How'd you like to take a walk, Green, with me and Quip and Jones?"

"I'd like it well enough to walk with anybody," came the rough answer. '* But I'm not allowed out-side this wretched yard." And Green went on to express his injured feelings in a manner too realistic for reproduction.

' You needn't swear about it anyhow," interrupted Tom, ;'and besides, Mr. Middleton has given you permission."

Green opened his eyes.

"What?" he gasped.

Then Tom repeated Mr. Middleton's message.

'Just my luck," observed Green, gazing ruefully at the letters he had cut. * If he sees those initials I'll lose my conduct-card again. I can't behave, to save myself."

Tom pulled out his own knife, and forthwith began working upon Green's carving.

'There!" he said presently. "If anybody can make J. G. out of that now he'll have to be pretty smart. Come on, Johnnie, and we'll have a fine walk."

Accordingly the four were soon outside the college grounds, an event which Green celebrated by put-ting a huge quid of tobacco into his mouth.

It was a gloomy afternoon. The morning had opened with a black mass of clouds low down upon the eastern horizon. With the progress of the day,

'1

« rr

they had been accumulating and spreading west-ward, growing thicker and blacker in their advance, till nearly half of the firmament was now veiled from the eye.

That's an ugly sky," observed Harry. There's lots of wind in those clouds," added Tom. It looks as though we'd have a big stormto-night."

" So it does," assented Alec, who did little elsein ordinary conversation beyond contributing thescriptural yea and nay.

" I aint afraid of storms," said Green.

'There's nothing wonderful about that," com,mented Tom. "What would you be afraid for?"

;'Some fellows get scared when they hear thethunder," explained Green; 'but I don't mind itone bit."

'I do," said Alec. "When the thunder begins,and I'm in bed, I always put my head under theblankets and pray."

'That's 'cos you're a coward," said Green loftily.' I don't fear going to bed in the dark nor nothin'."

:< In other words," remarked Quip, with a solemnroll of his big eyes, "you aren't afraid of any-thing."

'* Naw—I aint afraid of nothing."

'You're not afraid to blow, that's sure," put inTom, in a matter-of-fact tone. "All the same,Johnnie, I rather think you'd be scared if you knewyou had to die right off."

'I don't know about that," answered Green. ' Idon't expect to go to heaven anyhow."

"You don't?"

' Naw; I gave up trying to be good long ago."

102 TOM PLA YFAIR.

"At least, you might try to make the nine FirstFridays that Father Nelson talked to us about inthe chapel," suggested Tom.

Green stared at him heavily.

"He said, you know," continued Tom, "thatthere's a promise of grace to die well for any fellowthat makes 'em."

"I heard him; but once a month is too often for me.'

'Just think," added Harry Quip, 'to-morrow'sthe first Friday in November. Make a start, Crazy;it wont hurt you to try."

"I guess I'll not begin yet," answered Green, ashe proceeded to roll a cigarette.

"It would please Mr. Middleton a heap," Tomobserved.

'Yes, indeed," put in Alec.

" And it would do you any amount of good," addedTom. " Come on, Johnnie; you sneaked out ofgoing to communion last time the boys went. Youneedn't stare; I had my eyes open, and I saw youdodging. It's my opinion that you've been dodg-ing ever since you came back to college."

" Say, you didn't tell on me, did you ?"

'Not yet," answered Tom diplomatically—he hadnever entertained the idea of reporting Green to theauthorities; "and I wont mention it either. Nowyou'll go to-morrow, wont you?"

There was a short silence.

'Yes," answere Green at length, and speakingwith an effort, ' go."

Making their way ihrough the woods which girdedthe river, they presently arrived at a clearing uponthe bank,

TOM PLA YFAIR. 103

'Isn't it growing dark awful fast?" exclaimedHarry.

'Just look at those clouds; they're beginning to move faster and faster; and they're coming our way too," cried Tom.

4 Let's run home," suggested Green.

Borne on the wings of the storm, the dark masses in the east were advancing gloomily, rapidly, like a marshalled army. The wind which carried them on could be faintly heard, breaking upon the dread silence which had come over the scene round about them, as the ticking of a watch at midnight upon a nerve-shattered invalid.

Fascinated by the sweep of clouds, they stood, these little boys, with their eyes lifted towards the heavens.

"Ah!"

This exclamation which seemed to break from all simultaneously was evoked by a sudden change in the moving panorama. For, as they stood gazing, there dropped from the bosom of these clouds thin, dark veils reaching from earth to sky.

"What is that?" cried Green.

"I don't know, I'm sure," answered Tom. "I never saw anything like that in St. Louis. Maybe it's rain moving this way. Anyhow, the storm'll be on us in a moment. Just look how it's rushing towards us. It's too late to start for the college. Where'll we go to?"

And as they set about answering this question the clouds came nearer and nearer. The whistling of the breeze that one moment before had seemed but to emphasize the silence, had risen to an angry scream.

The four lads, wavering and irresolute, not know-

ing whither they should go for shelter, presented a striking tableau as they paused there in the open.

Tom stood with his legs apart and firmly braced. His hands were clasped behind his back; and with his hat tilted so as to show a shock of thick black hair over his forehead, and his mouth pursed as though he were about to whistle, he raised his eyes in an unblinking gaze upon the angry clouds. Next him was Alec, pale, silent, with an awe-stricken look upon his fair face. He had put his arm through Tom's, and clung to our little friend as a drowning man to a plank. Tom was Alec's hero. Harry Quip was on the other side of Tom, the usual grin still lingering upon his merry face, and his hands thrust deep in his pockets. Green, who stood in advance of these, had become intensely pale.. His fingers were quivering, his breath came in gasps, and he glanced over and over from sky to companions, from companions to sky.

The first drops of rain began to patter about them, while the wind keeping time with the movement of the rain sent the trees before them bowing and sway-ing in a weird dance, all the more weird for the un-natural darkness that had fallen upon all nature.

" Hadn't we better run ?" asked Tom.

'Yes," said Green, eagerly. "Come on."

"I'm afraid, Tom, I can't run," said poor Alec. 'I feel weak and dizzy, and I'm so frightened.'

"Harry and John, go ahead," said Tom. "I'll stay with Alec."

'No you don't, Tom " said Quip. "If you stay, I stay."

;'Come on, Quip," implored Green, "they can look out for themselves,"

"Go on yourself," said Harry, speaking with some asperity. ' You can take care of yourself, if you want to."

'But I don't want to be alone in this storm."

'Then stay here," came the curt answer.

'Halloa!" cried a voice, "why you're smart boysfor your age; you've chosen about the safest placearound here." And John Donnel, out of breath withrunning, emerged from the woods and placed himselfbeside Green.

'We came near running away," said Tom. "Wethought we could run through the woods and findsome house to stay in till the storm blew over. We'remighty glad to see you, John."

' It's lucky you stayed here. If the wind getsany worse the woods will be a dangerous place—fly-ing branches and lightning and what not!"

During this conversation, short as it was, rain andwind had grown worse.

'Ugh! we'll be drenched to the skin,"said Tom."Why, halloa!" he added, "Alec is sick."

Alec had pillowed his face on Tom's bosom, andbefore the exclamation was well out of Tom's mouth,the poor child fainted.

"Here, give me the boy," shouted Donnel (shout-ing had now become necessary as the ordinary toneof conversation). "I'll fix him in a trice." AndJohn, as he spoke, too4c Alec in his arms, carriedhim to a soft bit of earth, and depositing him gently,threw open his collar.

'Halloa, Green, what's the matter ?" bawled Tom,attracted by the strange motions of the frightenedboy.

"I can't stand here; I've got to run," came theanswer.

Donnel raised his face.

"Stay where you are," he said sternly; "if youwant to die young, run through those woods."

As he ceased speaking, there came a dazzlingflash of lightning, followed almost instantaneouslyby a terrific clap of thunder.

With a wild cry, Green dashed for the woods.

"Stop him, Tom," cried Donnel, jumping to hisfeet, "stop him; he's lost his wits."

Donnel, though many yards in the rear of both,had set forward in hot pursuit. As for Tom, hescarcely needed Donnel's bidding. Green had notfairly made a start when Tom was at his heels.

Terror, they say, lends speed. But poor Greenseemed to be an exception to this as to many otherrules. He slipped several times, and once was withina little of losing his balance and falling to the earth.Indeed it seemed as though Tom, who was runningat his best, would catch him before he reached thewoods. But as Green drew nearer the dangerousshelter, he regained something of his customaryspeed; and Tom, who had thus far gained upon him,began to lose his advantage; Donnel, meanwhile,was lessening the distance between himself and Tomat every step.

At length Green, in passing a tree that stood likea sentinel, guarding the main body of the woods,slipped again, and before he could well recover him-self, Tom had come within five feet of him. Then,just as the thoroughly frantic boy broke into hisregular speed, Tom sprang into the air, alighted onGreen's back, and bor>* him to the ground.

And while they were still rolling upon the drenchedsarth, there was a sharp crack, like the report of apistol discharged at one's ear, a strange swishingsound, a crash as of many branches beating againsteach other; and, twenty feet before them, there camecrashing to the earth a giant oak. As it fell, a twigstruck Tom in the face.

In an instant, though dazed and bewildered, Tom had sprung to his feet. But Green rose only to his knees; he was quivering with fear and beat his breast.

"Spare me! spare me!" he cried. * I'll go to con-fession this very night."

" G^t up, will you?" bawled John Donnel, his voice rising high above the noises of the elements, as he caught Green by the shoulders, and dragged him to his feet. " If you don't move away from here, you'll not have a chance to make a confession."

•

And without further words, John dragged him back into the open. Tom followed quietly; even his face, :t must be said, had paled a trifle.

And there they stood motionless as statues, silent and awed for two or three minutes; there they stood till in the swiftness of its might the wind had flown by them, till the clouds had moved on to the western horizon, and left the sky above them perfectly clear, till, in fine, the storm had ceased with a suddenness befitting its violence.

" Well, it's over and all is well," said John Donnel.

" I guess we had better run for college, John," put in Tom, "and change our things, or we'll get rheu-matism or small-pox, or something ugly. What's the matter, Green?"

Green pointed a quivering finger at the western Sky.

"It is coming back. Those clouds have stopped moving."

'I guess we can beat 'em," answered Tom. "John, I'm awful glad you came. We'd have lost our heads, if it hadn't been for you. How did you come to be around ?"

" I was hunting for snakes with Keenan, and we got separated; you can rely upon it that George is safe in college by this time. Now boys, for a run home. Are you all right, Alec?"

'Yes, sir," said Alec, who had risen to his feet while the race between Green and Tom had been going on, " but I'm afraid I can't run very fast."

' Here, put your arm through mine," said John.

"And your other arm through mine," added Tom, whose color had fully returned.

In a very short time, indeed, they were changing their garments in the dormitory.

Green uttered not a word till he was about to leave the room. Then he said:—

'Tom, if you hadn't jumped on my back and pulled me over, I'd be dead now. Ugh!"

'Yes," replied Tom, adjusting his tie with more than wonted precision; "and if I hadn't tumbled over with you, I'd have been killed too. I was scared that time, I can tell you. But, of course, you weren't scared." Tom grinned as he waited for an answer.

"Scared! I should think I was. Say, Tom, I was lying to you fellows about my not being afraid."

"You needn't tell us that," said Tom bluntly.

"But I'm going to change; see if I don't." And Green left the dormitory and went straight to the chapel, leaving Tom and Alec alone.

"Well, Alec," began Tom, who divined from the timid lad's face that he wished to say something," do you feel shaken ?"

"A little, Tom. Did you hear what Green said just after the storm?"

"What did he say?"

" He said it was coming back."

"Oh, well! you know he was most scared out of his wits."

" Tom, it is coming back."

" Nonsense."

"Well, I feel as though something were about tohappen. Wont you please pray for me ?"

And Alec caught Tom's hand and gazed into hiscountenance with a sweet pathos inexpressibly touch-ing. A beautiful face it was that met our hero's,nonetheless beautiful for the modesty which nearlyevery minute of the day veiled the eyes, and sentthe blood purpling the pale cheeks. Now, however,Alec's eyes were wide open and fixed, oh, so appeal-ingly, upon Tom's. And Tom, as he returned thegaze, was impressed with something which he couldnot define, but which brought home to him for thefirst time, that he was in the presence of a boy ofextraordinary holiness and purity.

"Why, of course I'll pray for you, if you want meto. What's up ?"

" To-morrow, Tom, I finish making the nine FirstFridays."

"Well, I don't see why you want any prayingfor. I need it bad. I've done a lot of things thatI hadn't ought to."

"Yes; but you've done a lot of good, too. I was

HO TOM PLAY FAIR.

so glad, Tom, when you spoke up to Green. Youknow how to talk."

'That's what I've got a tongue for. But it wasthat falling tree which fetched him. He'll behavedecently for a week, I reckon."

Poor Alec looked as though he would say more;but words and courage failed him. He again caughthis friend's hand, pressed it, then hurried from thedormitory with that indefinable expression whichTom had noticed before.

Tom continued sitting on his bed for somemoments longer.

'I didn't know that Alec Jones," he soliloquizedas he rose. ' I thought he was a little girl, but he'sa mighty good girl anyhow."

And with a grin on his face, he left the dormitory.

CHAPTER XL

THE NIGHT OF THE FIRST FRIDA Y IN NOVEMBER.

IT was ten of the night, and, though so late inthe season, quite warm and extremely oppressive.Above, the clear sky was gemmed with stars. Inthe west hung a thick, black cloud; it had beenmotionless all the day.

There was a hush over the dormitory. The feeblelight of the lamp at the entrance was utterly insuffi-cient to limn the countenances of the slumbererslying beneath the cupola; and so it would have beendifficult for any one to perceive that Tom Playfair,whose bed stood directly beneath the cupola, was

TOM PLAYFAIR. Ill

"wide awake. With the single exception of the nightwhen he undertook to exorcise Green, who, by theway, was now his right-hand neighbor, nothing likethis had ever happened to him before. To his leftlay Alec Jones; beyond him Harry Quip, and, lastof the row, John Pitch. These five were groupedunder and about the cupola. The other occupantswere at the further end of the room, separated fromthis row of five by a space of some thirty odd feet.It will be convenient for the reader to keep thesedetails in mind.

Tom, as I have said, was awake. Perhaps a senseof novelty reconciled him to the situation; for he layvery quiet. The subdued breathing of the sleeperswas the only sound to break the stillness; withoutthe winds were hushed, and no cry of man or birdor beast broke upon the brooding calm of the night.

For fully half an hour, Tom, from their differentmodes of breathing, endeavored to place the varioussleepers. He easily picked out Harry Quip's, and,with more difficulty, John Pitch's. At this pointhe grew weary of this new study, and cast about inhis thoughts for some fresh diversion. It was hardupon eleven o'clock, when he concluded to arise, goto a window, and count the stars.

As he was setting foot upon the floor, a silvery,sweet voice, with a sacred pathos in every tone,broke, or rather glorified, the silence.

'My Jesus, mercy!"

The invocation came from Alec.

Tom bent down and gazed into the dreamer's face.Even with the feeble light, he could perceive linesof terror upon the slight, delicate, innocent features.

With a gentleness which, on recalling the inci-

dent afterwards, surprised Tom himself, he lightlypatted the upturned cheek; and forthwith the facegrew strangely calm; a smile, tender yet so feeblethat the facial muscles scarce changed, passed overit, and from the lips came the whispered, ' SweetHeart of Jesus, be my love."

With his hand still resting on the sleeper's cheek,Tom stood gazing upon the radiant face in muteadmiration.

" Amen," he whispered softly to himself. " If everI get to talking in my sleep, I hope I'll do it thatstyle."

He removed his hand; Alec opened his eyes.'You're all right, Alec," explained Tom, bendinglow so as to whisper into the boy's ear, "You got ahollering in your sleep, and I just passed my handover your cheek. Go to sleep again. Goodnight."And he held out his hand.

"Good night, Tom." And Alec drew his handfrom the coverlet to clasp Tom's, displaying, as hedid so, his rosary twined about the fragile arm.Then very gently Alec fell into a calm slumber.Looking on such a face, it was hard to imagine thatthe world was full of wickedness and sin.

Tom waited till he felt sure that Alec was soundasleep. Then he murmured to himself:'I guess I'll count the stars now."

Walking over a-tiptoe to one of the western win-dows he looked out. He counted no stars that night.For the dismal, black cloud was now in motion, ad-vancing ominously, swiftly, in a direct line towardthe small boy standing in his night-shirt at thewindow.

"Whew!" whistled the would-be star-gazer.

" Green and Alec were right after all. It is comingback."

Even as he spoke, the awful whisper of the ap-proaching storm could be heard; a whisper thatlasted but for a moment, when it changed to a sigh,deepened into a groan, which grew louder, moreviolent, more threatening every second.

'It's getting chilly too," murmured Tom to him-self. ;' I guess I'll hop into my pants."

And very quickly indeed, he was fully dressed—sailor-shirt, knickerbockers, stockings, everythingsave his tie and his shoes—and, with his usual calm-ness, returned to the window to watch and wait uponthe turn of events.

The patter of the rain upon the roof could now bedistinctly heard, while far off from the east came themuffled thunder of some distant storm. In attempt-ing to take another look from the window, Tomhappened to touch a wire fastening for the window-curtain.

"Ouch!" he muttered, withdrawing his hand veryquickly; and perhaps for the first time since hismother's death, he became thoroughly frightened.A queer feeling had passed through his whole body.What could it be ?

There was something wrong about things, and themystery frightened him. He had received a sharpshock; but he knew nothing of electricity.

The beating of the rain, while Tom was still pon-dering, became louder and louder, and the boys be-gan to move uneasily in their beds; many, indeed,were now half awake. The wind, too, was howlingabout the house in a fury of power.

Tom had just reached his bed, when a loud bang-8

ing noise brought every one in the room from theland of sleep; and a gust of rain came sweeping in,thoroughly drenching Tom's bed. Ah! that ne-glected bolt. The door of the cupola had flown open,and was now flapping noisily against the lightning-rod.

As with noisy recurrence it opened and shut, Tomcaught a glimpse of the stars on the clear easternhorizon, and almost directly overhead that black,sinister cloud, hanging like a curse over St. Maure's.

Even while he was taking in this strange aspectof the heavens, the water had formed into severalpools upon the floor. Quip, Jones, Green, and Pitch,all of them with appalled faces, had grouped them-selves beside Tom. No wonder they were alarmed;the frightful banging of the door, coupled with thefierce beat of the sheeted rain, was an overtax onthe nerves of the boldest.

"Oh, Tom!" chattered Green," I'm glad I went toHoly Communion this morning."

;< So'm I," answered Tom. " Say, boys, I'm goingto shut that door, even if I do get a ducking. Good-by." And he made a dash at the ladder.

Unmindful of the rain which almost blinded him,lie succeeded at length in securing a hold on the door.But pull and tug as he might, the wind, now at itsheight, held its own; till at last, in a sudden lull,the door yielded to his efforts.

' Now, if I could only get my hand on thatbolt—"

He never finished this sentence. For as he wasstill groping about for the knob, the wind in a sud-den rise sent the door flying from his grasp. Therewas a sharp, clanging sound, and the dull noise of

some heavy object beating upon the roof; and, as thedoor, torn from its hinges, pulled the lightning-roddown from the cupola, Tom lost his balance, andwas thrown backwards from his perch. Happily forhimself, he was flung upon his bed, whence he rolledto the floor.

Two boys assisted him to rise, and gazed anxiouslyinto his face.

On that occasion Tom, far from being stunned,was unusually awake to every impression. His senseshad become sharpened; and as he rose to his feethe took in the whole scene. At the other end of thedormitory stood huddled together all the boys saveHarry, Pitch, Alec, and Green. The prefect wasjust advancing from the group towards them. Tomcould see all this, for the simple reason that a cas-socked figure—he recognized the President of thecollege—had just entered with a lamp that lightedthe whole room.

The two who had lifted him to his feet were Jonesand Green. Upon the face of Alec there still dweltthat sweet expression, brought from dreamland, butsoftened and beautified in a new way by concern forTom's safety. Green's face had strangely changed.All the roughness had gone out of it. Awe and pity—awe at the storm, pity for Tom—had touched itinto refinement.

All this, I say, Tom took notice of, as they raisedhim to his feet.

"You're not hurt, old fellow, are you?" inquiredGreen earnestly.

"Not a bit."

"Thank God!" murmured Alec.

"I'm glad I went this morning," said Green.

"Tom," said Harry, "we'll help you pull yourbed away."

"Oh, it's no use getting drenched the way I
am.1

"We don't mind that," said Green, and he andAlec sprang forward towards Tom's bed.

They had not taken two steps, when there came adazzling flash of light. Tom fell violently to thefloor, pillowed upon the body of some one who hadfallen before him, where he lay motionless, yet con-scious, and with a feeling as though every muscleand fibre of his body had been wrenched asunder—lay there gazing up into a sky now suddenly brilliantwith stars, into a rainless sky with not a cloud to marits tranquil beauty.

The storm was over.

And as he fell the President's lamp had gone out,and in the dazzling brilliancy of that awful flash hehad seen five boys standing under the cupola goplunging forward violently to the floor, while thesmell as of burnt powder and of ozone pervaded thewhole apartment. Then, almost simultaneously in-deed, came a deafening noise. To the President'sears it sounded like the explosion of a powder mag-azine at his side. But he knew that it was not anexplosion of powder; he knew too well that it wasthe thunder following the lightning flash which hadstricken down his boys before his very eyes; and, inthe dread hush and darkness that followed, the Pres-ident's voice, clear and firm, filled the room withthe words of sacramental absolution, as, raising hishand and making the sign of the cross, he said:—

4' Ego vos absolvo a peccatis vestris in nomine Patriset Filii et Spiritus Sancti. Amen."

TOM PL A YFAIR. 117

' I absolve you from your sins, in the name ofthe Father and of the Son and of the Holy Ghost.Amen."

The presiding prefect had, in the mean time, re-lighted the dormitory lamp (which had also goneout in the shock of the lightning stroke), and wasnow standing beside his superior.

'Boys," continued the latter, who in the dim light
perceived several moving forms, " take your clothes
on your arm, and leave this room quietly, one by
one. Go to the infirmary; the storm is now over,
.and there's not the least danger."

On occasions such as this the panic does not im-mediately follow the catastrophe. Between thetwo there is always a lull—a time when the imagi-nation of each is charging itself with the real-ization of what has passed, with the picturing ofwhat may come. That done, the panic takes itscourse.

The president had taken the right time for speak-ing. Had he lost his head for one moment, therewould have ensued, in all probability, a frightfulscene. But his calmness gained the mastery overall.Quietly, noiselessly, with pitiful faces, the boyspassed down the stairs. How eagerly he countedthem. It was the most trying period of his longlife.

Six passed.

Three more—nine.

Three more—twelve. The last was the prefect.

Then there was a silence.

His senses, then, had not deceived him. Five hadbeen struck by lightning.

He had relighted his lamp, and now hastened to

the other end. Tom, his eyes closed, lay with hishead pillowed upon Green's body; near him AlecJones, calm—so quiet! Beyond was Quip, breath-ing heavily with an ugly gash upon his face. Pitchwas in a sitting posture, murmuring incoherentwords.

'Tom!" cried the President, stooping down, andcatching the boy's hand.

The eyes opened.

'Yes, sir; I'm all right; what's happened?"

The president made a slight gesture, and bent overGreen. No need to listen for the breath that neverwould return. He moved over to Alec Jones, and astifled sob burst from his bosom. Green and Joneshad been instantly killed; had never heard the crashthat followed the dazzling stroke; had been calledsuddenly before that God whom they had receivedat the morning Mass into their bosoms. It was theFirst Friday.

Tom's wet garments had saved him. The elec-tricity had taken its way through his clothes insteadof through himself. But he did not know at themoment that he had passed forth free from the jawsof death; for not one of those now remaining in thedormitory, save the President, was aware that thepower which sent them stunned to the floor was theawful power of the thunderbolt.

CHAPTER XII.

TOM^S MIDNIGHT ADVENTURE.

« TJ ARRY—are you hurt ? "

1 1 Tom was bending over Harry Quip. Butthere came no answer. The president touched Tomlightly on the shoulder.

'Playfair," he said, "can I trust you to keepcool ?"

'Yes, sir! if you just tell me what's happened.There was a queer feeling went through me just now,and something seemed to burn my right leg."

' The house has been struck by lightning, and youreceived a slight shock. Harry Quip got a worseone, and Green and Jones are seriously injured. Youand Pitch might remove Harry to a bed over there;but don't tell him, when he comes to, what's hap-pened to the others, and be sure not to show him along face, or you'll frighten him."

;<Catch hold of his head, Johnny," said Tom.With tender care, they conveyed poor Harry to thenearest bed; while the president, still cherishing afaint hope in his heart, eagerly sought to discoversome signs of life in Green and Jones.

Harry, shortly after being placed upon the bed,gave signs of consciousness.

" Halloa, Harry," cried Tom, forcing a grin.

' Tom!' Harry gave a gasp.

"Yes; it's me; and you're all right, old boy."

" Wh—what's happened ?"

."
,
" An electric machine got loose, or something,plied our ingenious hero, " and spilled itself on topof us. They let you have it at fairs for five cents ahead."

But even this comic view of the situation failed towin a smile from Harry.

" Where's my leg ?' he gasped.

:< Both your legs are screwed on in the right place."

'No: my right leg's gone."

Tom caught the right leg and lifted it into full
vew.'

How does that strike you ? "

"But I don't feel it."

"Well, catch hold of it, then; it won't come off.You gave me an awful kick with it just a momentago."

"I'm choking," continued Harry.

" If you were, you couldn't talk."

"But I can't swallow. Oh! " And Harry lookedmore and more frightened.

" Who the mischief asked you to swallow ? It isn'tbreakfast time yet, and there's nothing to eat roundhere, anyhow."

The infirmarian, who had entered at the beginningof this conversation, and who, having satisfied him-self that Green and Jones were dead, had now cometo Harry's side, here broke in.

"Playfair, we want the doctor at once. Run down-stairs to the room on the next floor where the brotherssleep. They are dressing now to come up here andlend us help. Take the first one you meet, or theone that's nearest dressed, and tell him to hurry offafter the doctor: we want him for Harry Quip."

Waiting for no. second bidding, Tom, followed by

Pitch, hurried from the dormitory. Luckily theymet a brother who was just coming up the stairs:and as the house clock struck twelve, Tom deliveredhis message.

'I'll have the doctor here within half an hour,"said the brother, turning about at once.

'I'm coming along, Brother George."

" No: you'd better go to sleep."

" I couldn't sleep now, brother. Oh, please let mego."

Brother George made no answer, and Tom, takingsilence for consent, followed after him. As a matterof course, Pitch clung to his leader.

Once out of doors, they sped through the garden,and took the high-road leading to St. Maure's. Sud-denly their course was arrested, for a most unprece-dented thing had come to pass. There was an in-significant creek flowing past the college and downto the river. Ordinarily it was very shallow, butthe furious rain of the preceding day and the pasthour had caused it to swell into a muddy torrent.Worst of all, there was no sign of the bridge.

' The bridge has been swept away!' cried Tom.

'I wish I could swim," said Brother George.;'Boys, you remain here, and I'll go to one of thehouses on this side and get help."

Scarcely had he turned his back upon them whenTom pulled off his shoes, stockings, and sailor shirt.

'What are you going to do, Tom ?"

'Didn't you hear the brother say he'd swim it ifhe could. I can swim that far."

'Oh, but it's an awful current. You'll be carrieddown to the river."

Tom gazed at the swirling stream, apparently

some fifty feet wide, moving in all the swing of atorrent at his feet.

"I'll bet I won't," he said presently. 'Anyhow,I'm willing to take a risk for old Quip. Here,Johnny, just lend me your scap'lers. I haven't beenrolled in them yet; but it won't hurt me to wear 'em.I think I'd better start higher up so as to land abouthere on the other side."

Having put Pitch's scapulars about his neck, Tomran some distance up stream.

"Now, Pitch, good-by. Shake hands. It's arisk, you know. If anything happens, you send wordto my^father and my aunt that I had the scap'lers on."

Tom was decidedly of the opinion that this bit ofinformation would make up for anything that mightoccur. So, somewhat serious, yet light and bold ofheart, he slipped into the water.

He took one step forward, and found himself upto his waist; another step, and caught by the currenthe was whirled down stream like a cork. But thiscork had legs and arms, and struck out vigorouslyfor the shore. Vigorous as were his strokes, how-ever, he felt almost at once that he would in anyevent be carried far down stream before reaching theother shore. For all that, he struck out bravely,beating the water with over-hand stroke. Tom, atthis period of his life, was by no means an expertswimmer. He had attended a swimming-school sev-eral times a week during the last summer, and hadsucceeded in learning to swim a short distance andto float on his back. But he knew nothing of swim-ming with the current, and, in consequence, quicklyexpended his strength. Before he had gone two-thirds of the distance across he was worn out. But

his presence of mind did not desert him. Murmur-ing a prayer, he turned over on his back, and, mov-ing his feet gently, he suffered himself to be carriedalong. He had not drifted far, when his body camein contact with something a few feet below the water.Turning instantly he secured a hold on it with hishands.

" Hurrah! " he shouted to Pitch. " I'm all right.I've found the railing of the bridge. It's only abouttwo feet under water."

And clinging to this, Tom made his way hand overhand, as it were, to the opposite shore.

Dr. Mullan was not a little surprised when heopened his front door three minutes later upon a boyarrayed in the simplicity of undershirt and knicker-bockers, who was battering away at his door with alog of wood as though he would burst it open.

"Oh, doctor, our college has been struck by light-ning. Three fellows are badly hurt, and you'rewanted there right off."

"John! ' bawled the doctor, "saddle my horse atonce. Come in, boy; you'll need a doctor, too, ifyou don't look out. How did you wet yourself ?'

" I couldn't find the bridge, sir, and I tried to swimacross. I found it then, or I reckon I'd be in theriver by this time."

The doctor's wife, who had caught these words,now came forward, and kissing Tom in true motherlystyle—an action which Tom, in his state of excite-ment, took no notice of—drew off his undershirt,and threw her own cloak about him.

" That's just the thing, Mary," put in Dr. Mullan." Now get him a small glass of brandy, while Iput him to bed.

"Oh, I say," cried Tom. "I'm not sick: you gooff and take care of the fellows that need you."

Returning no answer to this expostulation, thedoctor pushed Tom into his own sleeping-room, andwithout further ceremony pulled off our young swim-mer's knickerbockers, and proceeded to rub himdown vigorously.

"Ouch," cried Tom, suddenly.

"Why, boy, you're burnt."

The doctor was gazing at a spot on Tom's rightknee about the form and size of the human heart.

;' I thought there was something- the matter whenI pulled off my stocking: that's where the electricitytook me."

' Were you struck, too? "

'I think so; I went tumbling over as if I wasparalyzed. That burn isn't much."

"It's good it's no more." And the doctor, whohad opened a medicine chest, applied an ointment tothe spot, bandaged it, and had Tom wrapped warmin his own bed before his wife entered the room withthe glass of brandy.

' Now, boy, these are your orders. You stay inthis bed till nine o'clock to-morrow. By keepingquiet, you'll escape the consequences of over-excite-ment and over-exertion. You understand ? "

'But, doctor, I can't sleep."

'You can, though. Mary, if this boy doesn't goto sleep in ten minutes, give him a teaspoonful ofthis. Now good-by."

The doctor, aided by the directions of Pitch andthe brother, easily found the bridge, and made thecollege in a few minutes. Jones and Green gavehim no trouble: they were beyond doctors' skill

— had been from the moment the bolt touchedthem.

But for the rest of the night he was busy nursingand warming and rubbing poor Harry's legs intolife.

Tom, meanwhile, under the influence of an opiate,slept a dreamless sleep, watched over with lovingcare by a gentle woman.

CHAPTER XIII.

IN WHICH TOM TAKES A TRIP.

AS this story concerns Thomas Playfair and onlyincidentally the history of St. Maure's, the readerwill be spared the sad details concerning the nightof the catastrophe, and of the ensuing days ofmourning.

Tom, whom we have to do with, was conductedto the infirmary Saturday morning by the doctor inperson.

"Brother," he said to the infirmarian, "here's aboy who's to get complete rest for the next seven oreight days."

Tom, who was standing behind the doctor and theinfirmarian, smiled genially, raised his right leg, and,while balancing himself on his left, waved 4t spas-modically.

"Just look at him," continued the doctor, turningsharply and catching him in the act; ' he's trying toknock his burned leg against something even now."

"No, I ain't," protested the discomfited acrobat,bringing his foot to the floor; " I'm not a fool."

Whereupon he resumed his smile: the rogue knewthat Harry Quip would be his companion.

"Of course, brother," pursued the man of medi-cine, "you are to diet him."

Tom's face fell.

" Diet me! with what, doctor ?'

"With a boat-hook," answered the grave practi-tioner without showing the least sign of a twinkle inhis eye. He added in a lower tone to the infirma-rian: " Three pieces toast and tea for breakfast, samefor supper, with beef-tea instead of tea for dinner."

Tom overheard him.

" I say," he broke in, " I'm not sick. I want to goto school, and keep up with my class."

"You can't go out for a week, sir; and if youdpn't keep your legs quiet, I'll not let you out fortwo weeks. Now, remember, young fellow, no hop-ping over beds, no skipping, no jumping about theroom, no running. When you have to walk, walkslowly. But the best thing you can do is to keepperfectly quiet."

"Oh, pshaw!"

Tom was disgusted. Even Quip, jolly as ever,though battered, could not reconcile him to his im-prisonment. Nor did he become more reconciled asthe days passed.—After swallowing his toast, he waswont to seek out the infirmarian.

"Brother," he would say, "I think I'm r^ady forbreakfast now."

" I just brought it to you."

"What! you call that a breakfast? Look here,brother, I'm paid for."

The brother would answer with a grin, and Tomwould turn away growling.

On Saturday of the following week he received aletter which elicited a whoop from him.

" What are you howling about now ? " asked Quip,who with the exception of a slight bruise and atouch of stiffness, was as well as ever.

"Read it yourself," cried Tom, tossing the letterto Harry, and hopping about the room in an ecstasyof joy.

Thus the letter ran:

ST. Louis, Nov. 6th, 18—.MASTER THOMAS PLAYFAIR:

Dear Son.—Have just heard from president of collegefuller details of calamity, and of your sickness. Hear, too, thatyou have been changing for the better—got more sense—morefaithful to your duty—study harder. Glad to learn, too, that youare brave, tho* far too reckless. Best of all, I'm told that yourcompany is good.

Although president pronounces you quite well, he thinks thata few weeks' rest and change might be safe, as nervous shocksare likely to leave after-effects.

As I wrote you last September, your uncle has gone to Cincin-nati, where, as he says, he is studying law. In a few days Ishall be compelled to go there on business, and your aunt hasalready made an engagement to see a friend there.

Start for Cincinnati at once. Will telegraph your uncle to meetyou at depot. Have advised president to procure you throughticket, and enclose you twenty-five dollars for pocket money.

Good-by till we meet, and God bless you.

Your father, GEORGE PLAYFAIR.

At half-past two that afternoon Tom, standing onthe platform of a car, waved his handkerchief to hisplaymates as the train shot past the college.

Kansas City was reached fifteen minutes afterscheduled time; and Tom, who had been countingfor the last three hours on a grand lunch at the rail-road depot, was obliged to hurry from his car to theCincinnati train in order to make connections.

But here his forced patience was rewarded.

* Ladies and gents! " shouted a fat little man, who

seemed to be in a perpetual state of breathlessness,

"a dining-car is attached to this train; and supper,

with all the delicacies of the season, is now served."

" How much ?" inquired Tom, catching the fatman's sleeve, and fastening upon him one of themost earnest gazes the fat man had ever encountered.

' Seventy-five cents cash without any chromo. Doyou want to come in for half price ? Do you takeus for a circus ?' The fat man was chuckling be-tween each word.

" Pshaw! Is that all ? Why, mister, I'd be willingto lay out five dollars on a square meal. You'regoing to lose on me this trip. I've got a whole weekto make up for."

' Come right along, then," said the fat man.

And Tom needed no second bidding.

A negro with an austere face and a white apronmoved a chair for Tom, and, handing him the menu,waited for the order.

Tom's brows knitted as he read the bewilderinglist—a sort of macaronic out of rhyme and metre.

'I say, couldn't you let me have a program inEnglish of this entertainment."

The negro, changing his austere expression notone whit, rattled forth—

'Chicken roast or boiled, chicken salad; eggsfried, poached, boiled, omelette with jelly if preferred;beefsteak, lamb, mutton chops, veal, ham, sausages;potatoes, fried, boiled, Saratoga chips; tomatoesraw, egg-plant, baked beans, apple and custard pie,coffee, cream, tea, and bananas."

"That'll do, I think," said Tom: "fetch 'em in."

The waiter changed expression.

" Fetch in which ? "'Those things you were singing out."

The waiter scratched his head.

' Look here," said Tom, confidentially. " I haven'thad a square meal for a week. A doctor's been prac-tising on me, till I'm nearly ruined, Now, you justgo to work and get me lots to eat; get me a goodsquare meal, and I'll give you fifty cents for your-self."

There wasn't a sign of austerity on the negro'sface as he hurried away. Tom was served with ameal fit for a starving prince. And he did it justice.

The negro, stationed behind him, could scarcecredit his eyes. Nothing equal to Tom's perform-ances had ever come under his observation. Tom,ignorant of the admiration he had excited, plied knifeand fork in a quiet, determined way, wishing in hisheart that the doctor and infirmarian could see him.It would be a sweet revenge.

"Come here," whispered the waiter to one of hisfellows; "this young chap won't be able to get up.He'll bust."

However, after three-quarters of an hour's steadyattention to the matter in hand, Torn arose quitecalmly (whereupon four waiters, who had been view-ing his performance from behind, and expressingtheir wonder in dumb shows, slipped quietly away)and, making a huge sign of the cross, returned thanksfor his meal.

'I said my 'prayers after meals' three times,"he remarked confidentially to the waiter as he gavehim one dollar and twenty-five cents, * because Ithink I got in at least three suppers."9

Tom ought to have been sick that night. Heshould have suffered intensely.

The doctors and story books are at one on thispoint. All the same, he retired early and slept adreamless sleep which lasted for over nine hours.

And if the recording angel put any one on theblack list for gluttony on that particular day, I aminclined to think it was the doctor, and not the patient.

CHAPTER XIV.

IN WHICH TOM GOES TO THE THE A TRE.

OHORTLY after six o'clock of the following even-O ing the brakeman, throwing open the door ofthe Pullman car, bawled out what sounded like4 Hydrostatic," but was really intended to conveythe correct railroad pronunciation of Cincinnati.

Tom seized his valise and hurried through the carinto the depot.

'Why, Tommy!' cried our old (or young) friendMr. Meadow, rushing up and catching Tom's dis-engaged hand, "welcome to Cincinnati; glad to seeyou. And you look so well! You've grown, too,and you're improved ever so much."

'I'm real glad to see you, uncle," said Tom, re-turning the hearty hand-shake with no less hearti-ness, "indeed I am. You've changed, too. Yourmustache is very plain now—isn't it ? And you'redressed awful stylishly. I'm glad I've my newclothes on, or I'd feel ashamed to walk with you.How do you like Cincinnati ?"

"It's a splendid place, Tommy," answered Mr.Meadow as they walked out of the depot and madetoward a street-car. 'The people are very nice;and there's more amusement here than in St. Louis."

Tom took a stealthy side-glance at his uncle. Oh,these little boys! Some of them read characters withan intuition which humbles the widest experience.

' Yes! but I thought you came here to study law."

"So I did; but I'm kept so busy that I haven'tsettled down yet."

' You look heavy round the eyes, as if you stayedup late, uncle."

'Yes; I suffer from insomnia a great deal," an-swered Mr. Meadow, puzzled to find that he wasannoyed under Tom's innocent analysis. ' Howhave you been doing since you left St. Louis?':

'Pretty well, uncle. I made a bad start; butnow I'm doing better. You see, uncle, I'm tryingto get ready to make my First Communion."

"Indeed!"

'Yes. I hope it will be the happiest day of mylife."

A few earnest, sympathetic words from Mr. Meadowat this juncture might have raised their mutualrelations to a higher level. But Mr. Meadow didnot understand boys. His influence on Tom, inconsequence, was bad. He said:

"Here's our car; jump on, Tommy."

His chance was gone. He noticed a strange ex-pression on Tom's face; it was as though the boyhad received a blow. Now, there was nothing in thewords of the uncle to produce this effect; but in ourmutual relations there is something more potent thanwords. Manner, expression, and sympathy, or the

want of it, are the chief causes that go towards gain-ing or losing our influence upon one another. Mr.Meadow felt that a wall of separation had at oncearisen between himself and his nephew; that theirintercourse hereafter was to be on the surface.

He fell into a train of reflection suggested by thisincident, and, while Tom, with the lively interest of aboy in a strange city, took note of everything in hisnew surroundings, the uncle maintained silence till,at a signal from him, the car stopped at a street-crossing.

'Here we are, Tom; jump off, and we'll be justin time for supper."

Walking to an adjoining square, Mr. Meadowpointed to a cheerful two-story building.

'* Is that your house, uncle ?" That's where I board; all the rooms in the upperfloor are mine."

As Mr. Meadow had remarked, they were in timefor supper, at which meal, owing to the fact thattwo young ladies with their father and mother werepresent, Tom was content to eat little, and contrib-ute his share to the conversation by an occasional:' yes'm " and " no, mem," which, as he directed eitherreply indiscriminately to either sex, did not serve toset him at his ease, though it sent the young ladiesinto a series of giggles, till Tom, through sheer forceof indignation, recovered both tongue and appetite, tothe admiration of all present.

After supper, Mr. Meadow proposed the theatre.Tom was delighted with the suggestion, and an hourlater both were seated in the pit of a close building,waiting for the curtain to rise.

Tom, it must be confessed, was somewhat aston-

ished at his surroundings. The audience failed toimpress him favorably; and the sight of waiters hurry-ing about with their trays did not suit his ideas at all.

" Is this a first-class theatre, uncle ?'

'Yes; that is, it's a first-class variety. Would youlike a glass of beer or soda before the show begins ?'

" Naw," said Tom, his disgust entering into anddistorting his pronunciation: and he wished at thatmoment that he were back at St. Maure's.

The curtain presently lifted, and for an hour orso he tried to enjoy jigs, comic songs, and what wasannounced on the program as a ;<screaming farce."But he found it weary work keeping amused. Theatmosphere, too, soon gave him a headache. Mr.Meadow seemed to be perfectly happy. Tom glancedat him curiously.

"I'm glad I'm not made that way," he thought."If this whole business isn't what Mr. Middletoncalls unhealthy, then I'm pretty stupid. It's coarseand vulgar."

"Say, uncle," he resumed aloud, as the curtainfell upon the ;< screaming farce "— screaming actorswould be truer—"I'm getting a headache, and, ifyou've no objection, I'll go outside and take a breathof fresh air for a while."

Now, Mr. Meadow was very dry, and desirousalso of conversing between the acts with a fewyoung men, whom he did not purpose introducing toTom. So he caught eagerly at the opportunity.

;' Certainly, Tommy. Here's a dollar to buy somecandy. Don't go far; and come back soon."

"All right, uncle."

Tom went out; as the next chapter will show henever entered the theatre again,

CHAPTER XV.

IN WHICH TOM IS LOST.

was at last free to follow his bent. From1 the moment he had left St. Maure's to the pres-ent he had had " no fun," to use his own expression.

Now that he was rid of Mr. Meadow, he was deter-mined to make the best of the opportunity. Nor didthe question of ways and means trouble him. In thematter of amusement Tom, like every well-consti-tuted small boy, was of unfailing resource.

"Say," he began to the ticket-seller, a I'm goingout: how'11 I get back? "

"You can take a carriage," said the facetiousticket-seller, "if you don't care about walking."

Tom returned his grin.

"Imeanhow'll I get back without paying overagain ?'

"Oh, here's a check, Johnnie. How are you en-joying the performance ?'

"It's made me glad to get out," and withoutwaiting for the ticket-seller's retort, Tom, satisfiedthat he had squared accounts, sallied forth into thenight, and cast his eyes about in search of a confec-tionery.

The street was brilliant with electric lights. Everyvariety of store seemed to be in the neighborhoodof the theatre. Two saloons across the way sand-wiched between them an oyster-house; and stretch-ing to either side were shops of many kinds, all openall seemingly driving a busy trade.

Tom took a long look at the saloons. He wasimpressed, not favorably indeed, with the number ofmen in each.

"Pshaw!' he muttered. ' It makes me feel liketaking the pledge for life."

He had scarcely made this reflection when hisattention was arrested by the sight of a small boy,who, with a bundle of papers under his arm, passedone of the saloons, and, pausing in front of the oys-ter-house, stood gazing in through the large show-glass.

Tom was growing lonesome. With a hop and abound he crossed the street, and noiselessly placedhimself behind the newsboy.

The object of his attention was a lad of little morethan eleven. He was neatly but scantily attired.The sleeves of his jacket and knees of his knicker-bockers were patched, and his shoes were open atthe toes. The face was quite beautiful, beautifulwith some hint of refinement, all the more beautiful,perhaps, that it was touched and softened by sad-ness. But the eyes—large and black—how eagerlythey looked into that window!

Tom was satisfied with the inspection. He puthimself alongside the newsboy, and set to staring inhimself.

" Paper, sir ? " said the boy.

" What paper ? "

" Post or Times-Star:'

" How much ? "

" Two cents for the Star, sir, and one cent for thePost, sir."

"You needn't talk to me as if I was your father,"said Tom. " I'll tell you what I'll do, Johnnie: I'll

take a copy of each and give you a dime for 'em ifyou'll tell me your name."

"Thank you, sir: my name's Arthur Vane," andArthur received Tom's ten-cent piece with unmistak-able signs of gratitude.

"And my name's Tom Playfair; just drop that'sir,' and call me Tom. I'm glad to meet a fellowmy own size. I haven't talked to a boy for threedays; and grown people are so tiresome! '

Arthur here smiled, and the twinkle in his eyeevinced that for all his sadness he was naturally amerry lad.

"I think," he put in, "that it might be better ifyou could get boys of your own class in life to talkwith you."

"Just listen to him," said Tom, apostrophizing theoyster shop, " talking to me as if I wasn't an Ameri-can—why, Arthur, I'm a Democrat."

"But your mother and father mightn't like it,"said Arthur, very much astonished with his new ac-quaintance.

"My father's in St. Louis," answered Tom, "and my mother's in heaven. And what's more, you're just as well up in talk as most boys of your size; and it's my opinion that you haven't been on the streets very long, either. I took a good look at you before I came up, and I'll bet anything you're not used to taking care of yourself."

'You're right, Tom: I've been supporting myself and little sister for only two months. Papa died when he came here, and left us only a little money."

"A little sister, too! "

* Yes, Tom; poor little Kate has be.en very sick,

but now she's almost well. She's in charge of kind sisters."

Instead of continuing the conversation, Tom caught Arthur by the shoulders and bending down stared straight into his eyes.

"See here," he began after a pause. "Can you remember the last time you got a square meal ? '

The lustrous-eyed boy with the pale, thin face smiled again.

' I had a pretty good meal yesterday. But to-day I've had hard luck. This morning I was stuck."

;< On the Latin verb or a pitchfork, or what ? "queried Tom.

Arthur laughed again.

" That's a newsboy's term, Tom: we're 'stuck' when we buy papers and have a lot left unsold."

"Oh, that's it. So you didn't get a square meal to-day ? " '

' I had a plate of soup and two pieces of bread at noon."

" How much ? ' asked Tom.

"Six cents."

"Whew! think of a little boy going around with six-cents' worth of provisions — say, Arthur, do you like oysters ? '

" Oh, don't I ? " exclaimed Arthur with enthusiasm.

" I thought you meant something by looking in through that window. It's the same way with me,"continued Tom, gravely. ' I'm uncommonly fond of oysters myself, and so are all my friends. Now I'll treat. You go right in, and order all you want, Here's a dollar. Is that enough ? '

" I'd like to take it," said Arthur, looking wistfully at the money, "But I can't. It isn't fair/1

"But it is fair," answered Tom. "You're worth a dollar to me, and more. O Arthur, you don't know how tired I am of hearing grown folks talking about elections and stocks and bonds. That's all I've been listening to for three days. It's terrible. It got so bad that I felt like praying never to grow up."

After further words, Arthur consented to take fifty cents. He was about to enter the oyster-house, when Tom snatched his bundle of papers.

' What are you up to now, Tom ?"

'I'll keep the business going at the old stand: while you're eating I'll sell." And without waiting for remonstrance, Tom darted away.

'Here you are," he shouted, putting in his head at the saloon to his right; "all the evening papers with all the news about the elections and stocks and bonds."

"Elections! where?" exclaimed a portly gentle-man, holding a glass in suspense.

' Don't know, sir. There's always news about elections in the paper."

The gentleman smiled, and, joining in the laugh at his expense, bought a paper, and insisted on several of his companions following his example.

Tom, richer by fifteen cents, repaired to the next saloon. Here he made the same announcement, and was sternly ordered out by a barkeeper all bang and jewelry.

Nothing daunted, he took a position at the nearest street corner, and exerted his eloquence on every passer-by. But he found this slow work. Five min-utes passed, and he had disposed of but one more paper

'I didn't get a fair chance in that saloon," he murmured. "I think I'll try it again."

He peered in cautiously this time, and, when the barkeeper's back was turned, rushed in.

' Last chance, gentlemen. Here are all the even-ing papers complete and unabridged."

The ^irkeeper, with an ugly word, sprang over the counter and made a rush at him.

Tom stood his ground, looking the enraged atten-dant squarely in the face.

" Which paper do you want, sir ? Times-Star or Post?"

'Get out of here, you beggar," cried the bar-keeper, pausing suddenly as he saw that Tom did not take to flight.

' You needn't call names: I'm not a beggar. I'm selling these newspapers for a little fellow who's half-starved."

The barkeeper glanced around and perceived at once that the popular sympathy was against him.

:' Give me a Star, Johnny," he said, and presently every man in the room was buying a paper. Tom's pluck had caught their fancy, while his declaration had touched their hearts. In a few moments he had disposed of his stock, and resisting several offers to take a drink," hurried away to rejoin Arthur.

He found his little friend seated alone at a large table with a plate of fried oysters before him.

:< I'm hungry myself," observed Tom, helping him-self liberally to Arthur's dish. " Order a dozen more, Arthur, and I'll help you eat them."

* Where are the papers ?' inquired Arthur.

'Sold—every one of 'em. I didn't have a bit of trouble, though I thought that the big barkeeper

next door would murder me. But he didn't: he bought a paper, and ended by asking me to take a drink."

'You don't mean to say that you got Clennam to buy a paper—the fellow to our right ? "

'But I did, though; and I sold over fifteen papers in his saloon."

' Well, you're the funniest boy I ever met. There's not a newsboy in the city dares go into his saloon. They're afraid of him awfully."

•' I was afraid, too," said Tom. " But when I saw him rushing at me, I just braced myself up to see what he'd do."

'Tom, I'd like to live with you all the time."'Glad you like me, Arthur. Go on and order more oysters."

'Thank you, I've had enough."

'* So've I. How are you on ice-cream ? "

'Let me treat this time, Tom. There's a nice confectionery right around the corner."

In this realistic age one must be careful not to tell the whole truth, lest one be convicted of exaggera-tion. So I pass lightly over the astonishing feats of Tom and Arthur in the ice-cream parlor.

As Tom paid the bill he glanced at the clock over the counter. It wanted twenty-five minutes to twelve.;' Arthur, I forgot all about him. Oh, gracious! ""Who!"

* My uncle. I left him across there in the theatre."1 Why, the theatre let out half an hour ago."'Then, Arthur, I'll tell you a secret."'What, Tom?' cried Arthur breathlessly, for he was impressed with his companion's grave face."I'm lost"

" Don't you know where you live ?'

'No; don't even know the name of the street.Uncle Meadow will be the maddest man in Cincin-nati. The fact is, we were having such a jolly goodtime that I forgot all about him."

'Well, you're the queerest boy I ever met."

'I don't see anything queer about it. I'm lost,And you've got to take care of me. That's all."

Arthur laughed musically; looking upon him nowone would hardly recognize the sad-eyed boy of theprevious hour.

' It's so funny, Tom, to hear you talking of beingtaken care of by me."

'Where do you sleep nights ?' continued Tom.

'I haven't any regular place since we gave uphousekeeping."

' Halloa! who gave up housekeeping ? "

" My little sister and I. Till she got sick, we hadtwo little bits of rooms in 'Noah's Ark.' "

" Noah's Ark! " ejaculated Tom.

"That's what the St. Xavier College boys call it.It's a great big tenement-house right across the alleyfrom the college; and in fact it does look somethinglike an ark. Well, little Kate and I were there andhappy as larks. She was just the best sister, andkept the rooms so bright and cheerful that I used tobe so glad to come home after looking around altday for work! She could cook and sew like a grownperson, although she's only nine."

Who paid for you ?' broke in Tom.Well, in the beginning we had a little over twelvedollars left by poor papa. But after two weeks wehad hardly anything left. Then I had to go to sell-ing papers and taking up ail kinds of odd jobs.

«(<i

And in spite of all, I could hardly scrape up enoughmoney to pay the rent. After a while we had hardtimes getting anything to eat. I didn't mind somuch for myself, but poor little Kate kept on gettingthinner and paler."

" Didn't you have any friends ?'

"No, Tom. We were strangers in the city."

"Then Kate took sick, didn't she ?"

"Yes, Tom; and a good woman who lived in thetenement got the sisters to take care of her, andnow she's quite well. But I don't know what to do.I'm not able to support myself; and I can't bear tothink of seeing Kate starving right under my eyes."

They were standing under a lamp-post during this conversation and Tom could observe the signs of tears upon his little friend's face.

" Well," said Tom, choking down his own emotion," we'll hold a council of war to-night before we go to sleep. Do you know any good hotel around here ?'

"There's a place across the street, the European Hotel."

Tom glanced at the building disdainfully. 'No; we want something first-class. We'll put up at the best hotel you know of."

"The Burnet House is about four squares away."

"That sounds better."

I think Tom succeeded in astonishing more people on that eventful night than, within the same period of time, any boy that ever came to Cincinnati.

On the register of the Burnet House he wrote in a large, bold hand:

"Thomas Playfair, travelling student," and he gravely added to Arthur's signature "merchant."

4 We want a first-class room, and breakfast at

seven," said Tom to the clerk, who had become un-usually wide-awake.

" Four dollars in advance for the rooms, sir," said that functionary.

"I didn't say rooms. We're not accompanied by our families. Here's a dollar for one room."

"Two dollars, sir," said the clerk, now as thor-oughly wide-awake as he had ever been in his life.

" There's the other dollar; you needn't mind about sending up shaving water in the morning."

The clerk laughed, and summoning a bell-boy, directed him to show the " gentlemen " number eight, second floor. Hotel clerks are men of large experi-ence in certain directions; hence, notwithstanding the late hour, and the fact that the guests were boys without luggage, the aroused official was so taken with the honest little faces before him that he allowed them the privileges of the house without further investigation.

I am bound to say, though, that our two friends availed themselves of a privilege not ordinarily ac-corded to travellers.

No sooner had the bell boy left them in possession of their room than Tom picked up a pillow from the bed and proposed a game of 'catch." Stationing themselves at opposite corners, the two tossed the pillow gently at first, till, growing interested in their work, they threw with not a little energy. As an agreeable variety, Tom got the other pillow, and before long they came to a genuine pillow-fight, hurling their downy missiles, and dodging about in a manner that sent the blood to their cheeks and caused their eyes to dance with excitement. The boy who has no heart for pillow-fighting is fit for

treasons, stratagems, and spoils; let no such boy be trusted.

The contest waxed fiercer—that is, merrier—each moment. Finally, Tom, pillow in hand, charged upon Arthur. There was a rapid interchange of blows, much movement and noise of little feet, and a sway-ing from side to side of the room, till at length with a well-directed blow Tom sent his antagonist sprawling upon the bed.

It was then they noticed for the first time that someone was gently knocking at the door.

" Oh!' said Arthur, turning pale, " we're in for it now."

Tom threw the door open and found himself facing a mild-eyed old gentleman, who seemed to be farmore frightened than Arthur.

" Good evening, sir. Won't you walk in ? "

"' I beg your pardon, young sir; but I thought therewas a murder or something going on in this room.I live next door, and I was awakened a few minutesago by a noise as of people struggling for life."

"It wasn't that bad, sir. There was a struggle;but it wasn't for life. My friend over there on thebed," added Tom, wickedly, "is very noisy."

The old gentleman now understood the situation;the light that shot from his eye and the smile thatcurled about his lips evinced that he too had been aboy in the golden long ago.

" Well, young sir, may I ask you as a favor not tomake any more noise to-night ? We old people can'tafford to lose our sleep."

"Certainly, sir; honest, I didn't think about wak-ing people up. I'll behave till morning, sir; good-.night."

" Good-night, young sir," answered the gentlemansmiling benevolently, "'and God bless you!'

" What a pity," said Tom as the door closed, " thathe's grown up! He must have been a jolly boy."

"Yes, indeed," assented Arthur.

" It's the old story, Arthur; folks get spoiled oncethey grow up. They haven't right ideas about fun.Now, if that old gentleman had been a boy, he'd havecome rushing in with his pillow."

uYes," assented Arthur; "and if all the people inthe hotel had been boys, they'd all have rushed inwith their pillows."

" Just so; and we'd have had a gorgeous time. It'sa mistake for people to live long. It seems to me ifa boy's good, the best thing he can do is to die whenhe's sixteen or seventeen. Of course, if he's a sin-ner, it's right for him to live and take his punish-ment like a man."

" Where did you get that idea, Tom ?"

"I don't know, but I've thought about it lots thelast few days. You see, if a boy doesn't do any-thing real bad, he's bound to be pretty happy; thenhe dies and goes to heaven, where there's just no endof fun, and gets saved hearing all that stuff aboutelections and stocks and bonds."

"Some boys have awful troubles, Tom."

" Well, the sooner they get to heaven the better.Just the same, I'm not anxious to die yet. I wantto make my First Communion. There were twofriends of mine, Arthur, struck down dead; but itwas on the First Friday and both were speakingabout having gone to Communion that very day.They're all right. Come, let's say our prayers, andthen when we get to bed I'll tell you all about it."

JO

And before these two lads went to sleep, they hadbuilt in the intimacy of an hour a friendship whichwe older folk find to be the work of many years.

CHAPTER XVI.

IN WHICH TOM ENTERS UPON A CAREER OF EXTRAVA-GANCE.

WHEN Arthur awoke next morning, he stared inno little surprise at Tom, who was standingbefore a mirror and surveying himself with evidentcomplacency.

' Why, Tom!' he called out, " are you a real boy ?or is the whole thing a dream ?"

" Yes," answered Tom, with his customary modesty,' it's a sure thing that I'm a real boy.

What are youstaring at ?'

"But you've got my clothes on."

' Yes; don't I look fine in them ? "

' You'd look well in anything, Tom. But in themean time, how am I to dress ?'

' Take mine," came the sententious answer, as Tomturned his back to the mirror and craned his neckin a vain effort to see how he looked from that pointof view.

" No, I won't, Tom; you've been too good to mealready. I'll not take another thing from you."

"All right; if you don't put those clothes on,you'll have to stay in bed for a while. I'm going toleave in about ten minutes."

'* I won't put them on."

'You've got to. See here, didn't you tell me lastnight that you'd take my advice ?"

"Yes; but then you know "

' Never mind the rest. My first advice is to puton those togs of mine. They're a pretty good suit;but I've another suit along with me that's just asgood."

Tom, as usual, had his way, and waxed enthusias-tic over his new friend's appearance.

"My! Arthur, but you look splendid. You see,you're rather skinny, and your own suit made it plainto everybody. Now you look like a young swell."

Indeed, Arthur's appearance had really improved.Even his face had changed for the better. The eyesshone with a joyous twinkle; the lines of misery anddistress had softened; the refinement and delicacyof expression were now quite noticeable.

Two months upon the streets! Who would believeit of that gentle boy ? Doubtless Arthur's guardianangel could have explained the mystery, and intothat explanation would have largely entered thesweet prayers and tender sympathy and elevatinginfluence of a dear little sister's love.

Tom did not hear any guardian angel say this, butit came home to him, ail the same, as he gazed uponArthur, who \vas blushing under his scrutiny.

;< Arthur," he added aloud, "I want your sister tosee you in good form. It will do her more goodthan all the quinine and paregoric in the world, whenyou walk in on her the way you are now. We'll getbreakfast right away, and then you'll bring me downto the depot, so's I can find my way to uncle's, andwe'll shake hands for a while. Then to-morrowyou'll come and pay me a visit."

'That's a nice plan, Tom; but you must comeand see my sister first."

" Me! " exclaimed Tom, shocked into the objectivecase. "Why it would spoil the whole plan. There'dbe no fun at all, when she'd see me rigged out inyour clothes."

"I'll tell her anyhow, even if you don't come.,and I'll fetch her round to see you, too. It's myturn now to have my way. You've got to come."

"But I never talk to girls. I don't even knowhow it's done."

"Pshaw! that's nothing. You know she's almosta baby."

" I don't like babies," said Tom, growing eloquent."One baby looks just the same as another; and ifyou don't say a baby looks just like its pa, itsmamma gets mad. Then babies don't do anythingbut scream and eat. They've no hair and no teethand no sense. The only thing good about a baby isthat it doesn't stay that way forever. It grows intosomething: but it's tiresome waiting."

" Kate has a full head of hair, a set of teeth, andlots of sense for her age. Now, Tom, I'll feel reallymiserable if you don't come."

Tom sighed.

" She's only nine ?' he inquired.Just nine a few months ago."Well, I'll go, Arthur."

Then Arthur wrung his hand and so beamed overwith joy that Tom became fully reconciled to whathe considered the coming ordeal.

And an ordeal it promised to be from the verystart. For when, an hour later, the two, having fin-ished their breakfast, entered the hospital, and werewalking along a vast corridor, a little girl with stream-ing hair and shining eyes came running toward them.

u

it

:i O Arthur," she cried, dashing straight at Tom,who ducked very cleverly, and looked as sheepish asit was possible for him to look, while the girl checkedherself and sprang back, blushing, and Arthur shookwith suppressed laughter.

"I—eh—eh—it's the other fellow, I think,"blurted Tom.

And the " other fellow " with great tact put an endto the awkwardness of the situation by catching littlesister and saluting her in true brotherly fashion,

;'And now, Katie," he said archly, "let me intro-duce you to the boy you were throwing yourself at.He's the best "

'Oh, I say," broke in Tom, "you needn't beginthat way; it's bad enough. I'm Tom Playfair andyou're Kate Vane. How d'e do, Kate?' And Tomshook hands with some return of his ordinary cool-ness.

" O Mr. Playfair "

'Tom," interpolated the young gentleman inpatched attire.

'Tom," she went on, accepting the correction;"but I really thought you were brother Arthur."

"Oh, it's all right now," said Tom. "I'm notused to being taken for a brother. You see I neverhad any sisters; and that's why I got so nervous."

And then, despite our hero's protests, Arthur in-sisted upon describing at length the adventures ofthe preceding night. It was an awkward time forTom. But, as he sat in the neatly-appointed roominto which Kate had conducted them, he bore it withwhat meekness he could summon for the occasion.

The little child who faced him was very like Arthur,with a beautiful and refined face, but so pale and

thin! Sickness had stolen the rosy hue of health,and left in its stead a pallor upon the delicate fea-tures; sickness had worn away the rounded cheekstill the face, lighted by large, beautiful eyes, was suchas lofty-minded artists dream and ponder, but fail toreproduce as angel forms.

'Tom," said Kate, when Arthur had come to anend, " I dreamed last night that St. Joseph was goingto help me and brother Arthur."

:< She carries his statue in her pocket," whisperedArthur, "and prays to him often."

'* I wish you'd pray to him, Kate, to get me outof trouble. I'm lost—and I think my uncle willmake it pretty hot for me. He gets mad so easily!'

;< My dream has come true, like in a fairy book.Do you like fairy stories ? I do. And,

Arthur, youlook so well now. And I've got some good news,too."

"What?" cried Arthur.

"Guess."

"A situation for me."

"Guess again. It's a letter."

"Who from?"

"From a lady in Danesville."

"Danesville! That's where our uncle Archer usedto live."

' You're getting hot, Arthur. What do you thinkit says ?"

;<Come on and tell me."

While brother and sister were speaking, Tom drewa railroad time-table from his pocket, and beganrunning his eye over it.

'* It says that Uncle Archer is the nicest man, andoh, such a lot of things. Here, read it, Arthur."And Kate produced a letter.

' Why," exclaimed Arthur, glancing at the super-scription, "this is a letter to Sister Alexia."

" You didn't guess that. Yes; she wrote withoutsaying anything to me; and, and—why don't youread it ?"

' Listen, Tom; you know our story.

" DEAR SISTER ALEXIA:

" There is a Mr. Archer in Danesville—a Mr. F. W.Archer."

"There, now! He isn't in California," exclaimedKate, her eyes dancing.

' He is in comfortable circumstances, and as good as he iswealthy. Everybody esteems him. He is now past middle age,has an excellent wife, but lost his two beautiful children, a boy ofthree and another of five, two years ago on a trip to California.His wife is a very sweet woman and very affectionate. They hadintended on leaving for California to remain there; but the loss oftheir two children brought them back to Danesville. Theirresidence is 240 Lombard St."

"Why, Kate," exclaimed Arthur, "this is news.It's almost too good to be true. Danesville is in thisState, and—and "

" Didn't mamma say that her brother was the bestof men? " broke in Kate. " And now we're going tosee him soon."

"Kate, I'll tell you a secret. When papa wasdying, he told me to take you to our uncle in LosAngeles. But after the funeral we didn't haveenough money, and I thought it awful hard. Butnow it's best we didn't go. I never told you papa'sorder."

"Halloa!" said Tom. "Here we are. Danes-ville is on the road between here and St. Mary's—one hundred and twenty miles from Cincinnati."

' How many days will it take to get there ?" askedKate, eagerly.

'Days! You don't expect to go there by street-car, do you ? It won't take more than six hours, andthere's a train starts at half-past eleven this morn-ing."

;'O Arthur!' And Kate clasped her hands andlooked anxiously at her brother.

; The next question," pursued Tom, " is, how muchhave you two got?':

'I've fifteen cents and a quarter with a hole init," answered Kate.

"And I," said her brother, "have eighty-fivecents."

'Well, I happen to be well off just now, and Ireally didn't know what to do with my money. Now, little girl, you just go and pack up your clothes and dolls and things like that; and if you don't hurry up about it you'll miss the train."

'Torn,"said Arthur, "how'll you find your way to your uncle ?'

;'Oh, there'll be no trouble about that. Once I get to the depot where I came in, I can easily find my way to the street-car uncle took, and I know just where he got off."

'But, Tom, where'll I write to you, to tell you how everything turns out ? "

' Send your letter to the Burnet House; afterward I'll send you my address."

In due time preparations for departure were com-pleted. Tom took possession of Kate's valise—it was very light; witnessed an affecting parting scene between the nuns and the little girl; and before brother and sister could fairly realize what a change

had come in their prospects, he had made arrange-ments for their tickets and seats in the parlor car, and given the colored porter directions concerning the little travellers which rather astonished that func-tionary.

Kate and Arthur cried on bidding their protector good-bye, and our generous friend experienced a dim-ness about the eyes himself, as he stood at the pas-senger entrance and waved his hand in farewell.

Tom and Arthur were not to meet again for several years. But their friendship defied separation. Two days later Tom received a letter from Arthur, en-closing twenty-five dollars, and giving a giOwing account of the cordial reception accorded them by his uncle. With this letter came a note from Mr. Archer himself, containing such warm expressions of gratitude as made Tom blush at every line. The correspondence thus begun continued for years, unti.1 Tom and Arthur met—well that belongs to another story.

So it was that our hero left the depot light of pocket and light of heart. He had but one dollar left of the twenty-five given him by his father. He took it out and gazed at it.

"Well, I've had fifty dollars' worth of fun; and now I'll go and buy a dinner, and after that I'll go back to Uncle Meadow; and for the rest of my stay here I reckon I'll have to be poor and honest."

With a sigh, Tom entered an oyster parlor; and when he came forth he had five cents left for car fare.

154 TOM PLAY FAIR.

CHAPTER XVII.

IN WHICH THE PRODIGAL RETURNS.

IT is nigh upon four of the afternoon. Mr. Meadow is pacing up and down the front apartment of his suite of rooms, taking huge strides, occasionally striking his clenched hands upon an unoffensive table bordering the line of his route, and ever and anon stopping to glance savagely out of window. Mr. Meadow mutters now and then between his clenched teeth words which are mostly profanity and severe criticisms of his lost nephew. In short, Mr. Meadow is very angry.

'I'll cowhide the wretched little brat within an inch of his life if I ever get my hands on him." This remark, with the adjectives a trifle stronger than here set down, issued from his lips as the last stroke of four came ringing through the air from a neigh-boring church, and Mr. Meadow made his periodical pause at the window front.

This time he gave a sudden gasp, his eyes bulged from his head, as far as the economy of his bodily frame would allow, and he did stare.

He recovered himself by a strong effort, made a remark which shall not be repeated, then dashed down the stairway, threw the front door open with vicious and unnecessary violence, and

Could that be Tom ? The figure walking up thefront steps looked more like a young beggar, and avery disreputable young beggar at that, Arthur

Vane in his proper costume looked like a gentlemanin comparison with Tom's present appearance. Ar-thur's hat on Arthur's head had at least been inshape—on Tom's it was crushed as though it hadbeen used as a substitute for a football. On Arthurthe clothes, though patched, had been neat; onTom they were splashed with mud, while one patchon the knee was torn, and a deep rent under thearmpit revealed what kind of a shirt Tom was wear-ing. But the wretchedness of his appearance didnot end with his garb. His face was swollen anddiscolored; and his upper lip was puffed out to aridiculous degree. Mr. Meadow had seen Tom inmany a sad plight, but the limit was reached on thisoccasion.

"You brat! you vulgar little beggar," roared theuncle, with an extra adjective, "come right in, andI'll lash you with a cowhide."

Tom paused half way up the steps, and tried tosmile. It was an awful failure. Probably he waswilling enough to smile, but his upper lip, the mostimportant part of his smiling apparatus, refused todo its duty: and so instead of smiling he succeededin distorting his face still more.

" Thanks, uncle," he made answer. " But I guessI'll not come in. I've been walloped enough."

" Have you been fighting, you vulgar little gutter-snipe ?' continued the enraged uncle.

'Yes, uncle," answered the " vulgar little gutter-snipe," backing dow»n a few steps in preparation totake to his heels should need arise, "but I couldn'thelp it, honest."

" Who whipped ? "

Mr. Meadow was a sporting man; his weakness

asserted itself, and Tom was quick to see hischance.

" See here, uncle, if you promise not to touch me,I'll tell you all about it."

" You young beggar, what did you do with yourown clothes ?'

"Promise not to whip me, uncle, and I'll tell youall about it."

" Were you robbed ? "

" No; but all my money's gone, seventeen dollarsand a half."

" Were you robbed ? "

"Promise not to whip me, uncle, and I'll tell youall about it. It's as good as a story."

Mr. Meadow took a step forward; Tom as quicklymoved down to the foot of the steps.

"Stay where you are, uncle, or I'll run."

"Where did you go last night ?' continued Mr.Meadow, less savagely, for the humor of the situa-tion was making its impression even upon him.

"Promise not to whip me," answered Tom, firmly.

" I'll see about that after I've heard your story."

" Honest, uncle ? "

"Yes, honest."

" You won't whip me till I tell my story ?"

" I promise."

" Cross your heart, uncle ?"

"Confound you!—yes."

" All right, then." And Tom ran up the steps withhis usual spryness.

4 Now, uncle, let me wash first; I feel awfulsticky."

Mr. Meadow deigned to supply the young gentle-man with a basin of water. Tom threw off his coat,

rolled back his shirt sleeves, and kept up a severeprocess of bathing for fifteen minutes without sayinga single word.

' Well," snapped his uncle, impatiently, " who wonthe fight ?" .

;t Oh, I've got to change my clothes yet. Thesethings are spoiled from Cincinnati mud. Whereverthere was a puddle, I was sure to step right into it.You see, uncle, I was chased."

" Who chased you? "

'Two dogs and—oh, wait till I change."

Mr. Meadow had to content himself for the nextfive minutes with grinding out remarks between histeeth, which, through a sense of decency, he did notwish to find way to Tom's ears.

At length Tom was apparently ready for his re-cital. With the exception of his face, he looked likethe boy of yesterday and the day before.

"Well, now, let's hear your story."

Tom took a sponge from his valise, wet it and putit to his lip.

"Ah!" he sighed in relief; "that's just the thing."

" Did you hear me, sir ?'

" Oh, I beg your pardon. You want the story ? "

"That's what I said."

" And you remember your promise, uncle ?"

"Yes, you brat!"

"You needn't call names. Well, uncle, I'm notgoing to tell you my story; then you can't whip me."And he removed his sponge and smiled hideously.

Mr. Meadow bounded from his chair; Tom madefor the door.

"Will you keep your promise ?" he asked with hishand on the knob.

'Yes; come in; I'll not touch you. Go aheadwith your story: I promise not to whip you in anycase."

;'Ah! that's a bargain. You know, uncle, papadoesn't want you to whip me; so I thought it was

fair to get ahead of you. Well, last night " and

Tom then narrated his adventures up to the momentof his leaving the oyster-house with five cents forcar fare.

"And then, uncle," he contiuned, "I thought howI could best please you."

'What exquisite consideration," growled the au-ditor.

'Wasn't it, uncle ? I knew you wouldn't like meto come back without a cent in my pocket; and be-sides I was afraid you might call me a lot of names,and lose your temper—and you did, uncle. Youswore dreadfully, and you said "

' Go on with your story," growled the affectionateyoung man. 'Tell me about the fight."

"I'm coming to it, sir. Well, then, I started towalk home along the street where those cars ran thatwe took yesterday. You see, uncle, I'd made up mymind to save that nickel."

'You've wonderful ideas of economy," snarledMr. Meadow, in parentheses.

4 Well, when I'd walked about two squares I cameto an alley. It was an awful rough-looking place,uncle. There were three fellows leaning against ahouse on the alley corner when I came along; andbefore I knew where I was, they'd got on the out-side of me, and shut me into

that alley. I neversaw three rougher-looking boys since I gave up goingto fires."

*' And did you knock 'em all down ?"

"Huh!! The wonder is they didn't knock medown first thing. The middle fellow seemed to bethe ringleader. He was the smallest, about my size.He had two teeth that stuck out so's you could count'em without trying. They were his higher teeth."

"Upper, you barbarian," corrected Mr. Meadow.

"Exactly. They were large teeth; larger thanyours, uncle, I really do "

"Go on, will you ?"

" Why don't you give me a chance? This isn'ta grammar class. Well, the fellow with the big teethsaid, 'Say, gimme chaw terbacker.'

"And did you hit him ?"

Tom looked at his uncle reproachfully.

«

* Do you think I'm a fool ? I said that I couldn'tspeak French, and the other two giggled. Then helooked so that I could count five teeth, and said inan awful savage way—just the way you were talk-ing to me a minute ago, when "

" What did he say ?' burst in the excited listener.

"He said 'Gimme chaw terbacker.' And then heused some words something like what you
"

" Go on—what did you do?'

"I said, 'I don't talk German either,' and thenbefore I could guess what he was up to he gave mean awful whack on the lip, and he struck out again.I dodged the second blow, and I got so excited thatlike a fool I struck back with all my might, and hewent sprawling. I struck him on the mouth, uncle,and when he got up he was spitting and coughing,and I could only count one tooth."

" And what did you do then ?'

"I couldn't do anything, uncle. The other two

grabbed me tight, and while the fellow who used tohave a loose tooth was choking and hopping round,and swearing whenever he could get his breath, theother two went through my pockets and got the silkhandkerchief Aunt Meadow sent me on my birthday,a small magnet, a pocket-knife, a lot of string, abroken jew's-harp, and my last nickel."" And didn't you make any resistance ?"' I squirmed and wriggled round, and when they'demptied all my pockets, I ran as fast as I could tillI turned the corner. And then I began to feel awfulbad about that nickel. It was real hard to have tocome home without it, so I turned back quietly, andwalked into a drug-store on the opposite side of thestreet. I sneaked in while they weren't looking thatway. The drug-store had a big window looking outso's you could see into that alley for a whole block.I told the drug-store man that I felt sick, and thatI'd like to sit down in his store for a while. Helaughed when he looked at me, and said, * All-right.'Then I pulled a chair over to the window, andwatched those three fellows for over fifteen minutes.They were fussing just awfully about the handker-chief. The fellow with the tooth didn't get that.Then they had a row about the knife, and the fellowwith the tooth came near having it knocked out andhe didn't get the knife anyhow. They gave him thestring and the jew's-harp; and then they had an awfulrow about the nickel. They tossed it up and yelled"Heads ' and 'Tails,' and shouted, and I don't knowwhat all, till somehow or other the fellow with thetooth got that. You ought to have seen him. Hejumped into the air and knocked his heels together

three times, and started out of the alley, just as proudas though he were a millionaire."

" And what did you do ?'

" I followed after him quietly; and when he'd gotoff about a square from the alley on a big crowdedstreet, I caught up with him, and touched him onthe shoulder. He gave a little jump, but he didn'tknock his heels together this time. * See here,' I said,'give me back my nickel or I'll yell for a policeman.'He put on a savage look, and said, 'Don't yer foolwid me, or I'll fetch yer one on de ear,' and I said,'If you do, I'll loosen your other tooth, and yell forthe policeman too. Now hand over, or I'll shout.'He looked around, and sure enough there was apoliceman turning the corner. He got pale, andhanded over that nickel."

"That wasn't bad," commented Mr. Meadow, for-getting his resolution to be stern and uncompromisingwith the young scapegrace. ' Then, of course, youstarted to find your way back."

"No, uncle; I began to think how bad AuntMeadow would feel when she learned what had be-come of her pretty Christmas present, and how badyou'd feel about that old knife which you gave methe time you bought a new one."

"Don't be sentimental," growled Mr. Meadow, indisgust.

Tom stared.

" So I thought I'd go back, and see what were mychances for the old knife and the pretty handker-chief. When I got there, it all seemed to be arrangedjust the way I wanted it. The two fellows weresquatting down on a board about twenty feet in thealley, playing at mumble-peg with my knife; and theii

fellow who was farthest had my nice handkerchiefflying round his neck. They were bigger than I;but I saw a good chance. I didn't stop to stare, butcame running up softly while both had their headsdown watching their game, and grabbed that hand-kerchief, and kept running right on through the alleywithout stopping to say anything."

' Good!' said Mr. Meadow, unable to contain hisenthusiasm. 'Goon."

'Well, they gave a yell, and before I'd got halfway down the alley there was a rushing out ofpeople from back gates, and two dogs came flying atmy legs, and a billy-goat got right in my way andwould have broken my neck if I hadn't jumped overhim, and the dogs barked and snapped, and the boyskept yelling, and the people kept crowding out, andjust as I got to the corner of the alley, a lot ofstones and things came sailing after me, and a pebbleor something hit me on the leg, and then I went intoan awful puddle, and came plump against a boy withred hair, and sent him sprawling."

Here Tom lost his breath.

' I don't know how I ever got out of that alleyalive. The last thing I did was to kick a bull-pupin the ribs; he howled like he was crazy, and then Iwas half way up the street. I looked round then,and found that they weren't chasing me. Then Igot off some of the mud and started for home. Andnow, uncle, I'm sorry and awful hungry."

And Tom looked at Mr. Meadow pathetically.

"Hand over that nickel, young man." For thefirst time since his return, the prodigal lost counte-nance.

"I haven't got it, uncle."

"Oh, you spent that too."

"No, sir, I—er—I gave it away."

Tom had become very nervous and awkward.

" Whom did you give it to?'

No answer.

' Did you hear me ?'

" To a poor fellow I met. Come on, uncle, and get me something to eat."

Tom did not reveal the whole story; there was some modesty in his composition.

When the " boy with the tooth' had surrendered the nickel to its proper owner, Tom had noticed the sullen face of the poor wretch lengthen in disappoint-ment. In a flash the words recorded in the sole entry in his diary, "Vinegar never catches flies," re-curred to him. He ran up to the boy, who, with his shoulders raised and his head depressed, was creep-ing away, and touched him lightly again.

"Keep off," cried the fellow, with a snarl: "you and me's quits."

"No, we're not," said Tom. "Old fellow, you need this nickel more than I do," and he pressed it into the lad's hand. "It's all I've got with me; but I wish it was more, and I'm sorry about that tooth of yours."

As Tom turned away, he left the poor little wretch gasping, mouth and eyes wide open, and the little brain within pondering over the only sermon that had ever came home to it.

Tom walked on, light of heart and happy.

"It can't do him any harm," he reflected, u and maybe it'll do him good."

Then some one touched his shoulder.

"Say," exclaimed the toothless one, almost out of

breath, for he had had some trouble in picking Tom out of the crowd, "say, Johnnie, I'll never act dat way again—never. Do ye catch on ?"

It was in order for Tom to improve the occasion by saying something pious and edifying. But Tom didn't follow the traditions of the book. He merely grinned, gave his penitent a hearty hand-squeeze, and said not one word.

This part of the story, as I said, he concealed from Mr. Meadow. But that gentleman inferred some-thing of it, and was so pleased with his inference that he gave Tom but a quarter of an hour's scold-ing which he salved with a twenty-five-cent piece and a good dinner.

CHAPTER XVIII.

IN WHICH TOM ASTONISHES AND HORRIFIES HIS AUNT.

IT is ten of the night. Tom has just arisen from his knees, and seems to find some difficulty in divesting himself of his sailor shirt. He is gazing very hard at Mr. Meadow through a sort of lattice-work formed by the bosom of his shirt, which is now concealing his little head. In this dramatic attitude he stands till Mr. Meadow gets into bed. Then Tom with a jerk brings the shirt back to its normal posi-tion on his shoulders, and says:

"Uncle, you've forgot something."

" What ?"

1 Why you forgot to kneel down before going to bed. You didn't used to do that when we lived in St. Louis. Hop out and kneel down."

"Mind your business, young man."

In answer to which Tom sat down on a chair and began to whistle softly.

'Stop that noise and come to bed."

Tom ceased his whistling, arose, walked over tothe sofa, and, throwing an overcoat about himself,lay back with his eyes fixed upon Mr. Meadow's as-tonished face.

Then there was a long pause, during which therecumbent uncle and nephew looked at each othersteadily.

" What are you staring at ? " growled Mr. Meadow,raising his head and leaning upon his elbow.

"I'm taking in your night-cap, uncle. It makesyou look so funny."

" Get off that sofa and come to bed."

"Not in that bed."

"Why not?"

"You didn't say your prayers. Suppose the Devilwere to come round to-night: he might get thingsmixed up, and take me for you. Then there'd be apretty how-de-do."

Tom was not entirely in earnest, but he spoke withfunereal gravity.

"If you don't come to bed, sir, I'll report you toyour father."

Tom sighed. Mr. Meadow had hit upon the bestmeans of subduing him. He arose from the sofa,slowly undressed, then going to his valise took out abottle containing holy water, which he proceeded tosprinkle over the bed, incidentally dousing the aston-ished countenance of his uncle.

Then with another sigh he retired. He intendedto sigh for a third time once he had composed him-

166 TOM PLAYFAIR.

self for slumber, but he fell asleep before the timecame for carrying out this pious intention.

Tom was unusually docile on this occasion. ButMr. Meadow's threat was not an idle one. Thatvery day a telegram had reached them, announcingthe coming on the morrow of Mr. Playfair and AuntMeadow. The one person in the world whom Tomfeared was his father; and he still remembeied, viv-idly too, their painful encounter, touched upon, orrather glossed over, in Chapter II.

Next morning, accordingly, Mr. Playfair and MissMeadow arrived.

Mr. Playfair unbent so far as to give his little boya paternal kiss; but his aunt's greeting was so warmas to disarrange her toilet very considerably. Thenholding her darling nephew at arm's length, sheanxiously scanned his features.

Tommy, dear," she exclaimed at length, "youmust have received an awful shock."

"No, I didn't, aunt, it was just nothing at all. Ifell down all of a heap, and picked myself up asgood as new."

Tom made light of the matter; he knew his auntfrom of old, and he had no intention of being pliedwith family medicines for a week.

' Roll down your stocking, Tommy, I must seewhere you've been burnt."

' Do you take me for a tattooed man ? " exclaimedthe young gentleman indignantly.

'Pull down your stocking," said Mr. Playfair.

And when Tom with commendable promptnessexhibited the red mark, as of a branding-iron, uponhis calf, Miss Meadow pulled out her handkerchiefand began to cry. Poor, gentle lady!

TOM PLAY FAIR. 167

"Oh, I say, Aunt Jane, don't," exclaimed Tom,earnestly. He was a warm-hearted little fellow, andunder a boyish mask of levity concealed the greatlove he bore his aunt.

In answer to this remonstrance, she threw her armsabout him again, and renewed the kissing and hug-ging till he blushed as a red, red rose.

4 Why doesn't somebody take notice of me thatway ?' queried Mr. Meadow, who felt that he wasbeing ignored.

" I think I'll pull up my stocking," said Tom, nowreally embarrassed. ' There's no use in making sucha fuss about it. People that cook get burnt a lotworse, and don't say a word."

" Tommy, dear," resumed Miss Meadow, who, hav-ing had her cry out, was now, after the manner ofher sex, thoroughly renewed, "you're not quite wellyet; you've lost color."

'Gracious!' exclaimed Tom, turning his face toa looking-glass. ;< Aunt calls me pale, when my facelooks for all the world like—like "

" A ham, or better still, an Indian in his warpaint," interpolated the agreeable young man of theparty.

"George Playfair," Miss Meadow went on, afterbestowing a withering glance upon her only brother,'just look at your boy."

" I have been looking at him these last five min-utes, Jane."

" Can't you see that he's badly shaken ?'

" He was pretty badly shaken when you got holdof him. But if you mean to say he's sick, I mustgive it as my opinion that he never looked better inhis life,"

168 TOM FLAYFAIR.

" Men have no feelings," exclaimed Miss Meadowwith unusual bitterness.

"They can see through a millstone, Chough, whenthere's a good-sized hole in it," said Mr. Meadow,grinning at his own wit.

"Now, Tommy, tell us all about that dreadfulnight. By the way, Charles," she continued, ad-dressing Mr. Meadow, " are there any lightning-rodson this house?"

"Two."

"Is that all?"

"I should think that's enough."

'You can't have too many," continued MissMeadow.

'We might attach a lightning-rod to Tom," sug-gested Mr. Playfair dryly. 'He'd present an inter-esting spectacle, going round with a lightning-rodsticking out of his hat."

;'George Playfair," exclaimed Miss Meadow, aris-ing from her chair, "if you had any heart in you,you wouldn't go jesting on that subject, after sucha terrific visitation!"

'Oh! if you wish, my dear, we'll have both light-ning-rods removed from this house."

Miss Meadow gave him a look—such a look!—then turned to Tom, and, with many a question,succeeded in extracting from her tortured nephe'Vsome account of the calamity.

'Wasn't he brave!" she exclaimed, when he haddetailed his experiences in crossing the creek. " Hemight have been drowned." And Miss Meadowcaught Tom to her arms again.

;'If the boy had had any sense at all," said the

TOM PLAYFAIR. 169

practical father, " he'd have felt around for thatbridge to begin with, instead of risking his life."

'Yes, Tom," added the genial uncle, "you werea fool. By the way, that swimming adventure ofyours reminds me of—"

Mr. Meadow was about to relate how he had oncesaved a drowning companion by reaching him along pole from the bank, when he was interruptby Tom's extraordinary gesticulations. For Tomhad at once raised both hands in air, and set hisfingers wriggling in a way that was little short ofdazzling.

'What's the matter?" exclaimed the narrator.

'Ten times," answered Tom. "You've told usthat story ten times in the last ten months. Giveus something new."

Tom intended to be facetious, but his impertinenceoffended his uncle, who forthwith proceeded to nar-rate Tom's adventures in Cincinnati.

During the recital Mr. Playfair's brow clouded.

;< I don't like it," he observed at the end.

"Don't like what?" cried the aunt. "Indeed,sir, you don't know what a treasure you've got.Few boys would give all their money and their bestsuit of clothes in charity."

' Yes, and few boys who are supposed to be gen-tlemen would stay out all night, and run into saloonato sell papers."

" I forgot, pa."

'And," continued the stern father, whose verylove for his son made him a severe judge, " it's verycharitable to give away clothes and money, butwhose were they ?"

1 70 TOM PLAY FAIR.

"You gave me the money, pa; and, besides, I onlyloaned it."

"And then," Mr. Playfair was resuming) but MissMeadow came to the rescue.

" Now, George, the idea of scolding your heroiclittle boy after a separation of three months! Youknow you'd have been sorry if Tom had acted anyway else. "

" No, I wouldn't, Jane. Tom should have goneback to his uncle in the theatre — "

"It wasn't much of a theatre, anyhow," put inTom, getting in return a savage scowl from hisuncle.

" And Charles would have taken care of the boywithout all this paper-selling and staying out allnight."

"Well, pa, I meant to do right."

"What's that place they say is paved with goodintentions?" asked Mr. Meadow.

'I'm sure you meant right, Tom, but you mustbe careful. Remember you're getting ready foryour First Communion."

Mr. Playfair, it may be remarked, was somewhatJansenistic in his ideas. All during Mr. Meadow'saccount of Tom, he had been deliberating whetherthe boy were of a fit age and disposition for receiv-ing the Blessed Sacrament. He loved his boy, butdid not understand him.

'By the way, Jane," he said, turning to MissMeadow, "if you wish to see your former school-mate before dinner, we'd better start at once. Ofcourse you'll come with us, Tom."

Hurrah!" cried Tom, regaining his spirits.at this point Miss Meadow failed hirrj.
'

TOM PLAYFAIR. 171

"Mr. Playfair!" she exclaimed dramatically, "willyou please look out that window?"

"I'm tired looking out that window, Jane."

"And do you mean to say that you are willing toexpose your son's precious life in the face of ablinding snow-storm?"

Miss Meadow was carried into exaggeration byher anxiety for Tom's welfare. It was snowingquite briskly, but by no means in such a way as tomerit her strong epithet.

"Pshaw!" cried Tom, "I ain't a girl."

'I don't see any particular risk," said the father.

" In his present debilitated state," continued AuntJane firmly, * it would be absolute suicide to letthat boy put his foot beyond the threshold."

' Do you take me for a wax doll ?" growled Tom.

But, despite all protests, Miss Meadow had herwill.

Presenting her nephew with a box of candy andthe " History of Sandford and Merton,"and caution-ing him to avoid all draughts and keep his feetwarm, the good little lady departed with Mr. Play-fair and her amiable brother, leaving behind her avery discontented young man indeed.

Tom spent fully half an hour munching candyand reading the initial chapters of the story; thenhe closed the book with a snap.

"Those English boys must be queer fellows, ifthey go round preaching sermons the way thatSandford does.* I'm glad he doesn't go to St.Maure's; he makes me tired."

That was the last of Sandford and Merton for

* Tom did the English boys injustice. Master Sandford, Itold, exists in fiption, not in England.

Tom. He presented the precious volume, beforeleaving Cincinnati, to the house cook.

The ensuing hour passed very slowly. He gavemost of the time to gazing ruefully out of the window,with his nose flattened against the pane. The snowcontinued to fall, and the street below had becomecarpeted in white. Tiring even of this, he at lengthtook to standing on his head and turning somer-saults; and he was thus putting himself into a hap-pier frame of mind, when there came a ring at thedoor.

Thinking that it was his father and aunt, he has-tened to admit them himself; but instead of findinghis relations standing without, he opened the doorupon a very small boy, with a very weazen face anda very large snow-shovel.

"Halloa!" said Tom.

'Would you like to have the snow shovelled offyour pavement, sir?"

'It isn't my pavement; and, besides, I'm not thelady of the house," explained Tom. "But, if youlike, I'll go and ask her."

'Thank you, sir," said the very small boy.

Tom returned presently, with the news that thelady of the house would put her hired man at it,later on.

'Thank you, sir," and the little boy touched hiscap and sniffled.Tom was touched.

'I say, little chap, wont you take some candy?"

'Thank you, sir." The small boy received thehandful of caramels with a smile.

'How much do you'charge for shovelling snow?"'pursued Tom.

" Twenty-five cents is the regular charge, I think,sir."

"What's your charge?'*

"I don't know, exactly. I never tried before."

" How does fifty cents suit you?" continued Tom,spreading his feet and with his arms akimbo.

"That's too much."

" Not for you, though. You're not used to thework, and it'll take you twice as long to do it as afellow who is used to it. That's why I'll pay youtwice as much."

This was Tom's first expression of opinion inpolitical economy.

The very small boy was presently working awaywith a will, while his smiling employer, standing inthe doorway, looked on with undisguised interest.

"Where's your gloves?" asked Tom, after a silence of at least five minutes.

" I aint got any, sir."

"Here,"cried the employer, returning from the hat-rack with his own, " come up here and put these

on.'

"Please, sir, I don't want them, thank you."

He was a modest boy, this weazen-face.

" Who asked you whether you wanted them or not ?You're in my employment now, and you've got to do what you're told. Hop up here and put 'em on.What's your name ?" continued Capital, as he handed Labor the gloves.

"Fred Williams, sir."

" Call me Tom, or I'll discharge you. I like your name. I knew a fellow named Fred once, and he wasn't a bad sort of a chap, though he was an awful blower."

174 TOM PLAYFAIR.

Fred smiled in an ancient way and, descending the steps, resumed his work. One moment later, a snowball took him on the back of the head. He turned his face to the door, but Tom, who was grinning behind it, was out of sight.

'I did it," said the honest but undignified em-ployer, after a judicious interval, as he came running down the steps. ;' Say, you're tired, aren't you?"

"No, sir."

'Yes, you are; let me catch hold of that shovel.I'll bet I can manage it better than you."

Aghast, the employee yielded, and Tom put him-self to shovelling till his back ached. He had completely forgotten Aunt Meadow's injunctions.

'There!" he exclaimed, throwing a last shovelful into the gutter, " now that's done for. Here's your fifty cents, Fred."

"Thank you, sir," said Fred simply. "It's for

mamma.1

'Take some more candy," said Tom.

'No, thank you. Good-bye, sir.""Hold on; let's have some fun."

Fred grinned.

' Just stand at that corner," continued Tom, " and we'll peg at each other. You ought to get a chance at me, because I hit you when you weren't looking,you know."

'I'd like to, but mamma's sick and I want to help her."

'If I had any more money," said Tom, "I'd get you to clean off some more sidewalks; but I'm dead broke."

The little boy was about to speak, when a sound not unlike a scream startled the two lads.

TOM PLAYFAIR. i?5

"Why, Tommy," continued Miss Meadow, turning the corner with her brother-in-law, 'you'll catch your death of cold. Go into the house this very instant. Aren't your stockings wet?"

"Of course they are; I've been shovelling snow.Say, aunt," he added in a low tone, as he brought his mouth to her ear, "this little chap's got a sick mother. Give him a dollar and I'll do anything you like."

"You will? Then I'll give him two."

Tom's promise cost him a hot mustard bath, but he bore it bravely for sweet charity's sake.

After supper, our hero actually did become ill.

He felt an uneasy feeling somewhere within, and didn't know what to make of it. Like the youngSpartan with the fox gnawing at his vitals, he triedto bear his misery with unchanged demeanor. Poorboy! a week's feasting following hard upon a week'sfasting had been too much for him.

Miss Meadow, who had been watching him allday with the eye of a detective, noticed a change inhis color. There was no imagination this time.

"Tommy, tell me the truth," she said, "you aresick."

"It's here, aunt," said Tom, laying his handpathetically upon his stomach.

Whereupon Miss Meadow put him to bed, placeda mustard plaster upon the place indicated, and,seating herself beside her boy, held a watch beforeher to time his misery. In ten minutes be beganwriggling.

"You've got to bear it, Tommy dear."

"I prefer the belly-ache," growled the impatientinvalid. He attempted to move his aunt by groans,

J76 TOM PLAYFAIR.

but she was obdurate. Then he begged for a glassof water, determined, once his aunt had left theroom, to fling the wretched plaster out of the win-dow. But Miss Meadow, with her eyes watchinghis every motion, backed over to the door and calledout for water.

'I think, aunt, you'd better take that rag off,"implored Tom, when the watch had gone seventeenminutes. 'I'm perfectly well, honest; and thatthing's burning awfully."

But Miss Meadow mounted guard till twenty-fiveminutes had elapsed.

He was cured. His aunt, bent on making assur-ance doubly sure, now produced a box of pills;however, when he protested, almost with tears inhis eyes, that he never felt better in his life, MissMeadow gave in.

When she returned to the room rather suddenly, afew minutes later, she was horrified to find the dar-ling boy dancing about the room, apparently in anecstasy of joy.

Tommy! you reckless boy! What are you doingnow?"

'I was celebrating," he answered, somewhat dis-comfited at being discovered,and highly astonished atseeing that his aunt had a coil of rope in her hands."Celebrating what?"

That old mustard plaster. I feel so good thatit's off. But I say, aunt, you're not going to tieme down, are you ?"

'No, Tommy; but get into bed, and I'll tell youall about it."

Curiosity gave Tom's obedience a generous amountof promptness.

Then Miss Meadow gravely tied one end of therope to the bureau.

" It's a heavy bureau, Tom; and it will stand thestrain."

The astonished lad began to fear that his auntwas losing her mind.

" What strain ?"

'Tommy, pay attention to me; if the housecatches fire, or gets struck by lightning, drop thisrope out the window and climb down. You're goodat climbing, you know."

" Do you really think, aunt, that the lightning ischasing me round the world?"

"We don't know what may happen," said thelittle woman. " There are storms and fires all overthe country. Now, goodnight, dear!" and she kissedthe unromantic youth.

Miss Meadow had not been gone five minutes,when she remembered that Tom's water-pitcherneeded replenishing. She hastened back, and, asshe entered his room, gave a gasp. He was notthere.

"Tommy!" she called.

"Yes'm."

The voice was from without. Ah! she saw it allnow, as with a suppressed scream she hurried overto the open window, following the course of therope.

Tom was half-way down.

" You wretch—God forgive me!—my dear Tommy,what on earth are you doing?"

'Testing your fire-escape, aunt. It's immense!"He delivered this opinion as he touched foot in theyard. No sooner had he relinquished his hold on

12

the rope than Miss Meadow hauled it up into the window with feverish haste.

"I say," he protested, "how'll I get back?"

"I'll open the door for you, Tommy."

'But you've spoiled all my fun; it would be jolly climbing up again."

Master Tom, nevertheless, re-entered by the side door; and slept without a fire-escape that night.

CHAPTER XIX.

IN WHICH TOM AND KEEN AN HOLD A COUNCIL OF WAR.

"TTEY! you fellows over there; you needn't try. 1 to dodge work; come on, now, and haulsnow. Harry, for goodness' sake, go and showConway how to roll that snowball of his here. Ifhe goes on that way he wont have it here in timefor next Christmas. I say, John Donnel, stir upJohn Pitch, wont you? There he is fooling aroundin a puddle of water with his old rubber boots, whenhe ought to be hard at work."

Such were the quick and various remarks thatcame from the mouth of Tom Playfair, some fewdays after his return from St. Louis, whither he hadgone with father and aunt to spend his Christmasholidays.

The events of the November night had made Tomextremely popular among his playfellows. All boysare at bottom generous hearted. Selfishness is thecrust of years; and the countless mean acts of cer-tain boys are in nine cases out of ten the result ofthoughtlessness, and in the tenth case, the fruit of false ideals and defective training. So, in thegeneral chorus of praise for Tom, there was not asingle dissenting voice.

For some days past there had been talk in thesmall yard of building a snow fort, and of invitingthe boys of the large yard to attempt its capture.Various details had been discussed, until finally,with the rejection of some and the acceptance ofothers, it was resolved to carry the matter intoeffect.

"Who'll be captain?" queried Conway.

"Keenan!" suggested Pitch. " He was captainlast year."

"Not this time," said George Keenan. 'Oneturn is good enough for me. I like to play secondfiddle now and then. It seems to me that our cap-tain for this year ought to be Tom Playfair."

"Playfair! Playfair!" was re-echoed on all sides,and with the least little touch of a blush on the partof Tom, and wondrous unanimity on the part ofhis playfellows, our hero was installed as captain ofthe small boys' snow fort.

With his usual energy, Tom set about constructingthe ramparts of snow; his orders went flying rightand left. He was an active superintendent; heinspected everything personally; and in doubtfulpoints consulted the experience of Donnel andKeenan.

"I say, John," he said, addressing Donnel, whenmatters were well underway, " how long did you fel-lows hold the fort against the big boys last year?"

"About eleven or twelve minutes. They stole amarch on us last year. Before dinner, we had gotover five hundred snowballs ready. While we were

in eating, some of the big boys stole them. Thattook all the spirit out of our fellows. By the way,we ought to get even with them for that trick. I'mgoing to try to think out some scheme. Yes, Tom;last year they put us to rout in eleven minutes."

'Pshaw! That wont go. We're not going toallow them to clean us out in that style this year."

'Aren't you, now? I don't know about that,"put in Keenan. " Some of those big chaps are justawful at throwing a snowball. Once Carmodypegged a snowball that took me square on the nose.It came in so hard, that I thought at first that mynose was driven through my head, and would comesticking out on the other side."

'Yes," chimed in John, " and once last winterwhen Ryan hit me in the eye, I saw so many moonsthat I thought I was a lunatic."

This excellent classical pun—excellent becauseso extremely bad—was lost upon Tom. It was lostupon George, too, who at that moment was seeminglyabsorbed in thought.

Tom," he said suddenly, "I've an idea. Comeover by the playroom; I think you're just the boythat can carry it out."

There was inspiration in George's face.

The two walked away together, and held a long,animated, but whispered consultation. Presentlythey returned to John's side.

'Now, the question is," began Tom, "to find outwho are the best throwers in the big yard."

'Let's see," said Donnel. "There's Ryan andCarmody and McNeff and McCoy (he uses ice balls,too; he's a mean fellow) and Drew and Will Clearyand Ziegler. That's all I can remember." As

George enumerated each name he checked it off onhis fingers and blinked his eyes.

"You left out two of the best," put in John Don-nel—"Miller and Arthur."

"Just nine," said Tom, as he walked away.

Donnel perceived that something was on foot; hiscuriosity was aroused.

" Say, George, what scheme are you and Tomhatching?"

'We're going to steal all the snow in the bigyard, so's to deprive the big fellows of ammunition,"was George's grave reply.

'Oh, come on! what's the idea?"

'We're going to make a bonfire in the fort, so'sto keep the boys warm and prevent the snow fromfreezing too hard."

John aimed a blow at George, which would havetaken that young wag in the ribs, had he not duckedpromptly. With a growl on the part of John,and a laugh on the part of George, the conferenceended.

Meantime, the work went on with ever-increasingenergy; so that, as the sweet notes of the Angelusbell announced the hour of noon, and the boys withbared heads paused from their work to renew theangelic salutation,—one of the sweetest memorialcustoms of St. Maure's,—they bowed their faces andbreathed their words in the presence of a fortgraceful in its way, and strong as boyish skill couldmake it.

It had been arranged that the storming of the fort should begin precisely at one o'clock. Contrary to the general custom on holidays, there was much talking and little eating at dinner; and even the

advent of the favorite pie aroused but little enthu-siasm.

Truth compels me to say that not a few of the boys shortened their customary after-dinner visit to the Blessed Sacrament on this occasion;—we are dealing with boys, not with angels.

While twenty or thirty of the stronger lads busied themselves in inspecting and strengthening the for-tification, the others gave themselves to the manu-facturing and storing away of snowballs.

These they placed within the intrenchments, which, I forgot to mention, were situated in the angle formed by a wing and a portion of the main body of the "old church building."

Precisely at fifteen minutes to one o'clock, Tom, assuming an air of coolness which belied his real feelings, presented himself to the second prefect of the large yard.

'Mr. Beakey," he said, politely raising his cap, "could you please tell me who is the captain of the big boys?"

"Captain!" repeated Mr. Beakey, banteringly. 'They don't need a captain to rout out you little fellows."

" Maybe they think they don't, Mr. Beakey; but I hope they'll change their minds. Well, if there isn't any captain, couldn't I please have a talk with some of the leaders?"

"Certainly,—not the least objection," answered the prefect, in an encouraging tone; for he per-ceived that Tom was strangely timid and embar-rassed.

"And eh—eh, Mr. Beakey," continued Tom, blushing and hanging his head, "could I please

have the key of your class-room, so's we can go up there and fix our plans? It wont take more than two minutes."

The prefect handed Tom the required key. " Oh, thank you, Mr. Beakey! and please, sir, will you ring the bell for the assault to begin as soon as I come down ?"

"Yes; anything else on your mind?"

'Yes, sir; just one thing more. I want to see Carmody, Ryan, McNeff, McCoy, Drew, Will Cleary, Ziegler, Arthur, and Miller."

"Are those the leaders?"

"I think so, sir," answered Tom modestly.

'You have their names pat; probably you'll find most of them in the reading-room, and a few in the play-room."

Tom sought them out at once. They were not a little amused at his proposition to hold a meeting; but good-naturedly yielded, and followed him over to the class-room building.

"I say," said Tom, as they trudged up the stairs, "how long do you expect us to hold the fort?"

" If you hold it five minutes, you'll be doing well," volunteered Miller, with a grin.

" Perhaps you may hold out fifteen minutes or so," remarked Carmody, with a view to encouraging the young captain.

"Well, I'll tell you what," said Tom; "if we stand it out half an hour, will you agree in the name of the big fellows to give up the fighting, and allow the victory to us?"

"Of course." "I should say so!" "Yes, sir," came the general chorus; and as they spoke

Car-mody winked solemnly at Ryan, Will Cleary put his

finger to his eye, and a general grin passed fromface to face.

"Well," said the object of this subdued and ill-concealed merriment, as he unlocked the door ofMr. Beakey's class-room, "if you'll walk in, we'llsettle everything in less than no time."

Tom stood holding the door open, with the keyin the lock, waiting in all innocence and politenessfor the wily leaders of the large yard to enter. Allentered, still grinning. Suddenly, Tom sprang fromthe room, and the door banged after him, whilecoming close upon the slam grated the ominoussound of the key turning in the lock, followed bythe quick patter of light feet down the stairs.

The hard-hitters of the large yard were prisoners.

•-

CHAPTER XX.

STORMING OF THE SNOW FORT.—MR. BE A KEY TALKS ATCROSS PURPOSES WITH THE SENIOR STUDENTS.

"/"\H, Mr. Beakey," shouted Tom a few moments\J later, " ring the bell, please—we've got every-thing fixed the way I want it. And—I came nearforgetting it—wont you please time us? The fightisn't to go beyond half an hour. If we last it outhalf an hour, we win, you know." With whichwords, Tom started off at break-neck speed forthe fort; and such progress did he make that hewas within a few yards of his intrenchments whenthe college bell gave the signal for the beginningof hostilities.

The sound of the bell, coupled with Tom's ap-pearance, drew shrill, hearty cheers from the littleboys, as standing, snowballs in hand, they impa-tiently awaited the onset.

By way of echo, a hoarser, deeper sound camefrom the large yard; it was the battle cry of thelarge boys, confidently moving to victory.

Scarcely had these raucous cheers been fairlyheard, when their authors, thus far screened fromthe eyes of the small boys by the intervening build-ing, appeared in full view, as they came rushinground the corner of the " little boys' dormitory."

Forthwith, a few balls began to fall harmlesslyabout the fort.

"They might as well send off sky-rockets," re-marked Conway.

"Boys," said Tom, "don't throw a single ball tillI give the word. Be sure not to forget. All youhave to do for the present is to keep your eyes openand dodge every ball."

Thicker, swifter, oftener, straighter, came thesnowballs; nearer and nearer the attacking party.

"Hi! hi! Come, clear out of that, little chaps!"shouted Fanning, who was well in the front of hisparty. "Come and put us out!" came the answerfrom Conway.

" Come on, boys," continued the energetic aggres-sor, "let's charge 'em."

Inspirited by Fanning's advice, the large boysgave a rousing cheer.

"Now, give it 'em," bawled Fanning, as he camewithin about fifty feet of the fort.

In prompt obedience to this order, a shower ofsnowballs made the air white; and two of the small

boys, each holding his hand to his nose, markedtheir way to the infirmary with a trail of crimson.

"Whoop-la! Now's our time," cried Tom, as thelarge boys stooped for a fresh supply of snow."Fire!"

As ball after ball whizzed into the ranks of thebesiegers, their expressions of enthusiasm, so multi-tudinous before, shaded off into blended expressionsof astonishment and uneasiness. Presently, how-ever, astonishment pure and simple stamped itselfon their faces; for before they had fairly begun tododge the well-directed balls of the small boys, theshrill cry of " Charge!" came from the fort upontheir startled ears, and presto! there issued at a runtwenty-five of the small yard's chosen sharp-shooters.

Whiz! whiz! whiz! whiz!

This was too much. Amidst the shouts and tauntsof the small boys, the crash of cymbal, beat of drumand blare of trumpet—all purloined from the music-room by the ingenious Conway—the large boys ofSt. Maure's turned tail and fled! Not all, however.

In the confusion of onset, Fanning and a few ofthe unterrified resorted to a manoeuvre. Quietlyslipping aside they allowed pursued and pursuersto pass, then suddenly advanced upon the fort.

But the smaller boys inside were thrilled with themartial spirit of their leaders; they fought bravely.Still, the issue could hardly be looked upon asdoubtful. Slowly but inevitably the hope of thelarge yard advanced. Fanning's voice was becom-ing "hoarse with joy." He hoped that in a fewmoments the works of the enemy would be his. Buthe reckoned without his host.

He was still urging his men on, forgetful of the

sharp-shooters in his wake, when Tom's voice roseabove the din.

"Hold the fort, for we are coming," bawled theyoung Sherman; and as he spoke he laid his handon Fanning's shoulder.

"Do you surrender?" continued Tom.

Fanning with his contingent turned, only to findthat he was hemmed in by twenty-five warriors bold.

'Never!" shouted Fanning, as with a vigorousshove he tumbled Tom over into the snow. "We'lldie first."

'Then die!" said Keenan; and forthwith twenty-four small boys fell upon the unterrified—outnum-bering them, I must say, three to one,—brought themto the earth, bound them, dragged them behind theintrenchments, oblivious in the mean time of thegalling fire of the main body of the enemy, whowere content to remain, however, at a safe distance.

From that moment, the fighting on the part of thelarge boys was tame. Deprived of their most skil-ful throwers, whose absence they had not noticed atthe beginning of hostilities, and without the leader-ship of Fanning, they displayed a " masterly inac-tivity."

Whenever the junior students issued forth for acharge, they had a capital opportunity of observingthe elegance and variety of the senior students' coat-tails.

In the mean time, the prefects and several of theprofessors stood looking on. Among them was Mr.Beakey. He had a quick eye, and it struck him,presently, that a number of the large boys wereabsent. Where could they be ?

His suspicions were aroused. Perhaps they had

taken advantage of his being a new prefect—hearrived in St. Maure's but a few weeks previous—toslip up to the village. Perhaps—dreadful thought!—they might come back to college intoxicated.Mr. Beakey was familiar with stories of boarding-schools, and he remembered some sad cases of youth-ful intemperance.

He gave a sigh, took out his note-book, and ran over the list of the boys. His face grew longer as he read and compared. Yes, all the leaders, the very boys whom Tom had asked for, were missing.

" This is too bad," he muttered to himself. " They are the last boys I would suspect of acting under-hand. I do hope they wont do anything to disgrace the college. They're all good boys, and it would be a pity to have even one of them expelled. It'sa pity I don't know the boys better. But 'perhaps they're about in some corner or other. I'll make sure of that point first."

Just then, Tom, on a grand triumphant charge, came sweeping past him. Regardless of the flying missiles, Mr. Beakey caught up with him.

"Playfair," he cried, raising his voice above the din, "do you know anything about Carmody, Ryan, and those other boys you asked leave to speak to ? Where are they ?"

Mr- Beakey's face as he spoke was clouded. Tom judged the expression to be one of vexation, and inferred, boy-like, that the prefect was not atall pleased at seeing his boys routed.

"I'll tell him the story," thought Tom, "after the battle, when he's not so excited, If I tell him now he'll give me a big scolding."

So he replied demurely:

TOM PLAY FAIR. 189

;< Mr. Beakey, wont you please excuse me ? But, really, I'd rather not tell."

This answer confirmed Mr. Beakey's worst sus-picions.

'There's no doubt about it," he muttered, as he made his way out of the thick of the fight. " These boys have stolen away to the village. But I do hope they'll not drink anything."

Mr. Beakey took out his watch. He started; it was two minutes beyond the half hour agreed upon. Hastening to his own yard, he rang the bell.

A great scream rose from the throats of a hundred small boys, as, in the full flush of victory, they charged their vanquished seniors for the last time. It was a disgraceful rout.

No sooner had the bell sounded than Tom quickly pattered to the class-room building, stealthily has-tened up the staircase, and under cover of the cries of victory without, and the growling of the prisoners within, unlocked the door. He then hurried away, entrusted Mr. Beakey's key to the care of a large boy, and returned to his proper yard,—there to receive congratulations and fight his battles o'er again.

In the class-room which he had just left, however, there were no congratulations exchanged. Carmody and Ryan were sulking in a corner; Ziegler was elaborately writing " sold again" on the black-board; Will Cleary was whistling the "Last Rose of Sum-mer," after the manner of a dirge; while Miller paced up and down between the benches like a caged tiger.

" Confound it!" burst forth McNeff. " I was never so badly taken in since I came here."

19° TOM PLAYFAIR.

'You haven't been here so long; you're young yet," was Ryan's consolatory reflection.

"This is a pretty how-de-do," growled Cleary." Every mule in the yard will have the laugh on us."

"I'll paralyze the first fellow that laughs at me,"said McCoy.

"Just imagine the grin on Fanning's face," mut-tered Carmody.

The task of imagining Fanning's grin seemed tobe attended with some difficulties, for it induced a silence that lasted for several minutes.

"Isn't that little wretch ever coming back to un-lock this door?" cried Arthur, at length. 'The fight's been over nearly an hour. Hasn't any one got a button-hook ?"

There was a sullen silence.

"Well, come on," continued Arthur, "let's go to the window, and catch some fellow's eye, and get him to open up for us."

"For goodness' sake!" cried Ryan, "don't. There'll be laughing enough at us as it is. But if the fellows once know we're here, they'll march up in procession to let us out."

"Well," said Ziegler, "I don't propose to stay here forever. I wonder couldn't I squeeze through the transom?"

'You might try," said Carmody encouragingly.'" And who knows but the key is still in the lock? It would be just like that brat of a small boy to leave it there, and forget all about it. Small boys are nuisances."

While Carmody was speaking, Ziegler had taken off his coat and vest.

' Now, boys, give me a lift," he said.

Eager hands came to his help—a trifle too eager, perhaps; for Ziegler was hurried through the aper-ture in such wise that he came down on the other side on hands and knees.

"You're a lot of lunatics!" he volunteered as he rose, "you'd think I was insured for a fortune, and had two or three necks to break. There isn't any key here."

'Try and break the door in," suggested McCoy.

"All right! Get away from the door, then," returned Ziegler.

He stepped back a few paces, and then made a violent rush at the door, catching and turning the knob as he threw the whole weight of his body against the woodwork.

The door flew open, and Ziegler flew in. His flying progress was arrested by Cleary, who was rendered breathless and brought to the floor with his friend on top.

While the two unfortunates were ruefully picking themselves up, the others broke into a ringing laugh.

;< Shut up!" roared Ziegler, when he could com-mand his breath. "You're a lot of fools! You might have known that door was unlocked."

"That's a fact," assented Carmody. "It's funny it didn't occur to you. You're a pretty sharp fellow, you know."

"Aw! tell us something new," snarled Ziegler.

"Oh! why doesn't somebody hit me hard?" apos-trophized Ryan. "We've been mooning in here over an hour and a half, and that door's been open over a century."

Slowly and sadly they went down the stairs, each one trying to get behind the other,—a feat in which

all, of course, did not succeed. On emerging into the yard, they breathed more freely when they per-ceived that no one was outside but Mr. Beakey, who had been anxiously scanning the four quarters in hope of discovering their whereabouts.

"Boys," said the prefect, whose suspicions were confirmed by their sheepish looks and blushing faces, "you're caught—there's no getting out of it."

"Well, that's so, Mr. Beakey," said Carmody, trying to be easy and failing; "we might as well acknowledge it. We've been stupid."

"So, you don't offer any excuses?" exclaimed Mr. Beakey, in astonishment.

:<Oh!—well—it was only in fun, sir," said Ryan, whose sheepishness had now grown intense.

"Only in fun!" gasped Mr. Beakey. "Fun! fun! that's not my idea of fun."

"Why, it's not so very serious, Mr. Beakey," said Cleary, in a conciliatory tone. ;* And I hope," he continued, 'you wont punish Playfair on account of it."

Mr. Beakey remembered Tom's embarrassment.

"What!" he exclaimed. "Do you mean to say that that little innocent was concerned in it?"

" Why, he was at the bottom of the whole matter," broke in Carmody, in astonishment at the prefect's obtuseness. :'And let me tell you, he's not so inno-cent, either; he's up to more tricks than any boy twice his size in this college—confound him!"

' Really," said the prefect, in a troubled voice,

' the case is far worse than I thought. Boys, I

didn't expect it of you. I thought you had more

sense.'

General sheepishness at its maximum. Some

grinning helplessly. Majority gazing at their feet.

'Frankly," he continued, 'I am very sorry on your account.

"Oh, don't bother about us, sir," put in Cleary; "we can stand being laughed at."

'Laughed at!" echoed the prefect in dismay;" do you mean to say that such things are matter for laughter to the students of this college?"

'Why, certainly," said Ryan, no less puzzled than the prefect. ;'And, in fact, I guess we'll have to laugh the thing off ourselves."

"There, now, that'll do," said Mr. Beakey sternly. ' I see that not one of you is in a condi-tion to talk sense. You will repent your words to-morrow, when you regain the proper use of your

reason.'

The boys exchanged glances of perplexity. For the first time, they began to suspect that they were talking at cross purposes.

"Come, now," continued the prefect, 'tell the exact truth. How long were you up?"

(Mr. Beakey meant uptown; the boys thought that he had reference to the class-room.)

"Over an hour," said Carmody.

"And how much did each one of you take?"

The boys again looked at each other.

"Do you mean chalk, sir?" ventured Ziegler. "I took a small piece, but meant no harm," and he produced from his pocket a bit of black-board chalk.

Mr. Beakey flushed with anger.

"There wasn't anything else to take but ink," continued Ziegler, "and none of us wanted any." 13

This made matters worse. Mr. Beakey now felt confident that the boys were quizzing him.

'* Enough of this nonsense," he said. "You need not make your case worse than it is by untimely joking. You have already acknowledged that you are fairly caught. I missed you from the yard be-fore you were gone five minutes—and you have shown some signs of sorrow; you have acknowledged that you were "uptown' for over an hour; your shamefaced expressions and flushed faces show the effects of your indiscretion—there's a clear case against you. So, now, you may as well out with the whole thing, and tell how much you took."

The astonishment that deepened on each one's face with each remark of Mr. Beakey culminated in a look of comic amazement; the misunderstanding was too ridiculous. Mr. Beakey's last question was the signal for a hearty burst of laughter.

"Boys! boys!" implored Mr. Beakey, "for good-ness' sake don't create a scene!"

Restraining his mirth, Ryan explained the misun-derstanding; and as he spoke, it was delightful tosee how the wrinkles and frowns disappeared fromthe prefect's brow, and how the firm-set, stern linesabout the mouth softened into the brightest of smiles.

'Well, boys," he said, when Ryan had detailedtheir adventures, "I acknowledge that I've made abig blunder, and I ask your pardon. I don't knowthe ropes yet, you see. But sincerely, I am gladthat I am in the wrong."

There was a whispered consultation among theboys; then Ryan spoke:

' Mr. Beakey, we want you to do us a favor. Youand that Play fair boy are the only ones that know

of the way we were taken in—we'll make him keepquiet, if you'll promise to say nothing to any oneabout it."

"You can trust me," answered Mr. Beakey, "nota soul shall hear of it from my lips."

'Thank you, sir," came the general chorus.

Tom was easily induced to hold his tongue on thesubject; so, too, was George Keenan (who had sug-gested the plot to Tom) ; and so the " true inward-ness" of the big boys' failure to take the snow fortnow becomes public for the first time.

CHAPTER XXI.

IN WHICH TOM MEETS WITH A BITTER TRIAL.

IN the events I have narrated as happening afterthe night of the first Friday in November, I havepurposely avoided enlarging upon the grief andhorror of that dreadful accident.

One would think, judging from what I have relatedof Tom, that our cheerful little hero had beenstrangely unimpressed by the tragic incident. This,however, is a wrong inference. True, Tom, bybeing sent to the infirmary, was wisely spared thesad sights incident upon the burial of his two friends.After leaving the dormitory, he never saw the faceof Green again,—face more beautiful and composedin death than it had ever been in the years of col-lege life. Nor did he ever again see the face of thegentle boy who had asked his prayers. Had heseen it, he would have recognized the same beautifulexpression which had thrown a halo upon the coun-

tenance when the boy had uttered " Sweet Heart ofJesus, be my Love."

Nevertheless, the accident had deeply affectedTom. He knew that his own escape from instantdeath had fallen little short of a miracle; and everynight from his inmost heart he thanked God thathe had been spared to make his First Communion.That Green had been taken away just as he hadconquered his passions and made a start for thebetter, and that Alec had been called to God on thevery day he had completed his ninth First Friday,seemed to Tom to be a wondrous manifestation ofGod's mercy. It was a lesson, too.

It filled his little heart with a burning desire toreceive Our Lord in the sacrament of His love.Among Catholic boys—as I have known them—suchfeelings and affections show themselves outwardlyin a somewhat negative manner. They do notmanifest themselves in deed and conversation, saveby increased carefulness in avoiding anything sinful.

Joke and jest, play and study, may go on in allseeming as before. But the change, for all that,may be radical and life-long.

It was a happy day for Tom when on the fifteenthof February the First Communion Class was organ-ized. I dare say that no small boy who ever attendedSt. Maure's set about the work of preparation asTom did. Each day he had his catechism lessonprepared with a thoroughness that was beyond criti-cism. Nor, in the mean time, did he neglect hisother studies. Indeed, owing to his long absence,it became necessary for him to apply himself veryhard, in order to put himself on a fair footing withhis classmates. Unfortunately, the semi-annual ex-

animations were upon him before he could repeatall the class matter he had missed, and when, on the22d of February, the class-standing was published,Tom stood at the foot of his class, with but sixtymerit marks out of a hundred.

'I hope my father won't get mad about it," heremarked to Harry Quip; and as he spoke he lookedquite serious.

'Oh! I'm sure he won't mind it," said Harry.'He knows you've missed several weeks."

'Yes, but pa's getting mighty strict. He thinksI'm awful careless. The fact is, we like each otherimmensely,but pa doesn't know what to make of me."

In these few words Tom had set down their rela-tions quite clearly. Mr. Playfair loved his boy;but as for understanding him, that was anotherquestion. Clearly, if Mr. Playfair had ever been aboy himself, he had either forgotten that circum-stance or he had been cast in quite a different mouldfrom his son. The wall of misunderstanding hadbeen rising higher between them ever since Tomreached the age of reason. Such relations betweenfather and son are not uncommon.

Tom's forebodings on this occasion were not with-out foundation. Several days later he was sum-moned to the President's room. On entering, hesaw at once from the reverend Father's face thatsomething had gone wrong.

"Ah! Tommy; how are you studying?"

"Pretty hard, sir."

"And how are you getting on with your teacher?"

"I like him very much. If he's got anythingagainst me lately he hasn't told me anything aboutit,"

"Are you sure you've had no trouble lately?"

"Yes, Father; I'm getting ready for my FirstCommunion."

' Well, Tom, I've very bad news for you."

"Anybody sick at home, sir?"

'No; it regards yourself. Your father is verymuch displeased with your bulletin."

"Oh, I got low notes because I missed a lot ofclasses. Mr. Middleton says I've caught upalready."

' Your father knew you had been absent, too, butthere must have been something more in your bulle-tin,—some remark which indicated that you werenot giving satisfaction; for your father sends meimperative orders to take you out of the CommunionClass at once."

A strange expression came over Tom's face.Every nerve seemed to be a-quiver. Till that mo-ment, Tom himself had had no idea of the ardentdesire with which he looked forward to his "day ofdays."

'Don't take it too much to heart, my boy," con-tinued the President, both touched and edified atthe way in which Tom received the news. "I havea hope that further examination will discover somemistake. You mustn't give up hope yet. I'll in-quire about your bulletin, and find out just howthings stand, as soon as possible."

"Thank you, Father," said Tom.

* In the mean time, offer your trial to God, myDoy. It comes from Him. His ways are not ourways. And when He sends us trials, He wishes usto hear up under them cheerfully."

1 ('11 try to swallow it, sir. But it's rough."

Tom went directly to the chapel, prostrated him-self before the Blessed Sacrament, and there prayedfervently. When he entered, he was dazed, bewil-dered; when he left, three minutes later, he wascomparatively calm. There is no sorrow that prayercannot soothe; and children's sorrows, God bethanked for it, are quickest to yield their bitternessto fervent prayer.

No one observing Tom playing at " foot-and-a-half," within that same hour, could imagine thatthe nimble lad, all gayety and motion, had just metthe second great sorrow of his life. The death ofhis mother had been the first.

A week elapsed before he was again summonedby the President.

"Well, Tom, things are looking a little brighter.There's been a grave blunder. Report was sent toyour father that your conduct had been 'highly unsat-isfactory. ' Now those words were put in your bul-letin by some clerical error. They belonged to someother boy's. I have just written your father howmatters stand, and I'm quite sure that all will beright within a week."

Tom grinned excessively, and, finding some diffi-culty in keeping both feet upon the floor, hastenedto leave the room; whereupon he danced all theway back to his yard.

And till news came from Mr. Playfair, Tom wasin great glee. How eagerly he hastened to thePresident's room to hear the final word! He enteredall aglow and smiling, but the glow gave way toashen whiteness and the smile disappeared instantane-ously. Something there was in the President's facewhich warned him that his troubles were not yet over.

"I've been a little surprised, Tom, by the tenorof your father's letter. He says he is glad to learnthat your conduct is so satisfactory, and that youare doing so well in your studies; but he adds thathe has been doubting for some time about the pro-priety of your making First Communion, on othergrounds '

" I used to give lots of trouble at home," explainedTom humbly. " I guess pa thinks I need moretime to reform."

"He is acting through love for you, Tom; hewants to make sure that you are well prepared. Hesuspects that your levity of disposition is a sign thatyou are too young."

"Yes," assented Tom sadly, "I'd be better off ifI could go around with a long face."

"However," added the President, suppressing asmile, "he leaves the matter in my hands."

Tom brightened at once.

'Judging from the drift of his letter, though, Ithink that he would prefer you to wait."

Tom's face fell again.

' Now, my boy, you have your choice. If youinsist, I shall allow you to rejoin the CommunionClass."

Tom thought for a moment, then suddenly a lightflashed from his eyes,—the light of an inspiration.

"Father, I'll tell you what I'll do. I'll give itup for this year."

He did not explain his reasons, but for the Fatherno explanation was needed. Tom had taken theside of strict obedience and of sacrifice.

"God will bless you for that resolution, my boy.Your Communion, when it comes, will be all

happier; and even if you have been disobedient attimes, the act you have now made will more thanatone. You have chosen wisely, and God's blessingwill be upon the choice."

Tom departed happy. But the pain and strugglewere not over. At times an intense longing wouldcome upon our little friend.

On the feast of St. Joseph's Patronage, when six-teen little lads knelt at the altar to receive for thefirst time their divine Master, Tom's eyes becamevery moist. One tear trickled down his honest face,and with the dropping of that tear all his sadnesswas gone.

There was no relaxation in his studies, meantime.Looking forward to his First Communion, he conse-crated every day to preparation; and so, when thelast examination came, Tom won highest honors inhis class, with ninety-nine merit marks after hisname.

Poor Tom! Between him and his Communionanother tragic experience was to intervene. Uponthis roguish little boy God seemed to have specialdesigns.

CHAPTER XXII.

IN WHICH TOM WINS A NEW FRIEND AND HEARS A

STRANGE STORY.

IT must be said in justice to Mr. Playfair thatTom's record during the last half of schoolpleased him very much.

Jndeed, he expressed his pleasure in such terms on

their meeting again that Tom blushed to the tipsof his ears.

" Say, pa, what about my Communion ?"

" You can make it, my boy, just as soon as thePresident allows you next year. Perhaps I was alittle severe on you, but it has done you good."

And, indeed, there could be no doubt about Tom'simprovement, though truth compels me to add thathe made things very lively indeed at home duringthe two months of vacation.

On returning to college, he had a long talk withthe President, the issue of which was, that Ton.should prepare under the reverend Father's personaldirection to receive his Lord at Christmas.

That Christmas was to be the turning-point inour hero's life.

September passed quietly. Towards the end ofthe month Tom came upon a new friend.

He was sauntering about the yard one brightafternoon, when his attention was caught by thefollowing dialogue:

"He's homesick!"

" He wants his ma!"

'Give him a little doll, in a nice gold-paperdress!"

These were a few of the remarks from John Pitchand a few others of the same ilk, addressed to atimid-looking lad, around whom they had rudelygathered. Just then Tom and Harry chanced to bepassing by.

" What's the matter ?" inquired Tom of the victim.

"He wants his ma, but you'll do, Playfair," vol-unteered John Pitch.

"You're a mean set, to be teasing a poor new-

comer, who hasn't got any friends," exclaimed Tom,his eyes flashing.

" Mind your business, Playfair," said Pitch." Yes, and you mind yours, and let the poor newkid alone. Come on, Johnny What's-your-name,and have a game of catch. Here, take some candy."Tom's new friend, James Aldine, said very little,but his eyes spoke volumes of gratitude. He was aquiet, olive-complexioned boy. His eyes, dark andheavily shaded, had a trick of passing from an ex-pression of gentle timidity to one of marked fear.Tom, who at once took a liking to the new-comer,soon came to notice this change of countenance, andas the days slipped by and their intimacy increased,Tom's wonder grew. He was puzzled, and, beingan outspoken boy, was only waiting a favorable op-portunity of satisfying his curiosity. At last theoccasion presented itself.

It was the second week of October, whei. he andJames found themselves alone on the prairie, fullytwo miles from the college. The average boy canmake an intimate friend in something under a week.The intercourse of these two had already gone be-yond that period, and Tom felt himself fully justifiedin remarking:

"What makes you look so scared, Jimmy?"

"Do I look scared?"

" Just as if you had been training a large stock ofghosts, and hadn't succeeded."

Jimmy shivered, and his face paled.

"Halloa! now, I say," cried Tom, clapping himheartily on the back; "what is the matter, any-how ?"

"Qhs Tom," and Jimmy's long-pent emotions

204 TOM PLA YFAIR.

escaped in a flood of tears, "I'm afraid of beingmurdered."

" What ?" gasped Tom.

" Just listen. You know where I live, about sixty-five miles from this place, on a large farm. Last yeara new-comer moved near us, named Hartnett. Hewas a short, dark, ugly-looking man, with bristlingblack whiskers. He lived all alone, about a milefrom our folks, and seldom said a word to anybody.One night, about a month ago, I happened to passby his house, when I heard a noise inside, as if someone were trying to shout, but couldn't; then I hearda tremendous hubbub, as if there was a scuffle;then the crack of a pistol, and then all was stillagain. In spite of my fright, I crept up to the win-dow, and, oh, Tom, how I was frightened! On thefloor lay a man in a pool of blood, and over himstood that dark man, looking still darker. I was sofrightened that I couldn't stir, and there I stoodwith my face against the window-pane. Somehow,I couldn't move. Then my heart gave a greatjump, when suddenly Hartnett's eyes met mine.At first he turned deadly pale, then he swore adreadful oath and made for the door. As he moved,my strength came back, and I tell you I ran downthe road at full speed; yet not so fast but that Icould hear his heavy breathing as he followed. Oh,it was awful—that run through the dark woods! Idon't think I'll ever be as frightened again, noteven when I come to die. Even as I ran, I couldtell that he was gaining on me; and I called to Godto help me, and prayed as I had never prayed before.At last his hand was on my collar, and he had metight. He pressed me to the earth with one hand.

TOM PL A YFAIR. 205

and with the other pulled a knife from his bosom.I shut my eyes and said what I thought was to be mylast prayer. Suddenly his grasp loosened. I openedmy eyes and saw he had changed his mind.'Boy,' he said, in a tone that froze my blood, 'kneeldown.' As I took the position, 1 ^eld me closely.'I know you,' he said, 'and you needn't fear I'llever forget your face; now swear never to tell whatyou saw in my house.' Then he put me through adreadful oath, and swore that if ever I opened mylips about what had happened that night he wouldkill me with most awful tortures." Here Jamespaused, and trembled in every limb.

Tom put his hands in his trousers' pockets, andstood with his legs wide apart. It was his methodof expressing astonishment.

'Gracious!" he said, "but he's a bad man! Yououghtn't to be afraid of him, though."

'But I am; it is not so much fear of him as ofmy conduct that worries me. Sometimes I wonderwhether I have to keep such an oath. Do you thinkI have?"

"I haven't got that far in my catechism yet,"said Tom; " but I can ask my teacher. Why, what'sthe matter?"

As Tom was speaking, a look of horror had comeupon Jimmy's face.

;'Oh, Tom, I've broken my oath. I've told youthe secret without thinking of it."

Tom was startled. His hands went deeper intohis pockets and his legs spread wider.

"Well," he inquired, after a few moments' reflec-tion, " you didn't mean to break your oath, did you ?"

"Honor bright, I didn't," protested James.

206 TOM PLA YFAIR.

"Well, then, it isn't any sin; because you can'tcommit a sin unless you mean to—that's what we aretold in catechism. But if I'd been in your place Iwouldn't have taken that oath. I'd have died first."

"Well, do you think I'm obliged to keep it?"

"I don't know about that. I'll tell you what:I'll ask the President about it, so's he won't knowthat I mean any particular boy. What do you sayto that ?"

"I think it's a good idea."

Before night, Tom had inquired of the Presidentand learned that an oath taken under compulsionwas not binding.

"But," said James, when this news was impartedto him, "what shall I do about it? Do you thinkit my duty to tell on him?"

"I don't know, Jim; you'd better think about it.Come on, let's play catch;" and Tom produced aSpalding league from his pocket. They were hard atit, when Harry came running up in great excitement.

"I say," he began, "have you heard what theRed Clippers have done ?"

"No; what?" inquired both in a breath.

"They have put up, as a prize, a fancy base-ballbat and a barrel of apples to any club in the yardthat plays 'em a decent game inside of a month."

The "Red Clippers" was the banner base-ballclub of the small yard, and the players were thestrongest, hardiest, most skilful and most active ofthe junior students. They were the constant themeof admiration among all the little boys,—an admi-ration not unmerited, inasmuch as the Red Clippershad over and over again defeated the best middle-sized nine of the large yard. A challenge, conse-

TOM PLAYFAIR. 207

quently, from their nine, was, in the eyes of all, anopportunity to win glory.

"I'll tell you what," said Tom, "let's get up aclub to beat 'em."

James Aldine smiled, " and looked at Tom asthough he doubted the seriousness of this offer.

"Get out!" said Harry in disdain. "We'll haveto grow several inches, and swell out in every direc-tion, before we'll be able to beat them."

'That's what you say," retorted Tom. "Butwe'll see about that. Now, look here! Harry, youcan curve, can't you?"

"A little," was Harry's modest reply.

"Very well; you'll pitch and I'll catch. We'llpractise together and fix things so as to fool someof those fellows. Joe Whyte may hold down firstbase; he's a good jumper, and isn't afraid of any-thing you can throw at him. Willie Ruthers canplay second base, and you, Jimmy, can try shortstop. Harry Conly seems to be a pretty good littlechap, and he can hold down third. Then, we canput Harry Underwood in right, he's a gorgeousthrower; Frank McRoy in centre, he's got long legs-and can cover a great deal of ground; and LawrenceLery in left, he's a good fly-swallower."

"Pshaw!" grumbled Harry. "All those fellowsyou've named are little tads. Do you expect tobeat the Red Clippers with them?"

"That's about it."

"Beat the Red Clippers!" reiterated Harry.

"That's just what I said, if we take a few weeksfor practice."

"Hire a hall?" said Harry.

"Just wait, will you? Now, you and Jim go

round quietly and get our fellows together, withoutletting any of the other boys know what's going on."

With but little delay, the boys in question werebrought together; whereupon Tom in a low voiceunfolded his plans. At first his hearers received theidea of beating the Red Clippers as a bit of unin-tentional pleasantry, but as Tom went on, theysettled into earnestness in such wise, that when hecame to a pause, all yielded the readiest assent to hiswishes, and despite Tom's modest disclaimer electedhim captain, manager, and trainer of the new club.

From that time on, Tom saw to it that his menwere practising constantly; and yet their trainingwas so unobtrusive, so "hidden under a bushel," asto excite no comment among their playmates.

After breakfast and supper, for instance, McRoy,Underwood, and Conly would take extreme cornersin the yard and give the whole recreation-time tothe catching of "high flies;" the basemen wouldpractise the stopping of "grounders" and the catch-ing of line balls; while Tom and Harry, with theprefect's permission, would go behind the oldchurch and employ their time at 'battery work."Tom was a plucky little catcher, and even if hefailed sometimes of holding a ball he was not afraidto stop it. His main idea in regard to practisingwith Harry was to initiate that young pitcher intosuch tricks as Tom's small experience could supply.

Whenever half-holiday came he and his men, in-stead of going out for a walk, remained in the yard.Then, when the play-ground was fairly well cleared,he would put his basemen on the bases, his pitch-er in the box, and his three fielders in turn at the bat.

It was a pleasing sight to see how deftly these

knickerbockered lads handled the ball. See thepitcher, bending his fingers into almost impossiblepositions round the ball! He is preparing to delivean " in-curve." Whiz! there it goes, right over theplate, whack! into Tom's hands; and the boy withthe bat wonders how he came to miss it. From theway Tom throws it at the second baseman, youwould think it was a matter of life and death. Butit is thrown too high; however, Ruthers seems tothink the catching of it to be likewise a matter oflife and death, for he springs into the air, brings itdown with one hand, and without stopping forapplause passes it on a low line to the first baseman.The first baseman is familiar with the short bound;he makes a neat scoop, then sends it daisy-cuttingacross the diamond to the short stop, who securesit on a dead run, jerking it into the hands of thethird baseman. How quick they are! how eager!The one week's practice has been magical in result.

"Good gracious!" exclaimed Willie, "but we canplay ball a little bit."

"You're right," said Joe as he walked in. 'Say,Tom, I think we can play 'em any time, now—rightaway."

'Not much!" said Tom emphatically. 'There'sa big thing we've got to look out for yet; if we fixthat we'll be all right."

'What's that?" was the general query.

'We've got to get used to their pitcher's delivery,so's to bat him easy. If we can't do good batting,they'll beat us badly. Now, I'll tell you what; I'vegot a scheme to bring the thing the way we want it.It's this: I'll bet any boy here the cakes for the14

2io TOM PLAY FAIR.

next two weeks, and the apples too, that I can holdhis delivery for half an hour."

The "cakes and apples," also the "pie," werefavorite stakes at St. Maure's. By these terms wasunderstood the daily dessert.

"I'll take you," said Harry, whose twinklingeyes gave evidence that he understood Tom's plan."And I'll give Keenan half the cakes if I win."

"Done,"said Tom, clasping Harry's hand, andholding it till Joe kindly "cut" the bet. "And I'llgo halves with George if I win. And what do yousay, Harry, if these boys here, who have heard usmake the bet, do the batting to see whether theycan bluff me?"

"I agree to that, too," answered Harry, with asolemn wink.

All now perceived the ruse and were delightedwith their parts. No matter who should win thebet, it would be a splendid opportunity for studyingtheir pitcher, and for getting some practice in batting.

After supper George Keenan was somewhat as-tonished to find himself waited upon by a delega-tion of yard-mates.

'What are you fellows up to?" he exclaimed.

"Look here, George," Tom began, "I want youto do me a favor. You see I made a bet to-day,while these fellows were standing around, that Icould hold your hottest balls for half an hour. Nowif you pitch your best and I win, you'll get my dessertfora week; if I lose, Harry'11 give you his for a week."

Most model boys, if we can believe the storybooks, are rather indifferent in regard to cakes andpie; but George was a model boy on lines of hisown—he jumped at the offer.

TOM PLAYPAIR. 211

"Why of course I'll pitch to you; that's fun for me.'

" Thank you," said Tom gratefully. ;' And I say,George, these boys will bat your pitching so as tomake it more real."

"Oh! that's all right," answered George, takingoff his coat, and stepping into the pitcher's box.

A referee was then appointed to time the carryingout of this novel bet; and the proceedings began.For some time Tom contrived to hold George'shottest balls with apparent ease, while the witnessesimproved their batting abilities. Strange to say,however, Tom, at the end of twenty-five minutes,began to show signs of weakening; and presentlycalled time. Harry had won the bet.

Tom then protested that he was sure he couldwin the wager some other time; and, as before,offered to bet on the result. Forthwith, Will Rutherstook him up, and it was agreed that on the followingday the test should be repeated.

In a word, Tom, by a variety of devices, succeededin getting his men an opportunity of studying and"solving" George's curves three or four times eachweek.

Nor was he satisfied, once they had caught the knackof hitting Keenan. He went further; he insisted ontheir batting so as to send it toward third base.He had a good reason for this, as the issue will show.

Thus, giving himself to study and to play withequal zest, and never losing sight of the sacredChristmas that was approaching, the month passedquickly and pleasantly for Tom; and almost beforehe could realize it, the day for the great base-ballmatch was at hand.

CHAPTER XXIII.

IN WHICH THE "KNICKERBOCKERS" PLAY THE "RED
CLIPPERS.11

HIGH Mass on All Saints' Day had just ended.In one corner of the small yard a knot of boyshad gathered together, and were indulging in ahearty laugh.

;<O Jupiter!" Pitch exclaimed, "won't we do 'emup!"

'They're pretty cool for little fellows," remarkedHarry Jones, the field captain of the Red Clippers.He was holding in his hand a note.

'What's the fun?" asked George Keenan, whohad arrived late on the scene.

'The best joke of the season, George," said Con-way. ' Go on; read it to him, Henry."

' Listen to this," said Henry, with a smile.

ST. MAURE'S COLLEGE,

Nov. ist, iS—.MR. HENRY JONES—

Dear Sir: We, the Knickerbocker Club of St. Maure's Col-lege, do hereby challenge the Red Clippers to a game of base-ball to be played on the afternoon of All Saints' Day.

Respectfully,

THOMAS PLAYFAIR, captain and c.

HENRY QUIP, p.

Jos. WHYTE, ib.

WM. RUTHERS, 2b.

JAS. ALDINE, s. s.

HENRY CONLY, 3b.

HENRY UNDERWOOD, r. f.

FRANK McRov, c. f.

LORENZ LERY, 1. f.

But George did not laugh.

"Those fellows," he said gravely, "may be little,but they are no slouches. As for ourselves, we havenot played a game the last three weeks, and someof you fellows need practice badly."

" Oh, pshaw!" said Pitch, " we need no practicefor them. I batted against Quip's pitching lastyear, and I can knock him all over."

Despite George's doubts, the Red Clippers decidedto play their opponents without preparation.

Soon after dinner, accordingly, all the small boyshurried from the yard to the base-ball field beyondthe blue grass, where they were presently swelled innumber by the arrival of the senior students, who,having heard of Tom as an "exorcist," and knownhim as captain of the snow fort, were anxious tostudy his methods in the national game.

At five minutes to two, Henry Jones sent a five-cent piece spinning in the air.

"Heads!" said Tom.

Heads it was, and the captain of the Knicker-bockers chose the "outs."

"Time! Play!" bawled the umpire, as GeorgeKeenan stepped up to the bat.

The ball that came from Harry's hands seemed tobe in a great hurry. It fairly crossed the plate, butwas too high.

"One ball."

Then came another ball, swift and low.

"Two balls."

The third ball was tempting, and just whereGeorge wanted it. But it was one of those deceit-fully slow balls, and almost sailed over the platesome little time after George struck at it. The

batsman had lunged vigorously, and as the resist-ance of the air was mild, he whirled round and waswithin an ace of losing his balance. Before hecould recover himself, another ball shot by, straightand swift.

"Two strikes," cried the umpire.

The crowd laughed; George tried to look easy,and Tom stepped up behind the bat.

George struck at the next ball, but he was tooslow, and walked away wearing the hollow mask ofa smile; while the crowd, always in favor of thesmaller boy, applauded lustily.

Shane next came to the bat, only to go out on afoul, captured on the run by Henry Conly. Pitchfollowed with an easy bounder to the pitcher, and,amid lifting of voices and casting of caps, the RedClippers took the field.

Harry opened the innings for his side by poppingup an easy fly back of the pitcher, and before reach-ing first base, changed his mind and went for a drinkof water. Tom now advanced to the bat and, aftertwo strikes, knocked a sharp grounder to Pitch, whowas covering short. As the ball went throughPitch's legs, Tom ran to second. Then arose ashout of triumph from the crowd, as Joe Whytedrove a low liner straight over third, earning secondfor himself and bringing in Tom. Willie Ruthersgave variety to this stage of the game by strikingout. Aldine followed with a high fly toward short.Pitch, and Conway, who played third, both ran forit; a collision followed, and ball, third baseman,and short stop rolled in three several directions.

"You idiot! What did you do that for?" Pitchblurted.

"Who? me?" inquired Conway, as he picked him-self up and began rubbing his head.

"Yes, you!"

'Oh, I thought you were talking to the ball! /couldn't help it. I wouldn't strike against yourhead for a fortune, if I could help myself."

Taking advantage of this altercation, Joe, whohad stolen third, ran home. The next batter, HarryUnderwood, knocked a vicious grounder between firstand second, but John Donnel was there and threwhim out with ease.

My base-ball readers must have already perceivedTom's motive in training his men to turn on theball. The weak points of the Red Clippers werethird and short.

In the second inning, after a three-bagger byDonnel, Conway made a clean hit, and sent Johnhome. Presently, Conway saw a good chance tosteal second; the baseman was playing far off hisbag. Just as soon, then, as the pitcher deliveredhis ball, Conway made a bold dash for second andthereby fell into one of Tom's snares. The short-stop of the Knickerbockers was there, caught theball from Tom, and touched the runner out.

In their half of the second inning, Tom's nine covered themselves with honors, and their opponents, especially Pitch and Conway, with errors. The third and fourth innings brought two runs on each side.

In the fifth, Pitch, who had lost his head, let sev-eral slow grounders pass him, while Conway dropped a fly and muffed two thrown balls—errors which, coupled with two base hits, yielded the Knicker-bockers four runs. In the sixth inning, consequently,

these two worthies were ordered to take positions in the out-field.

" If that's the way you treat a fellow, I won't play," growled Pitch, putting on his coat.

"And I want plaster for my head," added Con-way, putting on his.

"Let's not play any more to-day," said Donnel, at this juncture. "We're done up, and we might as well give in gracefully, before we begin fighting among ourselves."

The suggestion was good; the Red Clippers, beaten in the field, outwitted at the bat, and jeered at by the crowd, were indeed in no condition to continue. Jones perceived this, and wisely con-cluded to follow Donnel's advice.

Thereupon he held a short whispered consultation with Tom, apart, and, turning to the scorer, called for the score.

'Knickerbockers, 7; Red Clippers, 3,' roared the scorer.

Tumultuous applause from the sympathetic audi-ence, hand-springs and hand-shakes from the vic-torious players.

'Playfair," said Ryan, the captain of the senior club of the college, " I've been here four years, and, honestly, I've never seen a club better trained than yours. You little fellows deserved to win that game, you went about it so neatly."

Ryan's words voiced the general opinion.

Tom's training had indeed been successful. On one occasion during the game, the umpire called Will Ruthers out at second when he was manifestly safe; but not by the least word or look did Ruthers or any one of his side show dissatisfaction. So it

was during the entire contest, while Jones and Pitch and Conway made it disagreeable for the umpire by constant quibbling and growling, the Knickerbock-ers, to a man, cheerfully accepted his every ruling. This is but one point of their training; but it is a point which I enlarge upon for the simple reason that so few college teams set any importance upon it. And yet this point, if attended to, makes base-ball a training-school for wondrous self-command, and gives the game a dignity well befitting a nation's choice.

CHAPTER XXIV.

TROUBLE AHEAD.

TOM'S improvement was not limited to base-ball. In class and out, he advanced steadily. Noth-ing, perhaps, had so helped him as his choice of friends. From among all the boys of the small yard, he had selected as his chums Harry Quip, Willie Ruthers, Joe Whyte, and James Aldine.

Harry Quip, mischief-loving though he was, had a great amount of practical, common-sense piety. No one enjoyed a joke or a laugh more heartily than he, but he knew where to draw the line. He was easy of disposition; in fact, a superficial knowledge of him might bring one to think he was easily led. In regard to indifferent matters this was quite true. Harry would rather yield than quarrel. But when it came to a choice between right and wrong, he was firm as a rock.

One instance will give an idea of Harry's method on such occasions,

During the preceding vacation he was thrown inwith the boys of his neighborhood.

Shortly after his return from St. Maure's, he wasconversing with some of them, when one began nar-rating what he considered a very good story indeed.

Harry saw the drift of it. 'I say, boys," heinterrupted, "the air is getting too strong for mearound here. I guess I'll take a walk."

To his gratification, three of the little lads mus-tered up courage to leave with him. The joke wasleft unfinished, and whenever Harry Quip joinedthe boys the conversation was entirely proper.Indeed, before vacation had ended, the ethicalstandard of his companions had risen by manydegrees.

Willie Ruthers and Joe Whyte were bright, pleas-ant little lads, reflecting the virtues of their heroes,Harry and Tom.

James Aldine was something more than an ordi-narily pious boy. The younger students of St.Maure's College actually revered him, and calledhim the " saint." He was remarkable for gentleness.But his gentleness was made of stronger stuff thanthe term usually implies. His meek little wayswrought wonders upon Tom and Harry. Theyseemed unconsciously to catch his gentleness, andsoon joined with him in little devotions that touchedand refined their lives into spiritual beauty. Tomwas often overawed by Jimmy's piety.

"Say, Harry," he remarked one day, "that JimmyAldine's got more praying and piety in his littlefinger than you and I have in our prayer-books andwhole bodies put together. Did you notice him lastSunday after Holy Communion ? His face was a§

bright as—as—anything, and I watched him till helooked like a saint in a picture; and I expectedevery minute that a pretty gold crown would shinearound his head and a pair of spangled wings wouldcrop from his shoulders, and he'd go off sailing upto heaven, leaving you and me to fight it out, andeven then find it hard to behave half decently."

Evidently Tom had an imagination. Had hebeen older, he would have put his idea into verseand published it.

One of the first friendly secrets that Tom impartedto James Aldine was the story of his deferred FirstCommunion. James took as much interest in Tom'spreparation as Tom himself; and on recreation days,when they walked out together over the lonely prai-ries, he would speak so lovingly of Our Saviour in theBlessed Sacrament, that his companion, like thedisciples on the road to Emmaus, felt his heartburning within him.

On November the eighth two things came topass, both bearing closely upon the fates and for-tunes of our five little lads.

On that morning a cheering fire lighted up thewindows of Mr. John Aldine's home, on the outskirtsof the village of .Merlin. Within, a pleasant-featuredwoman was busily setting the tea-table. Beside thefire, a child, who had just emerged from babyhood,was critically and dispassionately examining intothe merits of a picture book.

A brisk step was heard without, the door opened,and a man entered.

"Papa! papa!" screamed the child, clapping hislittle hands with glee and running toward thenew-comer.

"Well, little Touzle," said Mr. Aldine, raisingthe child in his arms and kissing him, " and howare you, Kate ?" he continued, affectionately greet-ing his wife. ' We must be happy to-night. I havesucceeded well to-day in my law matters; and, bestof all, I have a letter from James."

' Hurrah!" cried Touzle, dancing about his papa'slegs, to the no small inconvenience of that gentle-man, who was trying to divest himself of his great-coat, " letter from Dimmy! how's brudder Dimmy ?Tell Touzle all about it, papa."

Mrs. Aldine, though not so demonstrative asTouzle, was no less anxious to hear the contents ofthe letter.

"Sit down, my dear, by the fire," she said, "andwhen you feel perfectly cosy, let us all together hearwhat our darling has written."

Mr. Aldine, be it observed, never opened theletters from his boy but with his wife beside him.It was a delicate attention, and a very small thing,it may be, but take the small things out of life, andwe have little left but murders and bank robberies.

'Well, here goes!" said Mr. Aldine, as he openedthe envelope and spread out the letter.

ST. MAURE'S COLLEGE, November 4th.Mr. and Mrs. John Aldine.MY DEAR PARENTS:—

A knock at the door, so sharp, so vicious, as tocause Mrs. Aldine to start violently, and Touzle tojump with great alacrity from his father's knee, hereinterrupted the reading.

"Come in," said Mr. Aldine.

Touzle. took refuge behind his mother's skirts, as

a short, dark, ill-featured man, with bristling blackwhiskers, entered the room. For a moment Mr.Aldine gazed at the stranger in some perplexity.

'It's Mr. Hartnett, who has called several timesin your absence to inquire for James," whisperedMrs. Aldine.

' Oh, pardon me, Mr. Hartnett," cried Mr. Aldine,advancing and shaking his visitor's hand. " Iought to know your face by this time. Sit down."

'Well," Mr. Hartnett made answer, as he seatedhimself, " I can't blame you for not knowing me, foralthough I have called on you several times I havealways missed you."

'I thank you, sir, for your goodness," said Mr.Aldine, " and especially for the interest which Iunderstand you take in my boy."

'Won't you take tea with us?" asked the wife.

'Thanks, with pleasure; it's chilly outside, anda cup of tea isn't such a bad thing in this weather.By the way, have you heard from the boy lately?You can't imagine what an interest I take in him.I met him once or twice and am convinced that he'llone day make his mark."

'We have just received a letter from him," saidMr. Aldine, highly pleased—as what father wouldnot be?—at these praises of his boy, "and, perhaps,if I read a little of it to you, you may not take it

amiss.'

'My dear sir," said Hartnett with much warmth,'you are too good; I shall be delighted. Touzle,you little rogue," he said to the child, "come hereand look at my pretty watch."

But Touzle, who had thus far persistently clungto his mother's skirts, was not to be tempted from

behind his intrenchments. With his great, roundeyes staring severely on Mr. Hartnett, he neitherspoke nor moved. It is said that little childrenhave an instinctive knowledge of good and bad peo-ple. Whether this be true or not, it is certain thatTouzle had decided views relative to Mr. Hartnett,and by no means favorable to that person.

" Here's the way the letter runs," said Mr. Aldine:

MY DEAR PARENTS :—I am so glad to learn that you arewell, and that dear little Touzle is happy—

"Hurrah!" cried Touzle in parenthesis.

—I am very happy here, and like the boys very much.Most of them are very good and kind, and only a few are mean.I like my prefects very much—my professor is just splendid. Ithink he can teach more in a week than most other teachers ina year. And now, my dear parents, I want to tell you some-thing I have long kept secret.

" Halloa! what is this?" said Mr. Aldine, knittinghis brows, and reading what followed to himself.He did not notice that Mr. Hartnett's face changedcolor, and that his right hand was quickly thrustinto his side pocket and remained there. For amoment there was silence, an awful silence—hadthe little family but known the thoughts of theirvisitor!

" Why, this is strange!" said Mr. Aldine, at length." He says that he is the only witness of a crimewhich he had sworn never to confess."

"What crime?" asked Hartnett.

'He doesn't say; but promises to tell me aboutit when I come to see him Christmas."

Mr. Hartnett's hand returned from his pocket, andwith a forced laugh, he said:

TOM PLAY FAIR. 223

"Oh, indeed! Perhaps it'll turn out to be a reg-ular romance." At the harsh merriment of the vis-itor, Mrs. Aldine could not refrain from shuddering.Touzle hid himself entirely from view.

"Well, it's drawing on late," resumed Hartnett,hastily drinking his tea, "and I'd better be going."Awkwardly enough he took his departure.

" Dear John," said Mrs. Aldine, as the door closedupon him, " I don't trust that man. Somehow I fearhe means us no good."

"You think so?" said Mr. Aldine, in surprise."I do, indeed."

" He's a bad, teaman," said Touzle, stamping hisfoot.

"Well, I'll keep my eyes open; that's all I cardo," said the strong-nerved husband.

Their suspicions would have been confirmed hadthey seen Hartnett standing a few yards from theirdoor, his clinched hands raised in imprecation upontheir happy home.

About midnight, Hartnett issued from his lonelyhouse, valise in hand, and set off rapidly down thepublic road. He was never again seen in Merlin.

At St. Maure's, on this same day, Tom was madethe happiest boy at college—and that is saying agood deal—by receiving from home a box contain-ing, among other things, a rubber coat, a pair ofIce-King club skates, and a fine breech-loading shot-gun for hunting purposes. Luckily it was recreationday, and Tom, having obtained permission of theprefect of discipline, joined the customary huntingparty, of which James Aldine was a member. Underhis friend's direction Tom learned very fast. Hiseyes were good, his nerves strong. To his great joy

224 TOM PLAY FAIR.

he brought down a duck on his fourth shot. Tramp-ing through the woods and over the prairies, stealingcautiously up to game under cover of tree and bush,and creeping along the margin of lake and river,the day passed quickly indeed; and Tom, with threeducks in his hunting pouch, returned to college jubi-lant. Before retiring, he had arranged with Harry,Willie, James, and Joe to go on an all-day hunt thatday a week.

CHAPTER XXV.

A JOYOUS GOING FORTH, AND A SAD JOURNEY HOME.

A MID-NOVEMBER morning, cold, blustering,gloomy, the day of the great hunt.

Shortlyafter breakfast, five little lads scampered to thegun-room, and arming themselves according to thehunting traditions of St. Maure's, set out across theprairie in the direction of Pawnee Creek.

"Well, I'm glad it's cold," Tom remarked as theygot clear of the college premises. ' A boy enjoyswalking more in this kind of weather. He doesn'tfeel like standing around doing nothing."

"And I'm glad it's cloudy," said Harry Quip," because we aren't in any danger of spoiling ourcomplexions."

" Every kind of weather is good," said James.

"Yes, even hot weather," remarked Willie Ruth-ers. " Dear me, there'd heaps of folks be drownedif it wasn't for hot weather, because no one wouldever learn to swim."

"Yes," said Harry, his eyes twinkling, "and on

the same principle I reckon there would be heaps offolks frozen to death in winter, if there was no coldweather, because folks wouldn't learn how to keepthemselves warm."

Suddenly James Aldine stopped walking.

"What's the matter?" asked Tom, who was im-mediately behind him.

"You are, Tom. Do you think I'm going towalk in front of your gun, if you hold it with themuzzle pointing where my brains are supposed to be ?"

"Oh, what's the difference? It isn't loaded."

"That's not certain. And, besides, I object to iton principle. My father has often told me never tohunt with any one who handles a gun carelessly.Here, now, hold it this way, resting on your arm;now, should it go off, you may bring down a cloud,if your gun carries that far, but you won't hurt anyof us."

'Pshaw!" growled Tom, as he complied with therequest, "I thought a fellow who knew as muchabout a gun as you wouldn't be afraid!"

"Just the opposite; the more you know about agun, the more respect you'll have for it. A child,if he knows how to use a gun, is the equal of thestrongest man. It is a dreadful weapon. One littleload in it may carry death to the bravest."

James spoke earnestly; his words made a deepimpression on Tom.

At this point the conversation was cut short bythe appearance of a rabbit, which James despatchedwith a skilful shot. Game was plentiful that day,and before noon Tom succeeded in bagging his firstrabbit, along with a plump quail, while James secured three rabbits and several birds.15

Thus wandering along the banks of the Pawneein the direction of the river, they stopped shortlyafter midday at the skirts of the woodland whichsweeps along, perhaps a quarter of a mile in width,on either side of the river, and partook of a homelybut hearty repast.

The boy who, after being on his feet half theday, can sit down to a meal without appetite is notworth writing about. Our little party are worthwriting about, indeed! Cold beefsteak, ham,bread, cakes, and apples disappeared with wondrousrapidity.

" My!" said Tom, " I wish we'd brought more!"

All echoed this sentiment.

"I tell you what; let's- fix up a rabbit," saidHarry; 'we can build a fire easily, and I'll cook."

The suggestion was favorably received, and in atrice James was preparing the rabbit which Tomhad brought down; Harry was lighting a fire, whilethe others collected sticks and dry leaves. Theyhad hardly put themselves to their interesting task,when snow began to fall.

'Hurrah!" cried Harry, jumping to his feet, anddancing about the fire, "we'll have a snow fort inthe yard to-morrow."

"Hurrah!" shouted the others, and all begandancing about the fire. There is an inexpressiblecharm in the first snowfall of the year, which glori-fies a boy; every tiny little messenger falling radi-ant, white-robed from the skies seems to whisper atale of glee to his responsive heart. Round andround the fire the lads danced, faster and faster,while thicker and larger fell the flakes. Theirdancing might have been prolonged indefinitely,

had not the embers given warning that more fuelwas needed.

"Hold on, boys!" cried Tom, who had just failedin an attempt to execute a hand-spring, "we wantmore wood, Jimmy; get your rabbit ready quick,'and off they danced in different directions.

By the time the rabbit was cooked, the groundwas hidden from view.

' We'll have plenty of fun going home," remarkedJames, as they again fell to.

" How's that ?" asked Joe.

'Why, we can track rabbits over the snow."

"Hurrah for King Winter!" shouted Tom withfresh exhilaration.

" I wonder when we'll have another meal as jollyas this?" queried Harry.

'Who knows?" This from James Aldine.

"I say," said Tom, who was too healthy a lad toindulge in conjecture, 'I'd rather be here eatingthis old rabbit, with the snow getting into my ears,than at a turkey and ice-cream dinner in the moststylish house."

No one seemed inclined to gainsay this statement;and a few minutes later, having done full justice totheir fare, they resumed their hunt, each one peeringin every direction to discover rabbit tracks.

As they pushed along, Tom noticed that James,who was lightly clad, shivered occasionally.

"Say, Jim, aren't you cold? Here, take my coat,I'm too warm for any use."

"No, no!" remonstrated James; "I'm used tobeing out in the cold."

But Tom whipped off his garment before Jameshad fairly entered his protest, and with his grandest

air of authority made his friend put it on. Then,clad in his sailor jacket and knickerbockers, thesturdy young Samaritan trotted on as comfortablein his light attire as though he were in the heatsof mid-summer. Genuine kindness is warmer thanany coat.

They were about two miles to the northwest ofthe college (two and one-half from the village of St.Maure beyond) when to their great joy they cameupon the long-looked-for tracks. On they ran withnew energy, but coming to the road, over whichmany vehicles must have passed, they were broughtto a sudden halt. The prints had become confusedwith the impress of wheels and horses' hoofs.

It may be observed, that the road lay between thewoods skirting the river and a long strip of landknown as the valley, which, stretching on eitherside of the railroad track, changed gradually intothe wild, rolling prairie.

Tom was for following the road, Harry for mov-ing through the valley on toward the prairie, whileJames favored taking to the woods. By way ofcompromise, they agreed to scatter, each followinghis own plan.

So Tom, followed by Willie and Joe, trotted alongbriskly some ten or fifteen minutes, when Joe, outof breath, begged him to slacken his pace. Tompaused, and suddenly, from right beneath his feet,a rabbit which had been concealed in the brushwoodscampered forth.

Bang! went his gun; the rabbit fell dead.

"Ain't I getting to be a great hunter!" roaredTom in undisguised admiration at himself. "Waitone moment, boys, till I load up again Here goes

for a deadner!" and he inserted his loaded shell.' There's five fingers of buck-shot in that,—enoughto kill six rabbits standing in a row."

"I say, Tom," said Willie, "it's getting dark!"

'So it is," assented Tom, taking out his watch.'Why, halloa! it's near four o'clock. We'd betterget ready to start for the college, or we'll come latefor supper and get fifty lines each from Mr. Middle-ton. Come on, we must find the other boys."

Vigorous shouting soon brought Harry to theirside, but shout as they might, James Aldine gaveno sign of being within ear-shot. Some minutespassed,—darkness was coming on apace. Joe Why tobegan to betray signs of nervousness, and WillieRuthers caught the feeling. Suddenly—it was anaccidental circumstance, but none the less awkward—all ceased shouting, and the hush of the eveningseemed to take grim possession of each. Tom wasthe first to break the silence.

'Well, I suppose we'd better take a trot into thewoods," he observed.

'Isn't it gloomy and silent under these trees?"said Joe, as they picked their way among the trees.

" Isn't it, though!" said Willie. " I feel as thoughI had the nightmare."

As they plunged into the woods they became moreand more solemn; their shoutings had ceased en-tirely, and, indeed, they hardly spoke above awhisper. The gloom and grim silence of the white-armed trees had exercised a spell upon them. Sud-denly they heard a sound that made their blood runcold; it was a groan.

'Good God!" whispered Tom, crossing himself,'but that sounded like Jimmy's voice. Come on,

boys softly. Don't step on any twigs, but pickyour steps. I'm afraid Jimmy's in danger, and Ihave reasons you don't know of;" and Tom, as hemoved forward, followed tremblingly by the others,held his gun at full cock.

Another groan was heard. Tom's face becamepale as death, but his whole expression was nonethe less determined. Bending low, and partiallyprotected from view by the bushes, they moved ontill Tom paused, his face alive with horror, stag-gered, but recovered himself and raised his hand tothe others in warning.

Judge of their terror, as, in obedience to Tom'sgesture, they ranged themselves beside him andgazed on the sight that had so stricken him.

In a pool of blood, its bright red color contrastingso frightfully with the white snow, lay James Aldine.Above him, a stained dagger in his hand, stooped aman,—dark, sullen, villanous, with the unholy lightof murder in his sinister eyes. He seemed to beexamining the poor child's features, as though tomake sure that he was dead.

As Tommy gazed, his expression changed fromhorror to determination. Making a slight gestureto his companions to remain quiet, he drew up hisgun and covered the stranger. Then, advancingstealthily to within a few feet of the villain, whowas facing in the opposite direction, he said in aclear, ringing voice:

" Drop that knife, or I fire!"

So sudden came the shock upon the stranger, that,as he turned, his nerveless fingers let the dagger fallto the earth, while his face assumed a look of themost extreme terror,

" Raise your hands above your head, at once, ofI fire," continued Tom, in the same inflexible tones.The gun, pointed direct at the man's breast, wasas steady in the child's hands as though it were heldby a statue.

The determined face of the boy utterly cowed theman. Up went his hands without delay.

"Now, sir, take that path right behind you andgo straight on at a steady walk till you come to theroad leading to St. Maure's; and I give you myword that if you attempt to move from the path,put down your hands, or turn around, I will shootyou at once. I know you, Mr. Hartnett [at thename the man's face put on new terror], and I knowthat this is not your first murder. Now, turn roundand walk straight on."

"Take down that gun," chattered Hartnett; "itmight go off accidentally."

" It will go off if you don't do what I tell you."

Completely mastered, the man turned and movi 1forward, keeping Tom's directions to the letter.Boy though his captor was, Hartnett perceived thathe was dealing with a man, as far as determinationwent, and a very determined man at that.

As Tom, preceded by his captive, moved towardthe village, Harry, Willie, and Joe raised Jamesfrom the ground, wrapped him in their coats, andtenderly bore him toward the college.

It were vain to attempt portraying adequately thestate of Tom's mind as he tramped steadily on afterthe murderer. His imagination never wandered;his whole being was fused into the determination tobring that man to justice. The road was lonelyand deserted; not a sound smote the stillness; the

minutes passed on into the quarters, but the steadytread of captor and captive beat equal and silentupon the yielding snow; the heavy gun covered itsobject as though supported by muscles of steel;sensation, fear, hope,—all were kept in abeyance toTom's present purpose. The blinding snow dimmednot his eyes, the cold stiffened not a limb. Whetherit was a minute, an hour, or a day that the sterntramp lasted, Tom could never have told. Hissenses, concentrated to a single purpose, were deadto all else till the village was reached, and crowdsof men came thronging around him and his prisoner.

Then speech and his normal activities returned.

"Arrest this man," he said; 'he is a murderer!"

Strong hands were laid upon Hartnett; Tom'sgun slipped from his grasp, a mist swam before hiseyes.

'My brave boy," said a gentleman, catching hishand, " you must be cold, and worn out too. Letme put my coat about you."

"Thank you, sir," said Tom.

Then he staggered, blood issued from mouth andnose, and he fell into the gentleman's arms senseless.

CHAPTER XXVI.

SICKNESS.

DR. MULLAN'S face was graver than usual as heissued that evening from the college infirmaryin the company of the reverend President.

' Both are critical cases, Father, and, indeed, Ihave more fears for that brave little Playfair than

for the other. Aldine's wounds are not necessarilyfatal; a good constitution will probably bring himthrough. But the little hero is in danger of some-thing worse than death. The strain upon his mind,the force of his emotions, the terrible ordeal towhich his most remarkable will-power has subjectedhim, have thrown him into a high fever. He mayrecover, but, even then, his mind may be impairedor his nerves shattered for life."

"God forbid!" said the President. "Do you con-sider it advisable to write for the relatives ofeither?"

"Well, it would be no harm to send for Aldine'speople; but as for Playfair, there's time enough.We had better wait till we see how his case turns."

Both little sufferers were in a private room, re-moved from the common ward of the infirmary.James Aldine, weak, pale, hardly conscious, waslying on his uninjured side,—now and then givingforth a feeble moan of pain. In another part of theroom lay Tom, his cheeks flushed with fever, hiseyes bright and wild. Harry sat beside him andoccasionally bathed his forehead. Whenever theinfirmarian approached, Tom would shiver withhorror, and would beg Harry, whom he called bythe name of some former acquaintance, to take thatman away, for he was a murderer, there was bloodupon his hands,—could they not see the blood?—there was murder in his every look.

About seven o'clock in the evening, when thecollege boys had been safely housed in their respect-ive study-rooms, Mr. Middleton, Tom's teacher,prefect, and dear friend, entered the room, and,strangely enough, Tom recognized him at once,

"Oh, Mr. Middleton," he cried, "will you helpme?"

" Certainly, my dear boy," said the prefect, grasp-ing the fevered hands entreatingly extended to him,u what can I do for you?"

"Come close to me," said Tom, 'I don't wantthem to hear it. See them all watching me," hecried, pointing around the room. 'They are all inthe crime. Stoop down, Mr. Middleton, I want towhisper to you."

The prefect bent low.

"They want to kill Jimmy, and they've poisonedme, so's I can't help him; but you'll take my place,won't you ?"

"Yes, yes, Tommy; rely upon it, no one shalltouch a hair of his head."

"And, Mr. Middleton, I'm going to make myFirst Communion to-morrow. It's Christmas, youknow, and I've waited—oh, so long!"

"Not to-morrow, Tom."

The fevered patient took no notice of this answer.

"Where is Jimmy now?" asked Tom, presently.

" There he is lying on that bed."

Tom raised himself and looked in the directionindicated. Then a strange, perplexed expressioncame upon him, as though the true ideas of whathad so lately happened were striving vainly tosquare with the wild vagaries of his fever. Ex-hausted by the mental conflict, he fell back and,still holding tightly the prefect's hand, closed hiseyes.

Toward nine o'clock that night, as Willie Rutherswas sitting beside the other sufferer, James recoveredfrom his stupor,

"Willie," he said, "how did Tommy come to besick?"

Willie told him the story of Tom's heroism, andof the high fever which the exposure and mentalstrain had brought on him. The listener's eyesfilled with tears of gratitude to his brave companion,but on hearing of Tom's great danger, his face grewtroubled.

"Tom is a real hero," he said, "and I shall prayfor him night and day, that he may get well."

Next morning all the students were unusuallysubdued. Gathered together in knots, Tom's brav-ery was the subject of universal panegyric; whileall, even the most flighty, were concerned at hisdanger.

At all times, Harry, Villie, and Joe were at theside of their friends. Nothing could exceed theirdevotedness. Ever and anon Aldine's face quiv-ered with pain, but there constantly dwelt uponit a gentle expression of resignation. The doctorwas satisfied with his symptoms. Tom's case seemedto trouble him more.

Toward evening of the second day after thehunting expedition, a lady entered and, kneelingbeside James, covered his face with kisses.

"Don't be troubled, mamma," said James, hold-ing her hand tenderly, "I am not suffering much;indeed I am not. Tom is in danger, and you mustpray for him."

Mrs. Aldine, who had heard the whole story,presently went over to Tom. The poor child, whohad been tossing restlessly all day, started up onseeing her, his face softened with joy.

" Qh, mamma," he cried, "why didn't you

to me before? Come to me, mamma, and stay withme always." He tenderly embraced Mrs. Aldine—his mother, poor child, was in heaven. 'Mamma,"he continued, "there's something I'm so anxiousto tell you. I'm to make my First CommunionChristmas, and you must pray for me that I do itwell. I used to be very wild at home, but I thinkthat I am not quite as I used to be. I've workedhard to change, and it is partly on your account,mamma. I know that you've been praying for meever since you went to heaven; and I rememberwhat you said to me just before you died. Theywant to poison me before I can make it. But poisondoesn't hurt me. I'm used to it now. I'm gladI'm sick. You can't fool me; I know I'm sick;and it's just as easy to keep from sin if you're inbed as it is anywhere else. Easier; I'd commitmurder, maybe, if I were out. I'd shoot—shoot—shoot- ' and Tom ended this strange monologuewith jumping up into a sitting posture and clinchinghis hands, while his eyes flashed in fury.

About sundown he changed for the worse. Heshrieked and cried, and could hardly be held downin his bed. Toward midnight the doctor was sum-moned.

"If his delirium lasts above twenty-four hours,his case, I fear, is hopeless."

On hearing this, James called Willie, Joe, andHarry to his bedside.

" Boys, I want you to join me in prayer," he said." I have made God a promise if He cures Tom. Itmay not be His holy will to cure him; but let usunite in prayer."

Led by James, the boys, in low, fervent tones,

recited decade after decade to the Blessed Mother;while Tom, hanging between life and death, wassoothed and restrained in his paroxysms by the kindhands of Mrs. Aldine and Mr. Middleton.

CHAPTER XXVII.

DEA TH.

IT was ten o'clock of the following day. Tom's raving had gradually lessened. As the hours wore on he became quiet, till at length, for the first time since the eventful Thursday, he fell asleep.

"His life is saved," said the doctor; 'but the danger to his mind is not yet over. All now lies in the hands of God."

;' So much the more reason for our praying," said James. " Come on, boys," he continued, addressing his three friends, " let us take heaven by storm!'

Morning waned into afternoon, afternoon shaded into night, and still Tom slumbered. Standing about his bed, Mr. Middleton, Mrs. Aldine, and the three boys anxiously watched the face of the sleeper.

A little after eight in the evening Tom's breath-ing changed. He opened his eyes. All stood with bated breath, awaiting his first words.

After gazing about vacantly for some seconds, he stretched out his arms, gave a low sigh, and said,' Good gracious! I'm all broken up!"

There was a smile upon every face; the tone was so natural, so like Tom.

' Tom, old boy, don't you know me ?" cried Harry, unable to restrain himself.

"I rather think I do. Why shouldn't I? But

238 TOM PLAYFAIR.

what's the matter with you all ? I'm not a museum, ami? You're all staring at me so! And where in the world am I, and what's the matter with my head? It feels as light as a balloon!"

"Do you know, Tommy," said Mr. Middleton, "that you've been sick for several days? Very sick, indeed?"

" Let me think," said Tom, passing his hand over his brow. "We were out hunting, and when we came to the place where poor Jimmy was stabbed—we—we—what did we do, anyhow? Did I fall down? And did that man try to murder me? And what's become of Jimmy?"

"Here I am, Tom," cried James, who was sitting np in his bed and literally brimming over with joy. "I'm all right, and so are you. You brought that murderer to jail. Don't you remember?"

"What—what did I do?" Tom inquired.

"Listen," said Harry, and with no little astonish-ment Tom heard his famous adventure narrated.

"Well, well, dear me!" he said at the conclusion," it may be all true, but there's one little question I'd like to ask."

"Ask away," said Harry cheerfully.

"Well, I'd like to know if I was there when I did all that?"

All laughed at the serio-comic way in which Tom put this query. In truth, his question, under the circumstances, was not extraordinary; nor is Tom the only one who has been puzzled by the mystery of his own identity.

"Tom," said Mrs. Aldine, when the invalid had heard a full account of his recent doings, "don't you know me?"

TOM PL A YFAIR. 239

'No, ma'am," he answered, with a blush, as he encountered the sweet eyes of a refined lady fixed upon his.

'While you were sick, you took me for your mamma; and, indeed, if the love and gratitude of one who has not the sacred name of mother can supply her place, I shall do it. I am the mother of James Aldine, whom you so bravely rescued." And stooping down, Mrs. Aldine tenderly kissed the little boy, as though, indeed, she were his mother.

To say that Joe, Harry, and Willie were happy, isthe mildest possible way of expressing their senti-ments; they were beside themselves. Their joywas threatening to develop into uproariousness,when the infirmarian very wisely ordered them totheir respective dormitories.

From that night Tom's improvement was rapid.He soon outstripped James in the race for health.While Tom bustled in and out of the infirmary,James kept his bed, his wound healing, but hischeeks growing thinner and paler day by day.

"I say, Jimmy," said Tom, about one week fromthe date of the crisis, "why don't you eat a decentmeal?"

'I'm not hungry, Tom."

"That's no way to do; eat, anyhow; you're get-ting thinner all the time."

'I know it, Tom; and, what is more, I believe Ishall never be well again."

' Nonsense! Humbug!" said Tom sturdily, thoughhis cheek blanched as he spoke.

'I do believe it, Tom, and I have reason. Thedoctor of late looks troubled. He complains thatthe wound isn't healing fast enough. And mamma

knows that I am in danger; for her face grows verysad when she thinks I am not looking at her; andonce, after she had spoken with the doctor, I sawher cry. But don't think, Tom, that I am anxiousto live; I had rather die, for I am ready. Should Ilive, dear Tom, the day might come when I shouldfall into some mortal sin. So far God has been sogood to me; He has given me a holy, pious mother,and very dear, good friends," he pressed Tom's handas he said this, "and, by His grace, has kept meout of all dangerous occasions. So I am happy atthe thought of dying now."

"Well, Jim," said Tom, with the tears starting tohis eyes, "I know you are ready, and I do wish Iwas as good as you. You've got the makings of anangel, but you mustn't die; I should lose my dearestfriend."

"No, no; indeed you won't," answered Jamesearnestly. * Please God, I shall be your friend inanother world. I would be of little use here; butthere I am sure I could help you far better. And,Tom, I am not sorry to die, for another reason. Idon't think I could ever be happy here below.I fret about things so easily. The least thing wor-

ries me.'

'Yes, that's so," admitted Tom; "you do fretabout things. I'm not that way myself."

Toward evening Mr. Aldine, who had been Easton business, arrived at the college, bringing withhim Touzle.

Touzle entered the sick-room dancing with joy,but on seeing his brother so pale and thin hesobered very much.

"Poor Dimmy is sick," said the child, running

his fingers through James's hair. "Where's thewed on your cheeks, Dimmy?"

"Somebody whitewashed me," was the answer;but Touzle was not convinced.

In December James was so weak that he wasunable to leave his bed. Tom had been about hisclass duties for several weeks, but whenever he wasfree he spent his time at the sufferer's side. As theboy drew nearer the grave, his spirit seemed to drawcloser to God. At times the light of sanctity flick-ered upon his face—such a light as nothing butexquisite purity and exalted holiness can enkindle.

Nor was Tom idle. Christmas was to be the dayof his First Communion. With all his resolute willhe applied himself to prepare for this august moment.Many an hour would he spend with James, speaking of the dearest of all miracles, the miracle of Our Saviour's ineffable love. At night, too, he would kneel long by his bed praying for love and grace; and the boys began to remark that instead of the dying saint Tom had arisen in his stead.

It was the eve of the great day. Just before retiring for the night Tom repaired to the infirmary to pay a last visit to his friend. The wan face of James almost glowed with joy at his approach.

"Oh, Tom, I'm so glad to see you," he said, "for I want to tell you the news. To-morrow, Tom, as you go to Holy Communion for the first time, I shall be receiving the last sacraments of the Church."

Tom was not dismayed; he had long expected this news.

"That is good," he said; "and I shall offer up all my communion for you."

"Thank you, Tom; you are too good. But I

116

wish now to tell you something else. Do you know why I expected to die from so long ago?"

"Why?" asked Tom.

'* Because when you were so sick I prayed and prayed, night and day, that, if it might be, God should take my life and spare yours. I knew you would be of some use in the world, Tom, but I would do little. So, Tom, you must try to do your work, and mine too; and that, you know, is little enough."

Tom was weeping.

4 I am very glad to die," pursued James. "At first, when I prayed to God, I was a little afraid of being heard; for I had hoped, Tom, to live long enough to be a priest, and to touch with my poor hands Our Saviour Himself. I intended to give my life to God; but God has come to take it before I can give it."

Tom was still weeping.

'Mamma," said James, as his mother came up and laid her head beside her darling boy's cheek, '* I know you do not refuse to give me up to God."

' No, my darling; if I loved you a thousand times more, He should have you."

"I'm so glad, mamma; to-morrow will be Christ-mas. Wouldn't it be nice were I to die then ? Then you would give me to God on the very day God gave Himself to you."

Tom was returning from the communion table, his heart beating in unison with the heart of his sweet Master, his radiant soul in the life-giving embraces of her Spouse. How the minutes flew, as he knelt in earnest commune with his loving Jesus!

He was a saint that morning—one of those little children whose souls are the glory of the Sacred Heart. How long, how fervent, had been his prepa-ration! But Tom now thanked God for the delay. His soul had been purified by trial. And now that the probation was over, Tom felt that he had been in God's hands. It was truly his day of days.

Thanksgiving over, he hastened to the infirmary. As he entered the room, Mrs. Aldine's sobs broke upon his ear. He hastened to the bedside, but the gracious eye of welcome was closed forever. A sweet expression, ineffably sweet, lingered upon the child's face, as though the body itself had, for one last moment, shared in the happiness of the liberated spirit.

'My God," murmured Tom from the fulness of his heart, as he threw himself on his knees beside the body, "Jimmy offered himself for me. Let me take his place in life. If it be your will, my God, I from this day give myself entirely to your work."

CHAPTER XXVIII.

AN ESCAPE FROM JAIL, AND THE BEGINNING OF A SNOW-STORM.

STILL Christmas morning! In a narrow room, lighted by one close-barred window, was Hart-nett, worn no less by confinement than by anxiety. His face had grown darker, his fierce eyes had be-come bloodshot; while his beard, nails, and hair, long neglected, imparted to his appearance an in-crease of loathsomeness.

Like a caged tiger, he was fiercely, doggedly pacing up and down the room. Occasionally he would pause to catch the interchange of greetings from the passers-by without. They were merry words; words beautiful in themselves, but colored into beauty more gracious than the dawn by the infinite Peace and Love that gave them birth; words that brought back again that undying song of the angels, that song of gladness, which, ringing down the ages, will move the glad echoes of the human heart till this world shall have passed away. " Merry Christmas! Merry Christmas!" The words few, the meaning simple. Yet, link them with the glad smile, the bright eye, the look of love, the warm pressure of the hand,—and what a wealth of meaning there is in the expression! It is the full-hearted utterance of human sympathy, kindness and love, raised into priceless value by the benediction of Bethlehem's Babe. But upon the prisoner's heart, long since attuned to the chords of anger and hatred, these words grated harshly. Muttering maledictions upon the authors of these cheery greetings, he re-sumed his weary tramp,—not blessed on this thrice-blessed day by so small a gift as one kind thought. By and by, a key from without rattled in the lock, the door swung open, and the marshal entered the room.

"Well, Hartnett," said the marshal, "your game's about up."

"What's happened now?"

The boy you stabbed died this morning. So to-morrow you're to be removed to the jail at the county-seat, if you're not lynched before you get there."

The prisoner wiped his brow with his sleeve, his breathing grew short, and an expression of abject fear started upon his face.

'What do the people say about me?" he gasped.

"There's not much said; they're rather quiet. But their way of looking makes me reckon that you won't get out of this jail more'n six foot before you're in the hands of a mighty mad crowd. But I guess we'll come a game on them. We'll take you off to-morrow before daylight, before folks know what's what."

'When are you coming for me?"

' Oh, about four in the morning. Anything I can do for you ?"

"No; I'll be ready when you come."

"Ain't you sorry that boy died?"

No answer from Hartnett.

'Won't you feel nervous-like to-night, with that boy's face before you in the dark?"

"See here, now," said the murderer, "don't try that on me. You needn't try to get me frightened. The boy is dead, and that's an end of it."

The prisoner spoke with vehemence.

"Well, I can't wish you a merry Christmas, but I do wish that you may come to realize what an awful thing you have—"

"Go away! Get out! Leave me!" shrieked Hartnett, his bloodshot eyes growing hideous with rage, and his fingers working in impotent passion.

"One moment," said the marshal, producing a pair of handcuffs; "here's a pair of bracelets you might as well try on."

" Now ?" exclaimed Hartnett, aghast.

"Why not?"

"Can't you wait till to-morrow?" he exclaimed, drawing back.

;'Come on; now's the time!"

" Marshal, I haven't asked you many favors since I've been here. Please let me go free till we start to-morrow; it's an ugly matter to have those affairs on, and I'd like to put it off as long as possible."

"Let's see," said the official dubiously.

"Why, I can't escape, man. Look at these bare stone walls—four ugly walls and a wretched, barred window; and that dismal low roof that I can almost touch with my hand."

'Well, all right," said the marshal; "but remem-ber, on they go the first thing in the morning. I'll leave them here for you to admire." And, carelessly tossing the handcuffs on the prisoner's bed, the marshal locked himself out. Had he seen the lurk-ing smile of triumph on Hartnett's face, he might have reconsidered his favor.

Hartnett listened intently till the retreating foot-steps had become inaudible; then, going to his bed, he turned up the mattress, and inserting his hand into a small opening, drew forth a slender, steel, saw-like instrument. After pausing to assure him-self that no one was near, he climbed up one of the stone walls of the prison, by means of hardly per-ceptible holes made for his feet, till his hands could reach the wooden roof. His first act was to jerk from the ceiling three strips of black cloth, which, on being removed, discovered three long, narrow chinks, plain in the sunshine, and needing only a fourth chink to make a hole abundantly large enough for his escape. The work already done had cost him days and nights of patient labor, his instrument

being small and, in appearance, unsuited for the purpose. He put himself to work now with re-doubled energy. Presently the beginning of the fourth narrow slit appeared. Half an hour passed; hardly a quarter of an inch was done, and two feet to be cut before three o'clock of the next morning. Hartnett grew nervous at the thought, and pushed his makeshift saw up and down with all his strength. Suddenly there was a sharp snap—his instrument had broken. In the agony of the moment Hartnett forgot himself, lost his hold, and fell heavily to the floor, where, with a smothered curse still lingering on his lips, he lay for some minutes stunned and helpless. But the sound of footsteps without soon brought him to his feet; and with an agility won-derful under the circumstances, he again clambered up the wall, deftly covered the betraying chinks with cloth, then lightly dropped to the floor.

For the rest of the day he passed his time brood-ing and sullen, now traversing his cell with hasty, impatient strides, now tossing restlessly upon his couch. Darkness at length came; the sounds of the day died away. Toward midnight, perfect quiet reigned. Hartnett's time had come. With the handcuffs in one hand he again mounted, with all his strength beat them against the part he had par-tially cut away. One, two, three heavy blows and the wood yielded a little. Another strong blow, and another; and his escape was secured. A moment later, he had gained the roof, leaped to the ground,—then skulked through the village, across the rail-road track, out into the great undulating, deserted prairie beyond.

Whither he was going he knew not. But, strange

as it may seem, no sooner was he free of his prisonwalls than an overpowering sense of terror cameupon him. Did he seek the lonely prairie of hisown choice ? That was a question he could not haveanswered himself. He seemed to be fleeing fromsome pursuing evil. It might have been the bitterwind of the chilling night; but there seemed to ringin his ear a dying groan; there seemed to dancebefore him a knife, dripping with blood; and thewild angry jargon of many voices haunted him asthough a horde of demons were at his heels. Thevery sky was dark and threatening; and strange,weird shapes, clad in the sable vesture of the dead,sprang up at every step before his startled eyes.Hour after hour passed away, and still he pushedwildly, madly on, his face quivering with fear andhorror. With the first streak of dawn his strength,thus far supported by terror, deserted him; andcoming upon a lone tree standing amid the vast sol-itude of the prairie, he threw himself beneath itsshelter, and losing his night's terror in the splendorof the dawn, fell into a deep sleep.

Let us turn from this wretch to the side of thedead child. His delicate, fragile hands clasped uponhis bosom and intertwined with the beads he had soloved in life, his face calm and serene and telling atale of beatitude immortal, he lay in his white coffin,surrounded by father, mother, and little playmates,subdued into unwonted gentleness as they enteredthe chamber where death had dealt his kindlieststroke. It was the morning after Christmas, andJames, it had been decided, was then to be buried.

"Not," said Mrs. Aldine, "that I am tired ofgazing upon the dear face of my angel boy, but
TOM PLA YFAIR. 249
because death in a house where so many boys aretogether would keep them in a sadness not suited tothe time."

Mr. Middleton, who had been James Aldine'steacher, spoke a few last words.

He told the students of the child Jesus; of Hishidden youth, and of His love for little children.Then he narrated, almost in the beautiful languageof the Gospel, the story of how Jesus, when He wasasked by the apostles who was the greatest in thekingdom of heaven, took a child and set him intheir midst. " And," he continued, " when I considerthe little I have seen of our departed brother's life,when I recall how earnestly, how devoutly, he soughtto love and imitate the Sacred Heart of Jesus, itseems to me that such a one as this must our DivineLord have chosen to stand in the midst of Hisapostles."

Slowly and solemnly the students, in ordered ranks,devoutly reciting the rosary as they moved, walkedfrom the college toward the graveyard, which laya mile or so out upon the prairie. As they nearedthe newly-made grave, snow began to fall in largeflakes. Before the burial services had concludedthe storm became blinding in its intensity. Mr.Morton, the prefect of the large boys, was alarmed.

"Boys,"he said in a loud voice, as the grave-diggers were completing their task, and the studentswere about to start for the college, " I warn you, onperil of your lives, not to disperse on the road back.This promises to be a terrible snow-storm, and wereyou to lose your way, death on the prairie might bethe result. Form into ranks as before and I willput two boys who know the prairie best at the head."

250 TOM PLA YFAIR.

It was very happy of the prefect to have takenthis decisive measure. At first some of the youthfulwiseacres grumbled, but when, with difficulty, allhad arrived safely at the college, it was generallyacknowledged that any other course might have ledto the loss of life.

CHAPTER XXIX.

END OF THE SNOW-STORM.

WHEN Hartnett awoke he found himself coveredwith snow, and, hastily rubbing his eyes, dis-covered with dismay that he was alone on the track-less prairie in the face of the fiercest and mostblinding snow-storm that had ever come under hisexperience. Starting to his feet, he pushed vigor-ously ahead. But whither was he going? He couldnot tell; mortal eye, were it ever so strong andsteady, could not have pierced the snow-veil whichstretched from earth to sky. Yet he must go on.To stand in such a storm were to perish. As hestarted out upon this enforced tramp, the snow wasalready ankle-deep; after an hour's weary walkingit had deepened several inches. But it was a trampagainst death, and as the echo of the last night'shorrid voices rang in his memory, he pushed on asthough the whole demon-world were at his back.Several hours passed, and finally the wanderer cameto a lone tree. One look, and he perceived that itwas the tree he had started from.

The wild, horrid explosion of curses that burstfrom his lips fell idle upon the dreadful solitude,but to his distorted fancy they seemed to be re-echoed

by a million hideous tongues; and more affrightedthan ever, he set forward again. Travel had nowbecome very difficult. At times he would fall intoa snow-drift, and on one occasion he was almostsuffocated before he could free himself. As theafternoon advanced, a feeling of languor stole uponhim; his senses were losing their sharpness. Thisbut terrified him the more, for he knew that, shouldhe give way to this weakness, he was lost. On hewent, then, with the desperation of despair; on, on,till darkness closed about him; on, on, till the rudewind rose and howled and hooted after him, andthrew itself against him; on, on, till the voices ofthe night were changed into groans and shrieks anddirges; on, on, till, weary, frightened, hopeless, withhis stubbly beard and hair encrusted with ice, hisface numb with cold, he fell and stumbled oversome earth slightly raised above the level,—fell insuch a manner that the raised earth served as a pil-low for his head. The feeling of languor had nowbecome a positive force; he would not rise again—let hell or heaven do its worst, he cared not. Againthere rang in his ears a wild shout as of demon tri-umph. Despair forced him once more to open hiseyes. Looking straight before him, he saw—couldit be?—a little child, clad in white and standinglooking down upon his face. Hartnett's eyes startedin terror; an expression as of the damned came overhis features, and with a low groan he fell backsenseless.

The day following the storm Tom with hisfriends obtained permission to visit James Aldine'sgrave. As they approached, Harry observed:

" Look at that tombstone standing up right beside

Jimmy's grave. It stands there all in white, likethe ghost of a child."

'* If I were to see that in the dark," observed Joe,' it would almost scare me to death."

"My God! look here!" cried Tom.

Tom had just removed a layer of snow fromJimmy's grave, revealing to all the head of Hart-nett, pale in death, but horrible, despairing, ghastly,—resting on the grave of the child he had murdered.

CHAPTER XXX.

CONCLUSION.

rPHE early history of Tom Playfair is told. On1 the day he made his First Communion, he maybe said to have "made his start" in life. All theevents dating from his first introduction to thereader — delay, disappointment, sorrow, disaster—all had converged into the shaping and perfectingof that "day of days," into the moulding of a noblecharacter.

Tom had met with two tragic experiences beyond the lot of most boys of his years and condition in life, and he had borne them bravely.

He had suffered, moreover, a bitter trial,—none the less a trial that it was in part self-imposed,—and his act of obedience had purified and strengthened him.

But he was still deficient; the evil effects of his unequal home-training had not been entirely effaced. About him there still lingered a touch of forward-ness, and the shadow of a boyish irreverence toward

his elders. Mr. Meadow's influence had woven it-self into his very texture. To borrow a schoolboy's expressive phrase, he was somewhat "fresh." He united in his character great physical and great moral courage, but the sweet modesty and gentleness which impart a lustre to perfect bravery were yet to come. He was a manly boy; the manliness was rough at the edges.

On the last day of the school year Tom tapped at Mr. Middleton's door to exchange a few words of farewell.

" Ah, Tom; I'm glad you've come! You're always welcome, but now— So you're going?"

"Yes, sir; and I've come to ask your pardon, Mr. Middleton, for all the trouble I've given you. You know, sir, I can hardly help wriggling; and it's so hard to keep quiet four hours a day, when there's such a good chance for a little fun sometimes; and then, sir, I've got to talk sometimes,—I can't hold in."

"Well, Tom, /haven't complained, have I?"

"No, sir; that's the way you make me feel mean. You're so patient. If I were in your place, I'd raise a row, sure."

"If I have been patient, I have had my reward; for I'm glad to tell you, Tom, that your improve-ment in conduct and in application has been so steady that it could be noticed almost each week."

"Thank you, sir," said Tom, blushing.

Like most generous, noble-hearted boys, he was a hero-worshipper; and from the time of the memorable interview between himself and Mr. Middleton, on the day that Tom and Pitch smoked together, his professor had been his hero. Tom had been con-

quered by kindness,—a conquest, it is scarcely neces-sary to say, no less creditable to the victor than to the vanquished.

He had issued from that interview Mr. Middle-ton's disciple; and a faithful disciple he had been. No wonder, then, that his chubby cheeks colored with pleasure at these kindly words of commenda-tion.

"You remember, Tom," continued Mr. Middleton, fixing an earnest look upon the little lad, 'you remember that letter I sent your father, nearty two years ago ?"

"I shall never forget it, sir."

"Well, I ventured on a bold prediction in it, and I have not been disappointed."

Tom could have kissed the hand extended to him; in our American way, he squeezed it heartily.

441 must add, though," continued Mr. Middleton, "that you've lost a friend you could ill spare."

" Jimmy Aldine?"

" Yes; he had a gentleness and sweetness of dispo-sition which exerted a marked influence upon you for good. He was a true friend; you needed such a friend; so did Harry Quip.

You and Harry havehelped each other, too; but James Aldine had aninfluence that stepped in where yours and Harry'sstopped short. He was in a manner a visible guard-ian angel to you both."

" He was like the fairy prince I read about theother day when I was alone in the infirmary with asore throat and didn't know what to do with myself,"sighed Tom. " I got thinking of him when I wasreading. I miss him very much, sir. He was thenicest boy I ever met."

"Ah, Tom, if you could find another friend likehim!"

'Well, sir, I'm young yet, and there's no end ofgood boys in the world, if a fellow could only findthem out. Maybe there'll be lots of nice new boyshere next year."

'Pray, Tom, pray for another James Aldine."

"I will, indeed, sir."

And with a swelling heart he bade his teacherfarewell.

On that very day a Baltimore gentleman wasbidding farewell to his daughters and an only son,the "fairy prince," who were departing for Cincin-nati, to reside there with their aunt while theirfather was to spend the summer in Europe with hisinvalid wife. This was the beginning of eventswhich bore closely upon the conversation just re-corded and upon the after-life of Tom.

Knowing nothing of this, Tom prayed all vaca-tion for the new friend; and in September his prayerwas heard.

Those of my readers who are interested in Tomwill learn in "Percy Wynn; or, Making a Boy ofHim," how and under what circumstances he metwith his " fairy prince."

THE END.

Made in the USA
Monee, IL
03 December 2020

50767471R00070